GHOST DAGGER

A Mystery by Helen Currie Foster

To Amber!
Happy reading!
Helen Currie Foster

Chapter One

Hidden *Like* a Rabbit

Breathing hard, Alice crested the shoulder of the ridge below Ben Cathair, three hundred feet above the Scottish coast town of Broadview. She turned seaward to absorb the view. Broadview's harbor sparkled in the late August sun; beyond lay Luce Bay and the Irish Sea. Below, to her right, on the headland ending into a small cove, she could make out the ancient house and outbuildings of Hardie Farm—owned by Hardies from time immemorial and now by Kathy Hardie Greer, Alice's mother-in-law, called Gran.

No one had met Alice at Hardie Farm. Gran's daughter, Robbie, was driving Gran back from her heart appointment in Edinburgh. The three women had voted to meet at the pub for dinner—no cooking tonight. So Alice, desperate for movement after hours cooped up on flights to Heathrow and Edinburgh, had parked her rental car in the shed that served as Gran's garage, tugged on running shoes, and headed uphill to a favorite spot. Reveling in the smell of sweet green turf mixed with salt air, she'd crossed Gran's pasture to the stepping stones across the little Hardie River, watching trout flick their tails at her from a shady pool. The Hardie flowed off Ben Cathair across the Flemings' land, where it had carved a small glen, and onto Gran's farm, then ran down to the harbor. Gran's property line lay upstream below the glen. Alice walked Gran's fence on her way up. Just checking the fence line, like any good Texas property lawyer would.

Now she turned in a circle. Around her stood the Sisters—six standing stones, each taller than Alice. They stood on the close-cropped grass. Alice paced around the circle, running her fingers over each stone. Who set them here? When? Why? Suddenly jetlag overtook her. She chose the southwest-facing stone and slid slowly down it to the turf, pillowed by her daypack. She leaned her head back on the sun-warmed rock and gazed through half-closed eyes out across the sea, in the general direction of Ireland. All she could hear was the little trout stream far below, the Hardie, running across its granite bed. Otherwise, so quiet. Little daisies in the short grass. The sun dropped lower.

She woke, very cold. Thick wet mist cloaked the circle. Was someone yelling? She thought she'd heard "Stay away . . . Hardie

Farm!" Or had she dreamed it?

Alice struggled to her feet and moved to the edge of the circle, one hand on the nearest stone. In the heavy mist below, close to where the downhill slope dropped into the glen, for an instant she saw three figures—two men, one taller, one blockier, facing a third man of medium height. One waved a stick; one, a spade; one held something that looked to Alice like a brush cutter or weed cutter, but not quite. The mist rolled in and all three vanished. A loud echoing *crack*!; Alice thought, incongruously, of a baseball home run.

She stood paralyzed at the edge of the slope. What had happened? The wind blew and the blocky man, suddenly just visible in the mist, turned and stared uphill toward the Sisters. "Someone's up there. I'm going up!" The mist rolled back in.

Alice edged backward, then skirted the back side of the circle to the steep rockfall that ran up toward the top of Ben Cathair. At the start of the rockfall lay a house-high group of boulders covered with prickly broom. She saw a gap and squeezed in. She peered through the broom, focusing on the far edge of the stone circle.

A broad shadow holding a short spade with a long narrow blade appeared in the mist, looked around, took a few steps into the circle. From below she heard a voice: "Hey, come back down!"

The shadow swung his shoulders and his head from side to side, surveying the circle, stared hard toward Alice's gorse patch. She stopped breathing. Then he turned and disappeared. She heard heavy boots receding, then silence.

Alice squeezed back out of her hiding place. Dumb, she thought. What was she thinking, trying to hide with her back to boulders, in a spot where she couldn't get out in a hurry? Why had she hidden like a rabbit? Why hadn't she just stepped out to confront them?

Because they scared her.

Being scared made her mad. But when she mustered her courage and marched to the edge of the stone circle, she saw no one below on the slope. She heard nothing. All three men were gone.

She shivered, her shirt damp from the mist. What had she seen, or not seen? Heard, or not heard? She shook her head. A disorienting welcome to Scotland. She looked at her watch. Five thirty!

She wanted to talk to Neil Gage, the pub owner, before six, when the bar got too busy, about the sudden departure of Gran's tenant at Hardie Farm. He'd decamped before Alice arrived. Curious, she'd peered through the windows of the rental cottage, fearing a mess, but saw only a crumpled newspaper in the fireplace, a bag of trash by the door, knotted tightly closed, and one chair askew at the breakfast table. Gage had called Gran to say the man had left a note for her, and then added: "If I'm honest, I would say that when he stopped to leave that note, the man acted a bit unnerved."

What Kind *of* Voices?

The mist had lifted into a low cloud right above her head, leaving the slope visible part of the way down to Upper Road. She started down the muddy footpath below the Sisters. The path was public but crossed the Flemings' property, which began uphill from Gran's farm and included most of the northwest side of Ben Cathair.

Upper Road was still wreathed with mist when she reached it. The wet pavement disappeared as it ran east, crossing the top of the town. You'd have to be careful driving that way right now, she thought. She glanced to her right, where the Flemings' wide private drive left the intersection of Upper Road and Hardie Road. She saw nothing, no one.

Upper Road was part of the loop around Broadview that changed its name every time it changed direction. "Harbour Road" along the seafront, it became "Hardie Road" as it turned and ran uphill from the west side of Broadview and past Gran's farm. At the top of the hill, below the Sisters, it turned east, renamed "Upper Road," and ran across the top of the town, crossing another smaller stream, the Dorain, which flowed from the east side of Ben Cathair and across distillery property. Past the bridge Upper Road turned back downhill, renamed "Distillery Road," and raced the Dorain downhill to the sea, where the road completed its circuit, becoming once again Harbour Road.

Now, as she trotted down Hardie Road, the mist below lifted and the lower town came clearly into view. She ran past the drive into Hardie Farm, swung left over the little humpbacked bridge that crossed the Hardie at the bottom of the long hill, and made the turn onto Harbour Road and into Broadview.

Broadview's harbor, flanked by its two streams and two head-lands, faced west on Luce Bay, below the stony horn of Ben Cathair, in Galloway on the southwest coast of Scotland. The nearest big town was Newton Stewart. During the short summer, artists lined the sea-wall, trying to capture the heights of Ben Cathair, or the undoubt-edly photogenic harbor, sparkling with sails. Broadview attracted the quirkier sort of tourist—bird-watchers walking the headlands, otter lovers rapt and whispering in blinds at the Dorain Refuge just over the headland from Gran's farm, history lovers climbing up to the Iron Age hill fort and the ruined abbey with its supposed hermit's shelter. The town had acquired a rep with foodies, with sailboat owners phoning ahead for reservations at the Broadway Diner, whose chef had returned from Edinburgh with big ideas. Alice had visited Broadview numerous times—she and Jordie had brought the kids for Christmas and summer vacations. She enjoyed poking around the shops and galleries—all gray granite or white stucco—that spilled downhill to Harbour Road. But she often suspected the town kept its secrets, and that the same smiling locals who welcomed visitors might inhabit a very different town than their guests enjoyed.

Late on Sunday afternoon, this end of town was quiet. Shops were closed; the streets were empty. Sunset wouldn't come until eight thirty, even this late in August, but the sun was hiding behind cloudbanks over the bay. Alice shivered in the chilly damp, trotting past Abbey Antiques, Brow and Beauty, the Royal Bank of Scotland. Only the red-curtained pub windows at the end of the bridge cast a welcome glow onto the sidewalk, promising warmth inside.

Under the painted swinging sign of the Sisters Pub, Alice pulled open the heavy door, releasing the heady, centuries-old aroma of fermented and distilled beverages, plus an incongruous but welcome note of Thai curry. She headed for the bar, where Neil Gage stood polishing glasses. Behind the publican's ready smile, his blue eyes missed little.

"Alice MacDonald Greer," she said, extending her hand.

"Aye, of course." He put down the towel and shook her hand firmly. "Jordie's wife. I'm always sorry for your loss. That was quite a man, Jordie Greer."

Alice nodded. Jordie had disappeared over four years earlier when his helicopter, flying back from an oil rig, vanished in the North Sea. Alice and her children, John and Ann, lived with the vacant uncertainty left by a death without a body to bury. But her children found comfort with Gran during their university year abroad in Edinburgh. Gran fed them, listened to them, let them bring laundry to the Edinburgh house where she'd raised Jordie and Robbie, and shared her insider's view of Edinburgh. They now had formed lasting ties with their Scottish kin.

The ties that bind had brought her here.

"So, this writer fellow, that was renting from Mrs. Greer, only you know we all call her Kathy, he came tearing in last week just as I opened. I looked outside at his car. He'd just thrown in his bags, in a heap. The man didn't buy a last pint or say good-bye. He shoved this envelope at me, addressed to Kathy, and said, 'I'm leaving. No one should have to put up with voices of strange men at night, stomping around that old sheep pen doing God knows what. Tell her to send me my deposit.'"

"What kind of voices?"

"I did ask him about that, because if it's Broadview lads I'd like to know. He just said men. Not kids, anyway. Local accents, is all he said."

"But what were they doing?"

Gage shook his head. "The man acted deeply insulted, but apparently nothing actually happened to him. Who knows what he saw, or heard, or thought he saw or heard? I'm just sorry Kathy's lost a paying tenant for the cottage." He handed her the envelope, addressed only to "Mrs. Greer." On a plain sheet inside, written in emphatic script, she read:

Mrs. Greer, I'm leaving immediately. You owe me my deposit. Send it to me straightaway. No one can be expected to stay in a place with men roaming around at night with lights and tools, disturbing my writing and my sleep. Rural peace, indeed! You will agree that is totally unlivable and unsafe.
—Clyde Pendennis Creighton

The signature dwarfed the rest of the note: a John Hancock signature, underlined with a flourish. She showed it to Gage. "Did he make that name up?"

"That's how he introduced himself to me. All three names." He lifted his eyebrows comically. "If I'm honest I would say I got the impression he thought I should have heard of him, but I haven't. At any rate, I don't like this notion of men roaming around at night frightening folks."

She believed him. It couldn't be good for tourism. "You don't have any guess as to what's going on?"

He picked up a glass, started polishing it, but she glimpsed a cloud behind the shrewd eyes. "Not yet. If I learn anything I'll tell you. Now, what about something for you?"

She tried again. "Nothing similar on anyone else's property?"

"Not that I've heard. So far we've had no nighthawking around here."

"Nighthawking?"

"You know, trespassing metal detectorists. We've got a couple of local hobbyists but they'd never bother Kathy." He shook his head again, smiled. "What'll you have?"

"How about some Talisker. And Robbie and Gran—Kathy—will be here soon, for dinner." She'd called her mother-in-law "Gran" for nearly two decades, since the children were born. Even Jordie and Robbie called her Gran. Alice had promised back in June that she'd come to Scotland for two weeks in August, after her children reported that someone was upsetting Gran about her land—not a hard promise to keep, especially when the Texas hill country burned with August heat and Alice longed for cool air, mountain passes, wildflowers, a hint of fall in the air, readily available here. She hadn't counted on that confrontation in the mist, though.

She took her drink to a scarred wooden table in the nook by the fireplace. Even in late August, the fire felt good. Nighthawking, she thought. Not like the lesser nighthawks she sometimes caught in her headlights, swooping across dark Texas roads, bearing her favorite bird description: "cryptically colored." Well, maybe the tenant's marauders were similarly disguised . . . but she felt confident she'd find them.

The pub door swung back and forth; the place was filling up. As she analyzed the various customers, playing her usual game of guessing peoples' stories, Alice herself fielded some speculative looks. What did they see? Medium everything, thought Alice: medium height, jeans, brownish-blond hair highlighted with talent by her Austin hairdresser, along with some intangible details that informed them she wasn't local. Then the door opened and Gran, slight, smil-

15

ing, white hair piled high, made her way over to Alice, slowing to chat with various pub patrons as she squeezed her small body past the crowded tables. "Well, my sweet one," she said, kissing Alice's cheek, "it was an all right checkup. I'll live another day. What about you? How was the flight?"

"Cramped, interminable, but I had a window seat! It was clear all the way to Edinburgh. And we're set up at the distillery. Their new taster, Davie Dockery, can take my clients around on a tour this week. I mentioned your name frequently, of course." The "Beer Barons," owners of the Beer Barn roadhouse in Coffee Creek, Texas, had the notion of starting a malt whisky distillery and wanted Alice to help. Two of them, Bill Birnbach and Jorgé Benavides, had decided to fly over to Scotland while Alice was there. "We'll play a little golf, sip a little whisky," Birnbach said. Alice had agreed it was a good idea. "It wouldn't hurt to evaluate the Scottish competition before you invest in the whisky business, and see what you're up against," she said. But before they arrived, she needed to sort out what was happening at Gran's.

"Davie, is it? I remember when he was snitching the apples off my tree. I didn't know he'd gotten the taster job. Good work."

"Where's Robbie, Gran? And what can I get you?"

"Robbie hopped out of the car on the way into town and said she needed some hill work after sitting and driving all day. She said she'd take a fast walk on Upper Road and be here in a few. And I'd like a sherry, please. Neil knows."

Alice rose and headed to the bar. Gage already had Gran's sherry on the counter. His eyes met hers. "Thanks," Alice said, realizing he also treasured Gran.

Alice recognized the happiness that had washed over her when Gran walked in. She'd had no idea what having a mother-in-law might be like; she'd set out with fear and trepidation for her first meeting with Jordie's mum. But Gran's immediate acceptance of her American daughter-in-law, her laughing adoration of her tall son, and her kind welcome of Alice's parents had won over Alice so quickly, she felt she'd known Gran forever. Now Jordie was gone, but she planned to keep Gran. She sat, sipped her Talisker, and searched Gran's face. She hadn't seen her since last Christmas, in Edinburgh with the kids. Was there a shadow behind those eyes? But before she could quiz Gran—how was she *really*, after her near-death experience and heart surgery—Gran, in her usual fashion, was quizzing her.

"How are you, Alice? Tell me about life in Coffee Creek."

Alice found herself telling Gran she was fine most of the time. But she still missed Jordie—sometimes it just hit her. And she hadn't really gone back to church because she still felt too naked there, sitting by herself. Also, people looked at her with anxious sympathy, and were clearly afraid to say the wrong thing. She stopped. "That's exhausting, the sympathy. Yet I resent it when people don't ever mention Jordie, like he never existed. So they're damned if they do, damned if they don't. Right?"

Gran nodded. Been there, done that.

"Sometimes I find myself expecting him to walk in the door."

"Me too," Gran said. "I keep waiting for his voice on the phone, saying 'Mum!'"

"But." Alice took a breath. "Well, Gran, I've started seeing Ben Kinsear. He's an old law school beau."

"Is he interesting? Are you having fun?" Gran asked.

"So far." She was watching Gran. "He's met the kids and likes them. And they seem to like him. He's in Cambridge right now taking a summer course. I thought we might meet for a couple of days while I'm here, hiking somewhere. But sometimes it seems so soon."

"But Alice! What kind of woolly thinking is that?" She narrowed her eyes at Alice. "Are you aware the earth is whirling around and around on its spindle? It's over four years since our Jordie died! Don't you think he'd want you to have a life now?" She pressed Alice's hand. Brave words, Alice thought, but wasn't Gran looking briskly in her bag for a tissue now?

The pub door opened and Robbie blew in. Robbie, tall, with a halo of light curly hair, headed for the bar. Every customer she passed greeted her. Neil's smile broadened for her. She possessed the same irresistible force of personality as Jordie and Gran. Alice shook her head. This family! To Alice, Robbie still looked more like a fierce athlete than a successful landscape painter. She watched Robbie's strong freckled forearm set down her pint on the table. "Old Mortality for me tonight. Seems appropriate after a trip to the doctor." Robbie slid onto a chair and lifted her pint. "Here's to thirty more years, Gran."

They ordered dinner—Thai curry for all three, provided by Neil's wife. "And if she was somewhat lavish in the matter of chutney," Alice muttered to herself, hoping no one noticed. As they spooned up their rice, she repeated what Neil had said about Gran's feckless tenant, the author Clyde Pendennis Creighton. "'Deeply insulted,' that's how Neil described him."

"And he calls himself a writer!" scoffed Robbie. "Look at the man! Here he is, in scenic Scottish countryside, getting a wealth of great material from a couple of small-town hooligans, probably harmless! Yet he decides to leave and demands his deposit back! That's a bit like me, as a landscape painter, complaining if a stormy day in Edinburgh offers a vision of clouds blowing across Arthur's Seat! Seize the opportunity, man!"

"You'd be perched partway up the trail, sketching?" asked Gran.

"Back to the Difficult Tenant," Alice said. "You think he was fabricating? Exaggerating at least? That it's just harmless small-town hooligans, like you said?"

Robbie sat silent, then leaned forward. "To tell the truth, I don't. When I was coming back and forth last winter, getting the rental cottage ready, getting the roof repaired, putting in a new door and front windows, someone nicked the building materials and we had to get more. That happened twice. The second time they even hauled off some roof tiles. The builder swore it wasn't his guys. And I don't think he'd lie to me. Also, it wasn't all the materials, just some—just enough to make you have to figure out what's gone, and go buy more—a real pain. Like someone wanted to mess with us, discourage us."

"I don't think anything's gone missing since those building materials," Gran said. "Of course, in June came the Great Fishing Dispute."

"But now that's sorted," Robbie said to Alice. "In March, helping Gran's tenant move in, Robbie had seen a group of fishermen come splashing down Gran's stretch of water from the Flemings' glen. She'd warned them off Robbie-style, in no uncertain terms. In June, still recovering from heart surgery, Gran had opened a stiff letter from a Glasgow solicitor representing Samantha Fleming. He said his research indicated that Gran's property did not include the valuable right to fish the Hardie and that Gran should not hereafter interfere with the Flemings' fishing clients. After a spate of transatlantic phone calls, Alice hunted down Gran's own Edinburgh solicitor, who tut-tutted and opined in soothing tones, saying that he was surprised by and deeply regretted such a questionable performance by his Glasgow colleague. "I loved our man's letter," Robbie said. Alice nodded. The solicitor had produced a dry, measured, crystal-clear masterpiece pointing out that Gran's long-established heritable rights of property in her stretch of the Hardie included not only exclusive fishing rights but also the right to preclude any trespassing, including by guests of adjacent landowners.

"That was just Samantha," said Gran. "Robert Fleming would never have allowed that letter to be sent to me." But at the time Robert Fleming, Samantha's father-in-law, paterfamilias of the Flemings, lay dying in a Glasgow hospital, and now lay buried in the Fleming corner of the church graveyard on Upper Road. Gran's solicitor had made it clear that an action for trespass would follow immediately if another Fleming lodge guest presumed to come onto Gran's property to fish the Hardie. Alice hoped the Great Fishing Dispute would not revive.

"Angus told me he'd make sure the Fleming guests behaved," Gran went on. "He was furious when he heard about their letter. He knew I'd never made such an agreement."

"Who are we talking about?" Alice asked.

"Angus McBride, the ghillie for the Fleming family," Gran said. "They have hunters and fishermen in, at their lodge up on the side of Ben Cathair. Angus takes the hunters out, you know, and manages the fishing in their little stretch of the Hardie. It's at least thirty years he's worked for that family."

Robbie nodded. "But this is new, to have your tenant complaining about men with lights marauding around the old sheepfold." To Alice the so-called sheepfold, with its uneven walls, looked more like the remains of a fallen-down barn or storehouse, later repurposed as a pen.

"So, maybe treasure hunters?" asked Alice.

"Maybe. These days they're more scientific," Gran said. "Metal detectors and all."

"Surely now that Alice and I are here it'll stop," Robbie said. Looking at her broad-shouldered sister-in-law, who rowed the bracing waters of the Firth of Forth with a masters-level women's crew, Alice privately agreed that no one would mess with Robbie. Robbie rowed stroke and took no prisoners.

"You think I can't take care of myself?" Gran straightened her shoulders and scowled fiercely at them. "I'm back!" After half a year of denial about her condition before finally agreeing to heart surgery, Gran was very proud of her speedy recovery. "But this problem with my tenant . . . I must say that I really dislike the possibility that he's not exaggerating, that there really were men marauding around the farm at night. That's quite disappointing. I thought I could say 'finito' to worries for a bit after you straightened out the Great Fishing Dispute, Alice. But I guess whoever or whatever this is, it's not finished."

Chapter Three

A Surefooted Man

Robbie headed back to the bar for fresh drinks. More customers were crowding through the door, including a pretty girl with a tight grasp on her ginger-haired athletic six-footer. Alice again noted how many people greeted Robbie, how she nodded at them with a lift of her eyebrows. She waited as Robbie started back from the bar, ready to recount her afternoon vision on the Sisters. But across the pub, heads turned at the sudden hush, then at the muttered exclamations of a group by the dartboard. Shocked whispers rippled across the room. The dart throwers dispersed slowly to their tables.

"Found down in the river," she heard the man next to her say, plumping heavily into his chair.

"Was it his heart again?" asked his tablemate.

"Dunno, but there'll be an inquest, the way he hit his head."

"That'll be the rocks, I expect."

"But Angus was a surefooted man."

Gran spoke. "Angus?" She turned to the man next to her. "Did something happen to Angus McBride?"

"Yes," said the man. "He was found in the river. Dead. Below the bridge." Alice thought first of the little humpbacked bridge over the Hardie. Did this have anything to do with the men she'd seen below the Sisters?

Robbie was standing behind Gran with a glass in each hand. Carefully she placed the glasses on the table and slid into her chair. She said nothing. Her face looked frozen.

Alice turned to the men at the next table. "When did it happen?"

"This afternoon, apparently," said the man. "Neil here says he was here for lunch. Ordered his usual ploughman's." He jerked his head toward the bar.

Bread, cheese, and chutney; death for dessert, thought Alice.

"Who found him?" asked Gran.

"The minister at the church on Upper Road. Walter McAfee. He was walking his dog over by the distillery and saw something below the bridge."

The distillery. So, not below the Sisters. Alice took a breath, relieved. Perhaps this had nothing to do with what she'd seen.

"Poor Angus. How horrible," Gran said. "And poor Walter, finding him. Not that he hasn't seen death, many times."

"I wonder if Angus tripped," added the man. "He'd lost his stick. At least, it was found some distance from his body, according to the constable."

Stick?

"What sort of stick?" Alice heard her own voice, sounding high and wavery.

"Angus always carried his stick. Not a cane, but more walking-staff sized, with a silver knob. Didn't he always tell us it had been in his family for years? He was very proud of it, as I recall." The man turned back to his supper. Around the pub, quiet voices muttered, chewed on the news.

Alice and Gran and Robbie faced each other over congealing curry. Alice could not eat another bite, thinking of the wooden *crack!* she'd heard—or thought she'd heard. But that was above the Hardie, not the Dorain. Robbie had put her spoon down. Gran's sharp eyes looked at both of them and returned to Alice. Alice took a deep breath and quietly told Gran and Robbie of her nap, of waking to cold mist, the muffled voices below, the glimpse of three, then her undignified flight into the rocks, and seeing the fog-shrouded hill climber scanning the Sisters while she huddled behind a gorse bush. What she'd seen that afternoon, and what she might have heard. Nearly heard.

"Better tell the inspector," said Gran. Robbie stood suddenly, face closed, and headed for the loo.

* * * * *

Robbie reappeared, pale, and said she would walk home alone. Alice and Gran sat quietly, Gran finishing her sherry, and watched people talk with shocked faces about Angus McBride. As they stood up to leave, Alice's phone vibrated in her pocket. The message screen said, "Lost all balls. Texans do not get links golf. Canceling next two days and heading for you and Dorain distillery tomorrow. Any rooms in town?"

"Oh, mercy," said Alice. "They're getting here tomorrow!"

"Your people?" asked Gran.

"Yes! Jorgé and Birnbach! They've canceled two days of golf and are heading straight here." She looked around wildly. Bar, darts. Upstairs? "Can they stay here, do you think?"

Gran waved at Neil, who came over. "Kathy, what can I do for you?"

"Two things. First, if the inspector comes in, Alice would like to mention something he may need to hear about." Neil lifted one eyebrow and nodded. "Also, by chance can you put up two visiting Texas boys for a couple of nights? They've accelerated their arrival."

"I do, in fact, have two rooms available."

Alice heaved a sigh of relief and explained to Neil.

"Not a problem. So, the links golf did not agree with your lads?"

She managed a smile. "You can have some fun asking them about that!"

Whew. But what about talking to the inspector? And what about Robbie?

"Gran, Robbie seemed upset about Angus McBride."

"So am I. So are we all. As to Robbie, I suspect she had a crush on him. Most of her life."

"But?"

"Oh, at some point, you know, she married and it didn't really take. Then she divorced. I thought she and Angus might connect after that, but about four years ago he married Jennie. And he was older, and I don't know if he was even comfortable with the idea of Robbie . . . I mean, she'd grown up learning to fish from him, learning to shoot, learning how to tie flies . . . She's never told me what happened, and I won't ask. But he was a fine one, Angus McBride. Most of the time. Arbiter of the village, in a way. I must say, though, he was an inveterate investigator. For example, he somehow figured out who Davie was running with, in Glasgow, and extracted him from a bad situation. Angus got him back here, and apparently into a solid job."

At the bar Neil was talking to a tall unsmiling man in a khaki windbreaker, who looked straight at Alice, then said something to

Neil. The man left and Neil walked over to their table.

"Ms. Greer, that was Ian Walker. He's police inspector for the district. He wants to talk to you but"—he looked around at the crowded pub—"not here. Can you stop by? It's that whitewashed building just across the road."

So the afternoon that began with Alice hiking alone in the sun up the slope to the Sisters ended with Alice sitting in the inspector's office on a hard chair telling Ian Walker, whose eyes did not seem to blink, about the descending mist and the voices below. He offered neither tea nor a handshake, and certainly not a smile. All business, she thought, and not particularly happy to see a meddling volunteer.

"You could not see their faces?" His face was expressionless.

"No. The man who came up to the Sisters—I call him Blocky Man—he looked very muscular. He had on a dark windbreaker or anorak with a hood. But I couldn't really see because . . ."

"You were squeezing down in the gorse bushes."

"Exactly. He scared me." She hated to say that out loud.

"He was carrying something?"

"Yes."

"A gun?"

"No, it was a spade. The sort we'd call a drain spade at home."

"And the other one?"

"Taller. Pale jacket. He was holding something like a Weed Eater or brush cutter. That's all I could see."

"You did not see either of those two strike the third?"

"No, the mist rolled back in. I did hear a sort of *crack!*, like a baseball bat hitting a ball."

He looked puzzled. "Perhaps that sounds like a cricket bat?"

Alice raised her eyebrows and shrugged. She'd never grasped cricket, never seen a match.

"When you, um, exited your spot in the gorse bushes and went down the hill, you saw nothing? No men? No body? No car?"

"Nothing. Although the mist got really thick just as I was coming down the hill. I couldn't even see down Upper Road."

"You didn't hear anything else?"

"No." She thought again about the sound she'd heard. "Didn't you find Mr. McBride's stick somewhere near him? That was the word in the pub."

"We did."

"Was it broken? Or cracked?"

"We're still evaluating the scene."

No answer for her. But her imagination pictured Angus McBride raising up his stick in self-defense.

"When was he killed?"

The inspector shook his head.

"But he was found in the Dorain?" she asked.

"Mostly."

Alice raised interrogative eyebrows.

"He was face-down in the Dorain, with his feet still on the bank, and with head injuries of indeterminate cause. That's some distance from where you describe seeing those three men." He lifted his chin and looked at her, as if from a distance. "When you saw the three men below, how clearly do you think you yourself were seen?"

Slow sinking feeling. She hadn't articulated that to herself. "I don't know."

"And you're staying with Mrs. Greer?"

Her mother-in-law. Her own name too. "Yes."

"And you will be here this next week."

Hmm. "I'll be in Scotland for another week." She paused. "I should mention . . ."

"Yes?"

"My mother-in-law's tenant left suddenly this week, complaining of men tramping around Hardie Farm at night."

"Any description?"

"No."

"Name? Hair? Eye color? Nationality?"

"'Local accents,' the tenant indicated."

"Any indication the tenant's alleged experience has any connection with Mr. McBride's death?"

"Just what one of those men said—assuming it was Mr. McBride?" She waited but the inspector said nothing. "I heard 'Stay away . . . Hardie Farm.' I'm guessing it was 'Stay away from Hardie

Farm.' That could mean a connection with Mr. McBride's death, assuming that third man was Mr. McBride."

"And you also don't know which of the three uttered those words, do you. Well, guesses and assumptions aren't enough. This gives me really very little to go on. If you had more detail, possibly that might help."

"Isn't it enough to get started? The reference to Hardie Farm seems significant!" Alice said, frowning.

He stood. "We've got a lot on our plate just now."

She was excused, apparently. She stood too. They stared at each other for a long moment. Alice turned and stalked out. Just wait, she thought.

C h a p t e r   F o u r

Head Injuries
of Indeterminate
Cause

29

Alice walked back up the graveled drive that led off Hardie Road to Hardie Farm. Downhill, to her left, she passed the shed that served as garage, the barn, then the stone rental cottage facing up toward Ben Cathair. Uphill to her right stood Gran's house. It was after eight thirty. The sun had set but horizontal rays of light gleamed out from behind the western clouds, falling across the land.

Gran's farm sat comfortably across the lap of the broad headland that began at the west shoulder of Ben Cathair and ran down to the sea. Her pastures supported a small flock of sheep, speckling the green turf with white, and two elderly horses, a bay and a dapple gray, Robbie's childhood love, standing quietly in the fenced pasture that ended at the copse above the steep drop to a small cove and the sea. Alice crunched across the circular gravel forecourt toward Gran's house, admiring its beds of hollyhocks and roses. Gran couldn't say exactly how old the house was. "I think some bits are before fifteen hundred," she had said. "But most is late seventeenth century, with, of course, improvements. Plumbing! Electricity! Central heating!" The house wasn't overlarge or formal, though the entry hall always felt imposing to Alice. She pushed open the front door, inhaling the familiar scents of ancient wood, stone floors, and a few roses on the mail table in the hall—scents that immediately brought back her first visit with Jordie, and his eagerness for her to love the farm as he did. The stone fireplace stood against the rear wall, next to the back passage to the guest bedrooms, Gran's bedroom, and the kitchen. A carved wooden staircase ran up two sides of the hall, disappearing in the darkness upstairs. In the dim light from the windows over the stairs, old paintings and prints glimmered against the dark paneling. Alice imagined they'd hung in the same place for years. The doors to her left led to a drawing room, which Gran had turned into a library, and a formal dining room; the closed doors on the right led to the study and the coat-and-boot closet, full of raincoats and mud-spattered wellies. Along the back passage Gran had hung some of Robbie's landscapes—the schoolgirl's early paintings detailed and careful, the later ones daring and more abstract.

She couldn't hear any sound from Robbie's domain upstairs. At the farm, Robbie painted in an upstairs bedroom with north light, across the hall from her own bedroom. "I've let her take over Jordie's old room for her studio down here," Gran had explained. Gran slept downstairs, across from Alice, who had picked the guestroom with its own stone-flagged guest bath and child-size tub. No more double bed upstairs with Jordie.

Alice headed down the back passage in search of Gran and Robbie. They usually found each other in the kitchen, which ran across the entire back of the house, with windows by the back door and a bay window on each end. Jordie had added those windows years earlier so Gran could look northeast toward Ben Cathair, southeast to the morning sun, and southwest to the sea. Alice loved sitting by the small corner fireplace by the bay window, watching a glowing coal fire and the waves at the same time.

Silence. "Gran?" The kitchen door was ajar. In the long August dusk of the high latitudes, Gran was cutting pink-and-white stock in the garden with Queenie, her pudgy corgi, prancing around her ankles; Sue, the task-oriented border collie, was engaged in olfactory inspection of the four corners of the sheepfold. Sue trotted over to allow Alice to rub her ears. "I wish you could tell me what you smell," Alice said. "Who's been prowling around the sheepfold, Sue?" Sue looked at Alice and cocked her head.

Gran and Queenie approached. Alice took the flower trug from Gran, smiling at the clove scent of the stock. But Gran didn't smile. "What did the inspector say?" she asked.

"Not much," Alice said. "I told him about the three men, below the Sisters. He asked where I was staying and for how long. I asked him when Mr. McBride was killed. He wouldn't say."

"Ah," said Gran. "And was it his heart? Or his head?"

Alice shook her head. "The inspector said there were head injuries 'of indeterminate cause,' as yet. Also, he was lying with his face in the Dorain and his feet on the bank."

"How odd," said Gran. "The Dorain's deep enough to drown in, but you'd have to work at it. Face-down?"

Alice nodded. "And I told him about the tenant's scare, the men out here at night. He said none of that gave him enough to go on."

But Gran, preoccupied, said nothing more.

Alice looked up. The evening sky kept a pink duskiness, and now the moon, rising in the east, slanted its first long almost-gold light across Gran's garden and the old sheepfold that stood at the top of the pasture, outside the garden wall. Alice considered the sheepfold. The lowest stone courses were covered with lichen. Very solid, Alice thought, and very old, like everything here. Downhill the sea continued its soft eternal approach to the cliff, coming in, sweeping away, coming in again. So peaceful, and yet—suddenly she imagined the terror of a Norse invasion, in the eighth or ninth century, imagined looking up from the garden, the sheep, to see those fierce carved ships, heading into your inlet, men vaulting over the sides, racing up the hill—

Of course, Jordie might be part Norse. Who knew, here. She should ask Gran. But Gran had gone back into the house.

The moon touched the slate roof tiles of the little rental cottage. Dark, quiet, empty now. She went back into Gran's house and down the passage to the small guestroom with its narrow bed. She said her usual quick prayer for her children, thought of Ben Kinsear, wherever he was at the moment, thought of her brothers and sister, and fell asleep.

Chapter Five

Land *of* Humiliation

"Broadview. We are here, almost." Text from Bill Birnbach, the accounting genius of the Beer Baron triumvirate. "May we buy you a pub lunch?"

"See you in a few!" Alice texted back. To her relief, a brisk-voiced woman named Maggie Smith at the distillery had assured Alice that a guide was available for three visiting Americans.

Breakfast in the kitchen with Gran had turned into a slow, comfortable morning of coffee (Gran's was excellent) and "butt'ries"— Gran's addictively rich butteries, pastries baked in her vast red AGA and served up with homemade jam and gossip, to which Alice listened with interest. No one mentioned Angus McBride, though Alice felt he was haunting the kitchen table, like Banquo's ghost.

"Mind you, it's not really gossip," Gran said. "It's more the proper introduction to the history of the village, right?"

"Oh, yeah!" Robbie laughed. "The bookseller's skirt chasing, the rich family's kids' disasters, the shareholders' disputes at the distillery, and who got nabbed for poaching salmon."

"Well, I don't tell everything," Gran remarked.

"But now I'm prepared," said Alice, "to withhold my skirt from the bookseller's clutches." She had a plan. "Robbie, what about helping me with these two guys today? They're offering a pub lunch. The distillery tour's this afternoon. I'll call and say you're coming too. Then afterward we could see the town, take a walk, see the rest of Gran's farm?"

Robbie looked at Alice, looked out the west window toward the sea, then lifted her chin and said, "You're on."

"Thought you were going to say no."

"Well, it'll give me something to think about besides Angus. And I'm a bit curious. Jorgé and Birnbach, right?"

"Yup. Jorgé Benavides and Bill Birnbach."

"Why do you call Jorgé by his first name and Birnbach by his last?"

"Ha! I don't know. I call Birnbach 'Bill' to his face. But otherwise, talking to others, I have to explain which Bill I'm talking about, since the third Beer Baron is Bill Benke. Jorgé runs the music, and the new microbrewery's out at his family ranch. Birnbach's our financial man. His family came to Texas from Germany in the 1850s, fleeing the Prussian draft. Bill Benke's back in Coffee Creek, minding the store. His family's Czech and he's our brewmeister. Great combination."

"All married?"

"The two Bills are. Jorgé is not." And Alice didn't know why; Jorgé's effortless, smiling management of unruly crowds, combined with his astute perception of others' motivations, made him a town favorite. And viewed objectively, he was attractive. Still, she'd never felt it appropriate to ask him why he wasn't married. The congenial crowd manager had a very private side.

"And they want to start a distillery in your Coffee Creek, for malt whisky?" Robbie shook her head. "Such effrontery!"

"You think? Let's see how serious they are." After all, they'd run a roadhouse/music venue with great success for decades; now they'd opened a small brewery with open-air facilities. Of course, malt whisky might pose a greater challenge.

Robbie looked dubious indeed.

* * * * *

Alice felt particularly satisfied striding down the hill into Broadview from Gran's, with Robbie next to her. She felt she'd learned the shapes of the hills, the sound of the river, the taste of the salty breezes; she felt, for long minutes, as if she lived there. Today the sun competed with tall scudding cumulus clouds: one minute, the light was soft and gray; the next, brilliant.

"Big surf today," Robbie commented, pointing at the whitecaps out in the bay.

"Can you land a boat in Gran's cove?" asked Alice.

"You can. But if you're sailing out of the Broadview harbor, you have to weather the point on the north end of the harbor, then come about into the cove and then pull the boat all the way up the beach and watch the tides. It's too rough to moor, off her cove. So we keep the boat moored at the harbor. Let's walk that way, even if it's longer." Robbie threaded her way out onto the pier, pointing at an eighteen-foot navy sloop, mainsail neatly furled, bobbing quietly with its dinghy.

"I always liked her name, *Lark Arising*. It reminds me of that piece by Ralph Vaughan Williams, right?" said Alice. "'The Lark Ascending.'"

"I know that piece. My dad loved to watch larks above the barley fields, and Gran named the boat. Maybe your guys would like to see it, while they're here."

"I'll bet they would."

"Didn't Jordie ever take you out in the *Lark*? He probably tried to get you on an overnight. He loved to sleep in that boat."

Alice remembered Jordie's frustration at her inability to master port and starboard, her forgetting to call the ropes "lines," her perpetual shivering in the wet breeze. "Yes. Jordie took me out in it. He was determined to teach me to sail, or at least to train me as an adequate crew member. His idea was that for our first overnight outing we should sail all the way to the Isle of Man. I remember that trip as extremely cold and wet." Also she remembered Jordie's strong voice yelling commands and her frantic attempts to master her tasks.

"Of course!" Robbie laughed. "Sailing up here is not for the soft. Speaking of soft, these days I sometimes wear a wetsuit to row." Alice shook her head. Robbie going soft on her!

They doubled back to the pub. "Let's grab a good table," said Alice. "Looks like Neil's got a crowd for lunch."

"Probably all wanting to talk about Angus." Robbie pointed at the limited pub parking area. "What are those idiots doing?"

Alice watched. Loud painful sound of gears grinding on a minuscule blue Ford, as the driver lurched forward, then jerked backward, trying to wedge into the last parking spot.

"Ouch!" She heard the car hit the stone wall behind it. One man slowly unfurled himself from the passenger seat. Alice sighed. "Um, Robbie, those are my idiots. And after that parking demonstration, they were probably lucky to get here."

"Alice! Hey, Alice!" Jorgé Benavides, brown eyes laughing, walked toward them in polo shirt and windbreaker. Birnbach was still struggling to extricate himself from the driver's seat. "Alice! We drove all the way from Ayr and we're still alive! It's a miracle!" He threw his arms wide.

"Robbie, this is Jorgé Benavides," Alice said. "Jorgé, my sister-in-law, Robbie Greer." She watched Robbie appraise Jorgé as she shook his hand. Their eyes met for longer than Alice expected.

Then Birnbach caught up with them. Alice raised her eyebrows. "Tough trip? All the way from Ayr?"

"Hey, you try driving on the wrong side of a road that's no wider than the car!" he said. "Alice, I was sure you were going to have to bail us out of jail. We barely escaped hitting two monsters. We came around a blind corner and there planted in the road were these huge hairy things, completely blocking us. Enormous horns. You couldn't see their eyes under all that hair. Would they budge? They would not."

Alice looked at Robbie, but Robbie was still looking at Jorgé, who was still looking at Robbie. What?

"Right, Jorgé?" Birnbach said.

"Are you perhaps talking about Highland cattle?" Alice said. "Bouffant hairdos, with bangs? Fond of standing in the middle of the lane?"

"Monsters." Jorgé straightened his shoulders and smiled. Then, Alice noted, he glanced back at Robbie, at the sun in her hair.

"Robbie?" Robbie finally looked back at Alice. "Robbie, this is Bill Birnbach, the financial whiz at the Beer Barn," Alice said. Birnbach gave Robbie his best smile, spectacles twinkling in the sun. "And I feel a bit like a border collie, but shouldn't we grab a table? Our tour at the Uisge Dorain Distillery starts at two."

They ducked beneath the sign of the Sisters and into the noise and warmth of the pub. Jorgé and Birnbach eyed the bar, the tables, the patrons. "Nice," Birnbach commented.

"Are you offering your professional appraisal?" asked Robbie.

"Oh, you know, every bar has its own feel. You know right away, when you walk in the door, what the owner's like, what the vibe is," Birnbach said.

"Well then, what's the feel at your place? The Beer Barn, you call it?"

He glanced at Alice. "Hmm. What would you say, Alice?"

"Relaxed, humorous, welcoming, slightly on the loud side. Good music, always. Good smells from the kitchen. When you walk in, you think, 'I believe I'll have a cold beer.'"

"And what is it here?" Robbie gestured at the pub patrons.

Birnbach examined the bar and studied the patrons. "Steady. Confident. Reliable. No querulous voices. Also, the bartender has a border collie eye if ever I saw one. Looks like he could subdue any complainers."

"That's Neil Gage. He owns the pub. Come meet him. Alice, find us a table." Robbie pushed the two men toward the bar. Alice grabbed the corner table so her friends could survey the premises, then smiled and shook her head as her clients bellied up to the bar, plunging into earnest shoptalk with Neil Gage.

When they were finally settled with drinks and lunch on order, Alice said, "So. Lost all your balls, you said?"

Birnbach rolled his eyes and sighed. "Alice, this links golf—I lost more balls on the first nine holes than I usually lose in a year. The rough—can I tell you about the rough?—the rough looks like those Highland cattle! Gorse! Bracken! I think that's what they call it. Finally I just told the caddie to get me a new ball every hole. But even that wasn't enough. My little slice? Well, a little slice means you will never see that ball again. Now Jorgé—Jorgé didn't lose so many balls. But on the other hand, Jorgé really got his money out of the course."

"What he means is, I got to take more swings at the ball," Jorgé said, "because I hit such dinky little shots trying to get out of the gorse and the wispy grass on the rough. I believe I had to claim ten strokes just on the first hole. And after that, the caddies could barely keep a straight face."

"Come on, they didn't keep a straight face," said Birnbach. "They had to pretend they were coughing so we wouldn't see they were hee-hawing at the Yanks messing up on their course."

"How do you know?" asked Robbie. "Surely they didn't say anything rude?"

"Good point," said Birnbach. "Who knows what they said? We

would ask about the lie of a green. They would answer in Romanian, I think."

"It might have been Gaelic. Or Old Norse," Jorgé suggested.

"Or possibly Finno-Ugric. We would ask which club to use. They would say something in Pictish. Or ancient Armorican."

"Finally we went to fingers," said Jorgé. "We'd hold them up." He demonstrated, holding up five fingers. "Five iron? Then there'd be a long and surely helpful explanation from the caddie, with commentary. I couldn't understand any of it. Finally I resorted to walking over and holding out my hand for the recommended club. And—Bill, do you want to discuss pot bunkers?"

"Complete menaces! Not hazards, menaces!"

"Pot bunkers?" asked Alice.

"Pot bunkers. A round hole, say ten feet across, deep as I am tall, with very steep sides. Like a cooking pot. If your ball goes in there—" Birnbach shook his head, recalling defeat. "Multiple strokes. Meaning, I dimly recall, six. Not to mention the humiliation of climbing out in front of onlookers."

"Six strokes? What, didn't you use 'the Weapon'?" asked Robbie, curling her fingers into air quotes.

Birnbach looked blank.

"The Weapon, man. It's a special wedge for pot bunkers! Didn't your caddie suggest it?"

"He did say something like 'weepin,'" Birnbach said. "You think he meant 'weapon'? I just thought he was mocking me—saying my golf was something to cry over."

"You should use a nearly flat wedge and you must really get under it," said Robbie, demonstrating with an invisible club.

"Robbie, do you even have a handicap?" asked Jorgé.

She smirked at him. "Want to play a few rounds?"

"Watch out for Robbie, guys. Ladies' golf team at St. Andrews," Alice warned.

"Scotland. Land of humiliation," groaned Birnbach.

"I still don't understand how links golf could be so hard," Alice said, egging him on.

"Well, first of all, if you go out and hit your usual drive—as I did," Birnbach said, "my basic hard-won drive that soars up over the fairway? That I've worked on for thirty years? Well, on the front nine, the wind's in your face and catches your ball and sends it off into the gorse. But on the back nine, which I am proud we survived to finish, the wind catches your ball and sends it sailing into a pot bunker. Or, again, the gorse."

"So you have to hit lower shots," Jorgé said. "We finally picked up on that. But I'm telling you, it was pretty humiliating. And the worst was—" He glanced at Birnbach.

Birnbach picked up his glass of Uisge Dorain malt whisky, staring morosely into the amber depths. "I didn't just lose all my balls. I lost one of my clubs."

Jorgé chortled into his glass. Birnbach went on, "Oh, did we mention the sideways rain blowing in your eyes and down your rain jacket? On the third hole I took a mighty swing and felt the club flying right out of my hand. It disappeared over a sandy ridge into, yes, more gorse bushes. Our caddie had to pretend he was retying his shoes. But I could see his back heaving up and down. Laughing at me." He sipped his whisky. "So I said, 'Maybe I need some new rain grips on that club.' Merciful silence followed."

"We decided, what with the wind and rain and the gorse bushes and the pot bunkers, we might start checking out distilleries," Jorgé said. "So tell us about this Uisge Dorain Distillery we're seeing today. This is not bad stuff." He lifted his glass. "Very not bad. And I know uisge is water, but could you tell us what dorain means?"

Alice looked at Robbie, who leaned forward. "Uisge Dorain could mean water fed by streamlets, or could mean a place where there are otters. River otters. And both would be true of that stream. The distillery started, like many, in the 1890s, but had to stop production during the second world war, and wasn't really getting traction after that. New owners took over in the sixties and now it's quite well regarded, especially in the last ten years. The twelve-year-old has won prizes, and the sixteen-year-old is—well, I'm partial, but it's excellent."

"As good as Talisker Sixteen?" asked Alice, who had chosen ale but was herself quite loyal to the unfiltered Talisker from the

Skye distillery.

"Depends on your taste, and how much peat you want, but I'd put Dorain up against Talisker, and others as well," Robbie said. "The problem is Dorain's had such limited production. They've expanded now. You'll see when we're there—finally they've expanded the bonded warehouse, which is critical. You have to have enough storage to age the older whiskies."

Alice finished her smoked salmon and brown bread. Jorgé and Birnbach had ordered fish and chips and cleaned their plates. "All right, ladies," said Birnbach. "Let's check out Uisge Dorain!"

Wort, Wash, *Washbacks,* Beer

Uisge Dorain Distillery sat on the other end of town from Gran's farm, just below the point where Upper Road turned downhill and became Distillery Road, which ran past the distillery property and on down to Harbour Road. The distillery's name came from the little Dorain, which arose in bogs on the southeasterly shoulder of Ben Cathair, curled around a hill, found its way under the bridge on Upper Road, then ran through the distillery property. From there the Dorain made its short way through the neighborhood below the distillery, down to the harbor and into the sea.

Alice, Robbie, Jorgé, and Birnbach climbed up the residential streets above Harbour Road to the open gates of Uisge Dorain. Gray granite walls surrounded the complex. To the left stood a large whitewashed two-story building with a covered conveyor coming out of its side, leading across the grassy yard in front of them and up to a tower with a pagoda-like top. Jorgé sniffed the air. "Ah. The faint whiff of malt!"

Davie Dockery met them at the gate. Medium tall, sandy-haired, with the long-armed reach of a young Viking, he looked no older than Alice's son, John. "Hullo, Robbie," he said, blushing a bit but squaring his shoulders. "Maggie texted me you'd be coming too." Like the other workers they'd seen onsite, he wore a heavy dark-blue shirt with the words Uisge Dorain and a crest embroidered in gold on the pocket. He also wore olive-green leather shoes with white trim and crepe soles, visibly new. New shoes for his new job, Alice said to herself.

She introduced herself and Jorgé and Birnbach.

"So, Ms. Greer, I mean Ms. Alice Greer," said Davie, and smiled again at Robbie, the other Ms. Greer, "told our Maggie Smith in the office here that you two are interested in seeing the workings of the distillery, not just tasting. She said that you own a brewery and are thinking of branching into malt whisky. I hear that's a thing in America right now." He grinned. "We're a few years ahead of you but we're happy to give you a leg up."

"We really appreciate it," Birnbach said. "I hear we're lucky to have you showing us around. So thanks."

"That's right," Davie said. "I don't usually do tours, as I'm supposed to be shadowing Old Will. That's our stillman, Mr. William Galloway. I'm training to be the stillman when Old Will—I mean, Mr. Galloway—retires. But since Ms. Greer said you are very interested, Mr. Galloway suggested I talk to you."

"We've admired your product down at the Sisters Pub just now," Jorgé said.

"Our whiskies are in the running for some prizes this year," Davie said. "Our sixteen-year-old whisky. And another special one. Called Distillery Pride." He blushed again. You'll never make a poker player, Alice thought.

"You worked on that one?" Jorgé asked.

"No, but I'm working on the next," he said. "First, let me just point out our four buildings. The big white one"—he pointed—"is our main building. Then you see our pagoda tower. Behind the pagoda tower, the long granite building is our warehouse, where we store our product. Then, in this smaller building just to your left here, you'll find our tasting room at the first door, and on beyond it at the second door are our offices. No worries, we'll definitely stop at the tasting room after the tour. So, before we walk over to the main building, let's talk about the malting process. Now you know what we make our whisky from, right?"

"Barley," said Jorgé.

"Right, barley malt, yeast, and water," said Davie. "Our water here's very soft. The Dorain's just a short stream, flowing right down off Ben Cathair. In fact, right where you're standing, you can see where it comes off Ben Cathair and runs under the Upper Road bridge and down onto our property."

The four obediently stared up the hill, toward the bridge over Upper Road, and into the folds of the shoulder of Ben Cathair. Alice could see part of the stream banks below the bridge, and she shivered, thinking of Angus.

Davie went on. "The Dorain only crosses a bit of peat up in the bog below the eastern shoulder, so our whisky has a perfume of peat but not the strong peatiness you find in the island malts, from Islay or Skye."

"But how can you protect your water source?" Birnbach wondered.

"Well, it's a short stream. And over the years, our owners negotiated agreements with landowners to protect it, or even bought the land along the banks. See upstream? Our owners bought the land you can see up from here, along the banks of the river. That way our source stays clean."

Birnbach again: "What if your river gets low?"

"We have a well here, too, just in case. Okay, let's go look at the malting room." He led them down the sidewalk and stopped at the stairs into the main building. "If we kept going down the walk, you'd see the Dorain up close; it runs past the main building, then under a sort of water gate under our wall and back down through the town." They followed him up the stairs, and Davie opened a door.

"We're unusual in that we produce all our own malt. We used to have to buy some." He opened a door. They peered into a vast space covered with grain in golden waves and hollows across the floor. Davie waved at two sturdy blue-shirted men, each with square-bladed scoop shovels, who were examining and slowly turning over the barley on the row closest to the four visitors. They wore paper booties over their shoes. Looking across the room, Alice saw a row of hooks with four blue shirts hanging neatly on hangers by the rear door. "We let the barley germinate. It gets hand-turned as we try to get it to germinate evenly. Then we must dry it gently to stop the germination and then grind it into grist."

Jorgé took a picture. "How long does it germinate?"

"Five days, more or less. Till the germ inside is about this size." He held up a laminated picture of a barley grain cut in half. "Then we feed it up to the mesh floor in the kiln, and dry it on the floor, toasting it very gently."

"That's under your pagoda tower?" asked Birnbach.

"Right you are."

"How do you feed it up to the mesh floor in the kiln?"

Davie pointed to an alcove on one wall. "Over there's the beginning of our conveyor. We put the barley on and then it goes out of the building and over to the kiln and back. We can control how fast it moves. That conveyor is much older than I am but it still works."

"Tell us about the kiln. Do you add any peat to the fire?" Jorgé asked.

"Ah, that's the stillman's secret! Whether, when, and how much! I'll let you wonder about that. And I don't yet know all the answers, either. So now"—he led them off down the hall into a high-ceilinged room with five huge wooden tubs—"now we go to the fermentation room. We've ground up the dried barley into grist."

"Grist for the mill," said Jorgé.

"Right. Then we add hot water and mix it in the mash tun with water. The grist has to be ground just right."

"What do you mean, just right?" Jorgé asked.

"Ground enough to let us get the most sugar out but not turn it into stodge, like lumpy hot cereal. We mix it up three times, at different temperatures, progressively higher, so we can get as much sugar out as we can. We call our resulting solution the 'wort.' We cool the wort down to about room temperature in one of your heated American houses and then we add about a kilogram of yeast for every three hundred liters of sugar solution. Or so." He grinned at them.

Jorgé smiled back. "Family recipe."

"Right!" Davie marched them past big wooden tubs with lids. Alice tiptoed so she could look over the edge at the rotating blades. Davie went on, "Now we store the wort for a few days in the washbacks until fermentation is done. The yeast is converting the sugar into alcohol and carbon dioxide."

"What kind of wood do you use?" Birnbach patted the tub.

"That comes from your side of the pond. Oregon pine. Now, after we get our 'wash' or 'beer' up to about eight or nine percent alcohol, it finally goes to the still."

"Wort, wash, washbacks, beer," muttered Alice. "Sounds like a spell."

Davie walked them around the corner into a sparkling whitewashed space with two copper pot stills. Big windows looked out on the walk in front of the main building.

A collective sigh at the size and beauty of the copper pot stills. They gazed up at the long stems rising toward the ceiling from the

47

elegantly curved pots below.

"This first one's our wash still. The wash comes out at about twenty-five percent alcohol. Then we call it the 'low wines' and send it on to the spirit still." He pointed at the second copper pot.

"How'd you pick the shape of these stills?" Birnbach asked.

"Ah, you've been doing your homework. Well, as you know, the really peaty malt whiskies, as from Islay, use squattier pot stills which retain more of the oils and fats and esters. The taller, slimmer stills make for a softer alcohol with less of the intense flavors. Our stills are, we think, in between, and just right. It's all part of stillman knowledge, though, to keep the stills in the ideal shape over the years. But also, the stillman has to be sure that the low wines are distilled just enough and not too much, so the essential flavors are not lost."

He pointed to a wooden chest with glass walls and brightly polished brass fittings, with pipes visible within.

"The spirit and sample safe?" asked Jorgé.

"Indeed. Full marks! Here's where the stillman checks quality, by measuring temperature, density, and alcohol."

"Not tasting?" asked Alice, thinking of vineyards.

"No. Forbidden. All done by measurement and timing. The stillman must let the foreshots go through to get rid of the methanol. Then the middle cut is what he wants. The last bit, the feints, go back into the spirit still."

"And you're learning all that, Davie?" asked Robbie. "The timing, the percentages?"

"I'm thinking about it night and day. Old Will's even taking me with him to the stillman's association meeting tomorrow in Edinburgh, to introduce me." His face glowed. "Ready to see the aging room?"

"What do you use?"

"Of course the casks must be oak, which is breathable. First we use the charred oak casks from America. But then we use casks that have been used to age Spanish sherry. And since we're limited on space, we use smaller casks that allow for more flavor absorption by the spirits each year."

"How long?"

"Our sixteen-year-old is very special. We've got a few treasures older than that."

Davie now headed them out of the main building and behind the pagoda tower toward the warehouse. Alice moved up to walk next to him.

"So how'd you learn you had a knack for this?" asked Alice.

"Oh, I'd headed up to Glasgow after school. Tried a few things, caught on at a new restaurant called Angie's that was getting lots of buzz. I was bussing tables. One day, two prep cooks called in sick; Angie hauled me into the kitchen and got me started. I had to make her famous pumpkin soup. She liked the seasoning. I told her I'd put a little more coriander seed in it and a little less ginger. She looked at me funny and then all of a sudden I had a job as sous-chef. She figured out my strength was adjusting seasoning. She got me to work with her on a couple of new recipes. She asked if I wanted to learn wines, and I said yes. But just about then I had a couple of problems, and she knew I . . . let's say I was having some trouble in Glasgow with some blokes and wanted to get out of the city and go back home. She thought I could do something at a distillery. And that's about when the word came around that Old Will at Uisge Dorain might be thinking of retiring."

"What kind of problems?" Alice could not resist.

"Oh, some guys . . . were trying to get me into some schemes I wanted no part of. It was safer to leave, I decided." He made a face. "I ran into some pretty bad guys in Glasgow. I'm glad to be back in Broadview."

"Any girlfriend yet?"

He blushed. Poor guy—I should quit this, Alice thought. "There's a girl . . . but I think she's got her sights set higher than the likes of me."

Turning away with relief he headed up the steps to the gray stone warehouse, with its no-nonsense steel doors. Davie unlocked them and ushered the group inside. Alice shivered. The building was eerily quiet; the gray stone walls exuded chill. Cold gray daylight from high clerestory windows lit the rows of wooden casks, stacked three high, each labeled with the distillery's name and the date.

"Sorry for the chill, but it's Scotland, cool year round, and that gives some consistency to our aging process," Davie said.

"I'm guessing this warehouse never gets too hot in the summer," Birnbach said. "We're still deciding whether we'll want to air-condition occasionally, in Coffee Creek. Or go underground."

"It will take us a while to evaluate how our local temperatures affect the whisky," Jorgé said. "I expect over here it never gets so hot that the angel's share gets too big."

"Drunken angels," Robbie said.

They walked deeper into the warehouse. Halfway along, the stone walls became concrete. "This is the new part of the warehouse," Davie said. "We needed more space so we could build up some older vintages." Davie frowned as he peered past the casks. "Excuse me." He strode past the last row of casks, flipping on the bank of lights at the rear. His footsteps stopped. Silence. She heard his feet move a few steps on the gritty concrete. The lights clicked off. He reappeared. "Sorry. Just checking. All's secure. Well, not much to see here but these casks. We do have room to grow—sales and reputation both."

He so loves this job, Alice thought. She hoped John and Ann would find their work as absorbing as Davie found his. Now he was moving them back out, glancing at his watch; he re-locked the warehouse door as they marched out into the sunny yard behind the pagoda tower. Alice sighed, grateful for the warmth.

"As I said, I won't be taking you up to the kiln. We're in the middle of a run right now. But if you look up, you can see the steam escaping. That's because we're drying the malted barley before it gets ground." All five stared up at the gray pagoda roof atop the white tower.

"Now may I take you to the tasting room for a wee taste of Uisge Dorain?"

"Absolutely!" said Birnbach.

Davie installed them at a counter in the tasting room. A willowy, pink-cheeked young woman, nametag reading "Fiona Smith," bustled in from the back room and set bottles and a pitcher of water on the counter. Alice recognized the pretty girl she'd seen at the pub last night, with the athletic six-footer. Davie introduced her, admiration in his eyes. "Fiona, as you see, is a big draw for the distillery. She works at the Soup Plate on Harbour Road but sometimes she stands in for her mother, Maggie, here in the tasting room when Maggie's got lots to do in the office."

A portly, sharp-eyed woman stuck her head out of the back room, then came out. Alice felt Robbie stiffen slightly, next to her. "I heard my name! Now that Fiona's here I'll just say hello and get back to the office." Maggie picked up her purse from beneath the counter and waved at everyone, then trotted out the tasting room door, fat calves flashing. Alice looked back at Davie, who was gazing at Fiona. Oh, yes, he was smitten. But Fiona? Fiona tossed her head, ignoring Davie, and fluttered her eyelashes at Jorgé and Birnbach as she set four glasses on the counter.

"We start with the twelve-year-old," Davie said. "If you like, you can add just a drop or two of water. This water's from the Dorain, so you'd be adding a drop of the same water we made this whisky with." Davie handed around the four small shot glasses. The four visitors inhaled.

Then Robbie laughed.

"What?" said Jorgé.

"Your faces look like you're studying for an examination!"

"Hey, we are! Plus, I'm trying to see how much peat Old Will added," Jorgé retorted.

They all sipped, staring thoughtfully into their glasses.

"Now, keep that taste in your mind, like, and try this. This is our sixteen-year-old." Davie handed around new glasses.

A few more cautious drops of water. Four sets of nostrils began sniffing.

"Mmm. Deeper," Alice said. "But almost sweeter. Yet not sweet. More aromatic?"

Robbie's phone buzzed. She looked at it. "Damn. I must go meet Inspector Walker, about Angus."

"Oh, it's so sad about that poor man!" Fiona spoke from behind her counter.

"Who?" said Davie.

"Angus McBride, of course! Do you not know he's dead? Found

51

in the river just here!"

"Who is Angus McBride?" asked Birnbach.

"The ghillie for—oh, thirty years!—for the Flemings, above town," said Fiona. "Found in the Dorain. Practically right here! Off the road and below the bridge above the distillery."

Alice caught a movement. Davie was clutching the counter, face white. She thought he might faint. "When?" he said.

"Yesterday afternoon," said Alice.

"They say he might have hit his head on a rock, but at the pub last night I also heard maybe someone hit him," said Fiona. "But no one could say who would have done it." She looked at Davie. "Davie, are you all right?"

"I'm just—I didn't know," he said. "I thought I saw some guys below the bridge late yesterday when I was here. In fact"—his eyes turned to Fiona—"three guys. But—not Angus!" He looked out the window up toward the bridge. "Sorry, I'd better go." He looked again at Fiona, started for the door, then came back and shook hands in a hasty way with Alice, Birnbach, and Jorgé. Alice's hand was damp when he finished. He hurried out the door, toward the main building.

Robbie looked at her watch. "I've got to go too."

Jorgé said, "I'll walk you down to talk to the inspector." Robbie lifted her chin, gave him a smile. They left.

Birnbach bought a bottle of the sixteen-year-old whisky for Gran's larder, and another to take home. "It's for research purposes, of course," he explained.

Alice and Birnbach walked back downhill toward the village, watching a fishing boat make its way back into the harbor. "Wonder what that's like," Birnbach said. "Depending on the sea every day."

"Our ancestors lived with it. Yours, crossing the Atlantic from Germany to Galveston. Mine, leaving Devon and Scotland and landing in Philadelphia. Can you imagine how you'd feel, after living in a leaky smelly wooden boat for weeks, finally to disembark in the New World? Finally to come up on deck, clutching your belongings, ready to stand on solid land and breathe the air of a new continent?"

"My German forebears boogied up from Galveston to the hill

country and never went to sea again, except for one who joined the navy and served under Nimitz in World War II. But these people, they still know the sea."

"The island nation. Hang on." Alice called Gran and asked, "Anything for us to pick up for tonight?"

"I've dug the new potatoes, and there's a lovely fish," Gran answered. "And plums. But can you bring some bread and some cream?"

"Why aren't we taking you all to dinner?" Birnbach asked once she had hung up.

"I want you to see Gran's farm, and she loves to cook. So we need to pick up the cream!"

She and Birnbach poked around the shops on the harborfront, visiting the two bakeries and choosing a loaf. At Broadview Village Stores (Alice loved this grandiose name for the small cluttered grocer's shop) she found a glass jar of clotted cream, and Birnbach picked out flowers and a bottle of wine for Gran. "Tell me about your Gran," he said.

"She's late seventies. She had two children, Jordie and Robbie. Robbie is seven years younger than Jordie. Gran's husband was an engineer, and helped build the Erskine Bridge over the Clyde, west of Glasgow. Gran's very smart, very intuitive. Great with kids. My two, John and Ann, adore her. They would never miss their weekly dinner with Gran while they were in Edinburgh. She understands their loves, their classes, their worries, and isn't eager to offer advice. She's seen a lot, both joy and sorrow. She's not easily rattled. Or maybe—"

"What?"

"Honestly, she's always been so stoic, it's almost as if she's already prepared, like she's got second sight. But surely not!"

"You're so rational, Alice."

"Hmm. Mostly. You don't want an irrational lawyer, do you?"

"Nope."

Chapter Seven

Still Alive

Birnbach asked Gran for an apron and moved easily into a spot at her counter. "What can I do?" Gran put him to work destemming parsley from her garden and chopping onions for the fish stuffing. When Alice slipped out of the kitchen, he and Gran were debating the best way to serve trout. Outside, Jorgé bent over in the garden, digging carrots and knocking the dirt off them.

Robbie sat on the stone wall that separated Gran's garden from the lower pasture, facing the ocean, still as a statue.

Alice climbed over and sat next to her. "How was it?"

"The inspector's not happy with my story about where I was before I met you for dinner last night."

"Gran said you just wanted a brisk walk. And why would the inspector be worried about you? You don't mean you're a suspect?"

"The inspector seems to think so."

"But why, Robbie?"

Long silence. Far below in the sunset, light waves curled toward Gran's cove. Sheep made their sheepish noises. A lark fluttered high up, singing, then fell out of the sky, swooping back down to the pasture.

"Oh, Alice. It's a long story. The inspector says a witness told him she—he said she, though he didn't mean to—she saw me having a fight with Angus a month ago, on the Upper Road. And it's true. I was. But to understand it?" She looked for a long moment at her sister-in-law. "Alice, I had a fling with Angus, right before I divorced. I wasn't very rational. The truth is I'd always been drawn to Angus; he taught me to ride, taught me to fish, taught me to shoot, taught me to track. I really had a crush on him. I was in heaven when Gran would bring us down here between school terms. But nothing happened, until the summer I was getting divorced. I don't know how to explain it. I was sad. My marriage was over. No kids. I felt like such a failure. I took a week off, came down here, ran into Angus. And I just made a dead set at him, Alice. But guess what. He was very willing. And then I got skittish, thinking this was like hooking up with my father. And he never went to university, he's a ghillie, I could just hear what the townspeople would say, what my

56

friends would say."

Alice thought, What is this? A drawing-room comedy? If you loved him, did it matter?

Robbie went on. "Okay, I'm not proud of this, Alice. I went back to Edinburgh, changed jobs, started teaching art, started painting again, got a grip. Angus came up to Edinburgh and I told him it wouldn't work. He said I'd made a fool of him, and that he wouldn't forget it. He turned and left. And I was furious—with him, with myself. I was so stubborn, and so was he. Then I heard he'd married Jennie."

"But what happened out on the road, then, this past month? Did you have a fight?"

"We did. I'd driven in from Edinburgh and needed a run, and there he was, on the Upper Road at the bridge. We walked down below the bridge a bit. He was in his 'do your duty' mode, telling me I needed to do my duty and be here with Gran, that she needed help. And that made me mad. And I told him to mind his own business. He said at least he knew his duty. And then we just stood there and I grabbed him and we kissed. Oh, Alice, that kiss." She stopped talking. Alice waited. Robbie took a deep breath. "You can't imagine what that kiss felt like. And I thought, I've missed all of this, I've missed Angus, because of my stupid pride. And when we separated after that kiss—we both knew we should not ever, should not—well, that was the last time I saw Angus."

"Does the inspector know this?"

"I'm guessing yes. You know how, depending where you stand, you can see Upper Road from the distillery grounds? That twit Maggie Smith, Fiona's mother—you met her today at the tasting room—was getting in her car in the employee parking lot. There's no love lost between me and Maggie Smith. I'm guessing from the inspector's questions that she saw us, though I don't know if she saw us kissing. But the inspector already had some sort of idea about me and Angus, because last winter someone made a crack about me at the pub one night—local boy, got drunk—and Angus went for him, outside in the street. The inspector intervened and talked to Angus, got him cooled off. But ever since, the inspector's given me some strange looks. And of course no one around here forgets anything, especially about Angus's high-handedness, so you know there's talk at the pub."

"Still, how can the fact that Angus defended you in a bar fight give you a motive for murder?"

Robbie said, "The inspector suggested I wouldn't want people in the village to know I'd had a fling with the ghillie."

Alice was unsure of her footing. What was life like in a Scottish village, where class mattered a bit more than in the States? Was the inspector's suggestion reasonable? "Well, Robbie? Would you want people to know?"

"I sure as hell wouldn't want his wife and child to know. How miserable that would be."

"But as long as it was only in the past . . . I guess it would still be embarrassing, but . . ."

Robbie said nothing.

"And did you tell the inspector you didn't even see Angus yesterday when you were running?"

"Yes."

"Does Gran know about this—this thing with Angus?"

"Not yet."

I'll bet she does, thought Alice.

"It's cold," remarked Robbie, closing the subject, standing up and climbing back over the wall. "Time for dinner." Alice watched her head uphill to collect Jorgé, who was triumphantly clutching his bunch of carrots.

Then Alice turned back to the downhill view of the sea. A lovely evening, chillier now, and still, with the cold smell of turf and the distant sough of the sea. Suddenly she felt such a wave of longing, for home, for children, for donkeys, for love—for what? For the ideal life that was never quite within reach? Jordie was long dead. Her beau, Kinsear, was somewhere in the south of England, but remarkably quiet. Her children were already halfway out the door; Ann was in Edinburgh, probably with her roommates or a boy, or singing somewhere, but not in a spot where her mother could hug her, smooth her hair. John was working in Austin, living with a buddy, driving out to check on the donkeys and (perhaps) party at the homestead. Never again would they sit in her lap, rapt while she read a story. Well, of course not. The illusion of safety, that's what she longed for: the illusion of the happy nuclear family, the perfect house, a tall wooden house in the trees, a gathering place where the screen door was always slamming as one more person came in, or went out—but of course, that perfect place only shimmered like a hologram in the past, where you tried to enter the picture but never could. And the hologram bore virtually no resemblance to her actual life.

Alice, get a grip! Of course children grow up. You did! And then we die. Even I will die, she told herself. But I'm not ready to believe that, and certainly the children will never die. Yet even Jordie, the benign bear, as she had seen him once in a vision she would never report to anyone, even the indestructible Jordie was dead, and of course Gran was older and frailer now, and Robbie had two new frown lines between her eyes. And Angus McBride, whom she might have seen down the hill in the swirling fog—well, he was dead. And she wished that the inspector had shown more interest in Alice's tale of the three men in the mist. Didn't that at least point to an explanation as to what happened to Angus McBride?

The sunset was gone; dew had fallen on her sweater. Shivering, she lifted her legs back over the cold granite wall and ran uphill and into the warmth of the kitchen, where Gran, sherry glass in her hand, was entertaining Birnbach with tales of the village. Jorgé and Robbie had commandeered the chairs by the kitchen fireplace and rearranged them, facing the fire, with their heads together in deep conversation. Alice poured herself a glass of Bordeaux and began to set the table.

* * * * *

After dinner, as of one accord, the four decided to return to the pub.

On the little stage by the bay window, a dark-haired, bright-faced young woman was tuning a violin. The young man with her, guitar slung around his back, was setting up a chalkboard sign:

SEAHEART! The room began to buzz with excitement.

"Oh, good!" exclaimed Robbie. "I hoped you'd hear them!" Seaheart, she said, were local favorites. "Just wait until you hear her fiddle."

And at that moment the young man said "Culum's Reel" into the mike, and the fiddler, petite and powerful, drew down her bow and fiddled until the room was made of music. Alice closed her eyes, almost inhaling the racing soprano notes of the violin, and then heard the guitar begin its counterpoint.

"Wow," whispered Jorgé. Alice nodded, watching Neil Gage, by the bar, watch Seaheart. Well, her clients and Neil shared a profession, didn't they? Managing the Sisters, and the Beer Barn. Offering local food, local music. Tying the community together. The musicians played until Alice thought their hands must ache. She smiled inside, reveling in the Scottishness of it all. Oh, the joy of music, and particularly harmony, and more particularly the deft little vocal ornaments the Scots and Irish added to their favorite old songs, and most particularly the unselfconscious way their audiences pitched in, singing softly the songs they all knew by heart.

"Here's one for all of you lovers," said the young man. "Of course it's our own Robbie Burns. But she"—and he nodded at the fiddler—"she wrote the tune." The fiddler led the way, and the young man sang, eyes closed, face lifted:

Lang hae we parted been, Lassie, my dearie,
Now we are met again, Lassie, lie near me.

Alice closed her eyes, deeply moved by the deepest, barest chords of human longing, the age-old yearning for love. The candid voices were twining now:

Near me, near me, Lassie, lie near me;
Lang has thou lien thy lane, Lassie, lie near me . . .

Alice composed her face, not ever wishing all to see her inmost self. But yes, long had she "lien thy lane" and she wondered if Kinsear felt the same.

Then, after a pause, the young man strummed for a moment, looked up and said, "This one's for our Angus, and his Jennie," and began picking out the first notes of "Wild Mountain Thyme." By the end of the introduction, when he lifted his tenor voice and sang, many in the pub were humming, and by the time he reached the refrain, the entire room was singing: "And we'll all go together, to pull wild mountain thyme, all around the purple heather, will ye go, lassie, go?" Robbie, Alice perceived with pleasure, was singing a lovely harmony a third up from the melody line. Gran would have loved the elegy for Angus. When the music stopped, no one spoke for several seconds. Robbie's eyes had a faraway look.

Then her own heart skipped a surprised beat. A dark-haired young man was, unmistakably, lifting a glass to her from a table on the far side of the room. After a moment Alice nudged Robbie. "Don't look, but who's the dark-haired guy by himself on the other side of the room?" After a moment Robbie surveyed the pub and looked back at her sister-in-law. "John Dougal. Local salmon smoker. I've heard he used to be sweet on—someone from around here. Watch out, Alice. The last few years, he's Georgie Porgie."

"Kiss the girls and make them cry?"

"That seems to be his modus operandi. I always liked him, but he got an edge on him after things didn't work out."

They stayed in their seats, with another round from the bar, until almost closing time. Then Neil Gage caught Robbie's eye and motioned her over. They talked for a moment. When she returned to the table, Alice saw lines of—anxiety? anger? both?—in her face. Finally Robbie said, "Neil heard that Angus was still alive when he was dumped in the river."

Jorgé and Birnbach overheard. "You mean he was left for dead? And died in the river?" Birnbach grimaced. "Sounds an awful lot like murder."

Alice said, "I expect they're still trying to find out what happened." No need to frighten her clients, no need to mention the nocturnal invasions of Gran's farm or her own interrupted vision of the three men below the stone circle of the Sisters. She and Robbie left the two men to their rooms at the pub and headed home.

🐎 🐎

Chapter Eight

Make
a Clean
Sweep

That night something woke her. Her narrow bed looked out to the pasture and the sheepfold. Had she felt a flash of light? She had. Two men stood partly illuminated in the sheepfold. One had dropped a lantern, which shone on their legs. She caught a glimpse of Sue, ears back, crouching, snarling. Then the light went out.

Furious, Alice jumped up, scuffled into her shoes, threw her sweater over her nightgown, and raced for the kitchen. She heard Queenie behind her, scrabbling down the stairs from Robbie's room. At the kitchen door she grabbed Gran's broom and slipped out onto the flagstone path, silently closing the door. Now what? She crept closer, broom aloft. "Hey!" she yelled. "What the hell are you doing? Come out!"

Flurry. The thumping feet of two men, one taller and one broader, racing toward her, one waving a spade, the other carrying an awkward long device with a disc at the end. Starlight reflected off the metal. Alice regretted her choice of a broom. She dodged wildly behind the clothesline pole, screaming "Robbie!"

Horrible strangled cry as the taller man's neck struck Gran's clothesline. He bounced backward and fell to the ground, writhing. The other man yelled "Get up!" and yanked at his arm and kicked at Sue, who snapped and lunged. A light popped on inside. Robbie charged out the back door, Queenie barking at her heels, and turned her flashlight on the fleeing men.

"What the hell, Alice?"

"They were in the sheepfold, with a flashlight. Woke me up." Alice blew out a big breath, glad to see her sister-in-law.

"You were going to, what, make a clean sweep of it? With that?" Robbie nodded at the broom Alice still clutched. Then they heard an engine start down by the gate on the drive.

"Let's get them!" Robbie raced to the shed for her little Prius.

Alice tossed the broom toward the door and ran after her. She saw brake lights go on downhill, but no headlights. "There they are! They're running dark, no lights."

"They'll have to show their brake lights. We'll make 'em," Robbie said. "Hang on!"

Alice later said that the car chase in *Skyfall* paled in comparison to Robbie's death-defying race along the harbor and over the headland on the cliff highway, chasing occasional red flickers of brake lights. They lost the lights in Whithorn and gained a determined constable, who pulled them over outside Newton Stewart. "Driving to the public danger!" he bellowed, glaring at Robbie, still in her pajamas, and Alice in her sweater and nightgown.

"We were chasing those two burglars!" Robbie said. Trespassers!"

"So you say."

But he let them go with a warning to turn the car around and go straight home to bed.

Robbie grinned at him as he put his notepad away. "Damn, that was fun!"

"I'm sure. However. Did you not see their license plate, these so-called burglars?"

"Maybe the last digit is zero," said Alice. "Pretty sure, but I don't have my lenses on. And it was a blue van, not overly big."

"You didn't know these two men?"

"No," said Robbie.

"But one—one ran into the clothesline and might have some bruises on his throat. Or a cut," Alice added.

"I'll make a note of it. Go along home now." The constable watched, hands on hips, while Robbie turned the Prius around.

* * * * *

"So the tenant's marauders were real," Robbie commented.

"Yup. Poor man. He must have dreaded nightfall after their first incursion, waiting for strangers to come poking around with flashlights."

"And anything else?"

They looked at each other. What had the men carried?

"One had a spade," Alice said.

"I think the other had a metal detector," Robbie said.

"I'll bet you're right." What she'd seen in the mist wasn't a Weed Eater, then. "So, they're nighthawkers."

It was nearly four, and the high-latitude dawn was turning the world from dark to gray. The two women prowled the sheepfold together. "They were digging here." Robbie pointed to the loose clods of earth at the inside corner nearest the house.

"But they left empty-handed," Alice said. "Thanks to my lightning-swift response."

"Hey, next time?" said Robbie. "Call me before you race out the door. Together we're invincible. We'll tie them up with the clothesline."

Alice nodded, smiling. But she was still angry: the temerity of these trespassers, thinking they could operate with impunity outside her bedroom window!

* * * * *

On Tuesday morning after the late-night chase, Alice stood by the bay window in the empty kitchen, looking down toward the sea. Gray mist hovered over the copse below the pasture. Gran, in her hooded rain jacket, appeared from the copse and lifted her head, turning back her hood. Then she started slowly uphill through the flock. The sheep moved a few feet this way or that as she passed through.

Gran looked so small to Alice, plodding through the pasture, angling toward the sheepfold. She glanced at it, then walked on by, heading for the three stone steps above it. Alice had never paid particular attention to the steps, which didn't seem to go anywhere. How old were they, anyway? Gran stopped on the first step. She looked down, appeared to take a breath, took another step up, stopped again.

What was wrong?

Alice jumped up, dropped her book in the chair, snatched her jacket off the hook, and trotted out the back door. Gran heard the door and turned toward her.

"I was just thinking of a little walk," Alice said as she neared Gran. But what she thought was, You look so old and small and tired and it scares me. "Want to stroll down the road a bit?"

Gran looked up, eyes crinkled. "Ha. You caught me. Looking decrepit."

"You didn't look as sprightly as usual, Gran."

"I wasn't feeling sprightly." Gran took a deep breath. Alice did too, inhaling the odd wet coconut perfume of gorse—the tropical sunscreen smell so at odds with heather and scudding clouds—mixed with the smells of sheep and mud and wet grass.

"What's up, Gran? It's about Angus? Or this place?"

"The latter. I feel guilty. I haven't told you."

"What?" Alice pulled open the heavy wooden farm gate and they picked their way across the cattle guard onto the gravel drive down to the road.

"About people pestering me to sell the farm."

"Who?"

"A sales agent for the Flemings. He keeps calling."

"How long has he been after you?"

"He first called me last October and said he had a client who wanted to buy my farm. He said the buyer was interested in the Fleming property; he wanted a Scottish place with a hunting lodge. But he wanted the land to run all the way to the sea, so he also wanted my farm. I said no, no, I'm not interested. Then he said the sale would protect jobs for people like Angus McBride. Yes, he mentioned Angus! And then he said that under a proposed land reform bill I might find the village organizing to buy me out for a more sustainable development, whatever that is. I got the feeling the agent hoped to put together a package that would make the whole deal more profitable for the Flemings. He drove down here but I refused to see him. He actually went to the pub and told Neil Gage I needed to sell. I heard that from Neil, of course. By then I was beyond furious. The man finally quit calling for a while. Then in June, there he was again on the phone! He called me when I was in the hospital."

Alice felt her blood pressure rising at the thought of the man harassing Gran in the hospital.

Gran went on. "He said the Flemings were really, really anxious to sell, but the buyer wouldn't buy without my land too. He said that with Robert Fleming so ill—this was before he died—Betty Fleming would feel better knowing she'd realize some income from the sale." Gran's voice changed. "That did not sound like Betty to me. Betty doesn't want to sell but she is quite ill. Neil Gage said he'd heard it's Samantha who wants the money. But I'm told it's not just Samantha—Robert's children and grandchildren want the money and don't give a fig about their family's land. Their three children almost never come up. But it's Samantha who's especially pushing them all to sell now."

"How'd you find that out?"

"Neil. At the Sisters." Gran fiddled with her bracelet. "He told me about this just before I went in for my heart operation. He mentioned that the agent came in one day looking harassed and said that the Fleming daughter-in-law was after him again to get the deal done, that the sisters and brother had apparently let her run the show, and she was making him dread the ring on his mobile. But then, Neil said, the agent got a bit confidential, leaned on the bar and started asking about my operation. Neil didn't approve, and when he asked the agent why he would ask such questions, the agent said, 'Surely with a dickey heart she won't want or be able to keep up the farm.'"

"What did Neil do?"

"He told the agent that he doubted anything would make me sell if I truly felt like keeping the place. He said I was born a Hardie, and Hardies were notoriously tough. Of course I liked that. But imagine the nerve, Alice, asking about my operation!"

Bad manners—like Samantha's bad manners in the Great Fishing Dispute. Alice thought Gran should worry less about a pushy agent with bad manners than about what had been happening at her farm. Bad manners were one thing; trespassing metal detectorists were another.

"I agree, Gran. You certainly don't have to fix life for the Flemings. If you don't want to sell, don't sell! And if you wish, we can think about a plan to make this work for your heirs."

Gran nodded. "The agent called again yesterday. He's got another potential buyer. He said the Flemings were really, really anxious to sell, and this buyer's Chinese, from Shanghai, but has business in London and lives there much of the year. Very posh, has homes in

Vancouver and Hong Kong. He wants a Scottish place to bring his clients. He likes the old lodge at the Fleming property. A Mr. Zhou."

"Does this man want to buy the Fleming property regardless? With or without yours?"

"The agent was vague on that."

"Well, Gran, do you want to sell?"

"No!"

"Never? Not even for a good offer?"

"This is Hardie land. I've told him I've no interest in selling."

"Okay."

"The thing is, though—" Gran stopped, pulling on a gorse branch, sniffing the yellow blossoms. "Who's going to take care of it when I'm gone?"

"Robbie?"

"I want Robbie to have it, if she wants. And if John and Ann are interested, I wanted them to have it, too. But what if they can't afford to keep it up?"

"Wouldn't be your worry, if you pass it on."

"I'm fond of this silly village. I wish there were some way the land could be useful to Broadview, and enjoyed by Robbie and John and Ann, but not saddle them with responsibilities they don't want."

"You can make it work."

"Right," Gran said. "But the thing is, really, I'm . . ." She turned and took Alice's arm.

"You're scared," Alice said, looking at Gran's face.

"I'm scared."

And that wouldn't do. It wouldn't do at all. Obviously there was more going on than a persistent agent. "Gran, let's go sit down."

So they walked back to the house to make tea. Gran sat at the table while Alice boiled water and found the requisite tea tray. Alice had learned early that in Scotland you could not just bring naked cups and saucers to the table; proper tea required a tea tray with all the accoutrements.

"Okay. What's up?"

Gran stirred her tea. "There've been three incidents, I guess you'd call them. The first was at the children's Halloween party at the church last fall, on All Hallows' Eve. That's Samhain, you know, the old festival. I'm always in charge of 'dookin' for apples,' which the children love the most. They get very wet. Anyway, the party was over and we were cleaning up. I was outside in the yard, getting ready to dump the water out of the tub. It was already dark, with just the church porch lights on. I bent over to grab the tub by its handles and suddenly someone shoved my face down in the water—I couldn't breathe, was trying to get my head back up but couldn't—and I heard a voice—a man—say, 'You'd better sell your place, old lady, or you'll be held down till you drown.' Then he pushed my head down all the way, over my head, and then suddenly let me up."

"Good God, Gran, who was it?"

"Of course I didn't see. He was gone. Whoever it was must have just slipped through the gate into the graveyard. I was sopping wet, half drowned, scared to death. I'd lost my glasses in the tub and had to grope around under the apples to find them. And I was freezing—the children had got me wet, they splash so, and the air was quite nippy."

"Did anyone else see?"

Gran shook her head. "It sounds silly and unreal now. I felt humiliated. Hair sopping wet, coat and dress wet to my armpits. I got my breath back, and started to get mad. I wiped off my glasses. I dumped out the water and lugged the tub and apples back to the door of the church hall. Then I stuck my head in and called Walter—you know, our pastor. He can be a bit dim. He looked at my wet head and said, 'Kathy, were you dookin' too?' I said 'No, did you see any strangers out there?' and he said, 'No, all members, but it was such a nice group, wasn't it? So delightful, all the children!' No help from him on the who-did-it score."

"Were his cuffs wet?"

Gran smiled appreciatively at Alice. "I do love you, Alice. You would even suspect my pastor. No, he was quite dry."

"Did you tell him what had happened?"

"No. I don't know why—I guess because he was inside with other people still there and I didn't want to alarm anyone."

Alice put the kettle back on, with a shiver of fear as she thought of Gran, held down in a tub of water, helpless. "Did you notice anything about the man? Did you grab at his hands, notice what he was wearing?"

"Yes . . . ," Gran said, "yes, I did try to grab hold of his hands, but they were up on my shoulders. He was wearing a tweed jacket, I think, with buttons on the cuff. You know tweed has a different feel, and I think I felt tweed when I tried to loosen his grip, but then he shoved my head way in."

What a bastard. But interesting, that he was wearing a tweed jacket. Which suggested— "What about his voice? His accent?"

"Well. Good question. He only said that one thing, in a low, hard voice. But he said it as if he was trying to sound classless. I think the 'old lady' sounded a bit too posh, like he was trying not to sound as posh as perhaps he was."

"Age?"

"I could not tell. But I can tell you one thing, Alice: he was wearing Hammam Bouquet. That's Penhaligon's. I know every one of their scents. Personally, I find that one a bit over the top, but de gustibus . . ." Gran's ability to discern scents was a family byword. Jordie had told Alice that when he was sneaking in late to their Edinburgh house, Gran could stand at the top of the stairs and tell where he'd been, "and, worse, what I'd been doing."

"And then," Gran said, "I made it to my car, drove down Upper Road, and was just turning left down Hardie Road toward the farm when a big car came up fast behind me and hit me hard on the left bumper."

"Hit your Defender?"

"Yes. The road is narrow up there at the curve. Whoever it was gave me such a blow that the car went partway off the road to the right. I managed not to skid off into the glen."

Alice squeezed her eyes shut. The edge of the glen was quite close to the road at that corner.

"Did you see who hit you?"

"No. Whoever it was just whizzed past me. It was a big SUV, bigger than mine. With the headlights off. And it was very dark, that night. Typical for All Hallows!"

"Gran, that was almost a year ago! You didn't tell us!"

"What was there to tell?"

Alice shook her head. Someone had held her head underwater in the churchyard, someone had tried to run her off the road, and her mother-in-law had maintained a stiff upper lip and said not a word.

"Also it made me feel like a scared old lady. Why didn't I get back on the road and follow that bastard and smash his car?"

"I know just what you mean, Gran." And she did, thinking of hiding in the rocks from Blocky Man. "I'll be right back. I just want to see what happened to the poor Defender."

Alice went out the kitchen door and walked downhill to the shed. The Defender's left rear bore a significant dent. Gran must have nearly gone airborne. The body paint was chipped and the dent was beginning to rust. Was there a bit of gray paint too? She couldn't tell. She returned to the kitchen.

"That's two," said Alice. "What's the third?"

"Alice. I feel so guilty. I should have told you yesterday."

"So tell me."

"The phone rang when you were touring the distillery. I had to say hello twice. Then someone said, 'You'd better sell the farm fast if you want your little Texas lawyer to make it home.'"

Alice bristled. Well. So who knew she was here? Anyone who'd been at the pub Sunday night, or at the distillery on Monday . . . "Was it the same voice as the man who held you down in the water?"

"I don't think so. The voice was muffled but rattled, like a piece of paper was over the phone."

"And you haven't mentioned any of this sell-the-farm stuff—the disgusting agent, the dookin' party, the dent on the Defender—because?"

"I don't want to sell. But I don't know how to deal with these people. That's not true: I can deal with the Flemings and their realtor any day. But invisible people? It's like boxing with ghosts."

Lord, thought Alice. At least the third threat's against me instead of Robbie or John and Ann. Because I am going to fix this mess. But what did a telephone threat about selling the place have to do with the men prowling around Gran's farm? Maybe that was a separate problem. On the other hand, surely to goodness the men in the mist were the same ones she had surprised in the sheepfold. But who could tell her the connection? No one in town claimed even to have seen them.

Except Gran's tenant?

"Gran, the deposit check for your tenant? Did you mail it?"

"I've written it with a note saying how sorry I am for his inconvenience. It's on the hall table waiting for the mail."

"I'm delivering it personally for you. Today."

Gran tilted her head, considering Alice. "Ah. You're going to find out what's going on here, aren't you. You've got the bit between your teeth."

Alice had to laugh. It was true, at least figuratively. But she had to ask again: "Gran, really, don't you ever want to sell? Honestly, don't you ever think you might want someone else to have all the responsibility?" Alice's clients sometimes admitted they had felt huge relief when they shed responsibility for family land, however beloved.

"No! My parents always said, 'Never sell the farm, we bought it too dear!'"

"What does that mean, bought it too dear?"

"My grandfather took out a loan, back before World War I. He and others in town borrowed money from the Flemings to build the stone pier at the harbor. They hoped it would become the ferry port for the islands, and for Ireland. Then after the war, when steel and boatbuilding collapsed, so did shipping. That left the pier, and building, practically empty. I wasn't yet born, so this is just a long-ago story to me, but my parents pitched in and worked their fingers to the bone. The Flemings were going to take the farm as well as my parents' share of the pier and the building, but somehow my parents and grandparents scraped together enough at the last minute to save the farm. And then my grandfather left the farm to my parents, 'the Hardie farm and buildings, the Hardie and its waters, the land, the house, and all that lies therein.' That's what the old will says. I've got a copy of it here in the house. And my parents left it to me the same way. 'The land, the house, and all that lies therein.'"

Funny drafting language, Alice thought. But what did she know about Scottish property law? Nada.

"No stories about how exactly they paid it off?"

"No. Mum just shook her head and said, 'Never let it go, Kathy.'" She smiled. "Mum would sometimes leave the garden, or the clothesline, and just stand by that sheepfold, looking down the headland toward the cove. I asked her once what she was looking at. She said, 'This place is part of my bones. My blood, my bones.' You remember my father was killed in an automobile accident? I was just married."

Alice nodded.

"After he died, the Flemings again asked Mum to sell the farm. Mum said no, she wouldn't think of it. She told me later that they were so poor after paying off the loan they lived in the kitchen, because they couldn't afford coal for the big hall fireplace—I don't remember ever seeing a fire in there, come to think of it. Too wasteful, probably. They only burned coal in the kitchen fireplace."

"Wouldn't it be fun to see a big yule fire, and put the Christmas tree in the hall?"

"It would! But the tree has always been in the kitchen. All my life!"

Odd, but true, thought Alice. She and Jordie had brought the kids for Christmas several times, and indeed the tree had always been in the kitchen.

Chapter Nine

Arthur's Heir

By midmorning Tuesday Robbie had loaded Birnbach and Jorgé into her car and was hauling them north to visit the Springbank, Auchentoshan, and Glengoyne distilleries. "That'll be fun for me," she'd told Alice, "and maybe you'll solve the whole mess while we're gone and figure out who killed Angus. Frankly, I'd like the inspector to quit looking askew at me. Or do I mean askance? Either way, I hate it."

Alice was relieved, not least because Robbie was driving, but also because she wanted her clients away from Broadview, however delightful they were. She intensely disliked having them anywhere near, much less involved, entangled, embroiled in a murder, particularly one potentially connected to her family. Plus, their absence would let her tackle the Difficult Tenant, as she now called him: she planned to find out who the marauders were, tie them up with a bow, and present them to the inspector, not just as trespassers but as perhaps responsible for Angus's death. She wanted Gran's face free of worry. She could not stay in Scotland forever . . . Silla was sending her the docket, emailing documents for Alice to review, reminding her of responsibilities to clients. She had just over a week to figure this out and catch the plane home. Time to act.

* * * * *

Clyde Pendennis Creighton answered his phone. Alice announced that she was heading his way, with Gran's check. "Shall I meet you at your place in Leith?"

"Can't you just mail it, for goodness' sake?" High, cranky voice, irritated.

"Oh, it's no bother, I'm already on my way. Your place in about two hours?"

"I am in the midst of writing my next novel, you know."

"Won't take long. Later, then." She hung up on his further protest. Then she called Ann. "Tea? Dinner?"

Ann was available.

Alice drove out of the farm with relief. At last she had a plan. She'd extract all available information from the Difficult Tenant and, as a bonus, check on her precious Ann. She never forgot her mother's comment about child-rearing when Alice confessed late-night worries after John and Ann hit their teens: "It's like Willie Nelson's song, honey; you know, 'You Were Always on My Mind.'" She headed out Harbour Road, climbed over the eastern headland, maneuvered the roundabouts in Newton Stewart and caught the A75 into Dumfries, then drove north to the A74, which led to the M8 into Edinburgh. She took the ring road, doubled back west along the water, and finally found herself in Leith, with its docks on the Firth of Forth.

From past visits Alice could navigate Ann's territory near Holyrood Palace, but Leith was terra incognita for her. Hands white-knuckled on the steering wheel, thanking the gods for public parking, she stashed the car in a carpark off Carpet Lane. Creighton's flat was in a pleasant stone building at the end of the street. So, not a starving artist. She'd checked him out online. Amazon showed a novel about five years old, with three polite reviews by readers. She'd read snippets online. The plot suggested self-revelation: a modern man, scholarly, sensitive, steeped in medieval history, concludes that he is actually King Arthur's descendant, but debates how to reveal this crucial knowledge to the world. Alice herself doubted that this character deserved Arthur's mantle: in the snippets she read, he came across as fussy and egocentric, unlikely to undertake knightly quests of benefit to any but himself. And wasn't that the author, really? Oh, Alice, she chided herself. You're judging Creighton before you even meet him. After all, the poor man paid rent for a refuge, and then . . .

She rang the buzzer on the stone porch. A wait. "Yes?"

"Alice Greer. Here with a delivery from Mrs. Kathy Greer." Another delay. The door buzzed and she pushed it hard before he could change his mind.

Well, so much for expectations. Clyde Pendennis Creighton was tall, dark haired, and conventionally handsome, though his mouth seemed too small. He looked down his nose at Alice over red reading glasses. Italian and spendy, Alice thought. He held out his hand for the check. Alice ignored the hand and sailed into the room, which was carefully furnished in mid-century modern.

"What a lovely view!"

"Yes, and as you see, I'm working." He gestured toward his teak desk.

"But I do want to speak to you about your experience in Broadview. May I sit down?" She did.

An upward glance of exasperation. The artist, always beset by the demands of the hoi polloi. He leaned on the mantel. "Yes?"

"Well, of course Mrs. Greer was quite concerned. She spent much thought on making the cottage comfortable."

"The cottage was adequate."

"And of course she wants people free to enjoy the property, the uplands, the glen, the views off the headland."

"The views are . . . pleasant."

"And she was delighted to have the author of *Arthur Redivivus* choose her cottage. She told me she is anxious to learn when your new book will be out. And will the main character return?"

He preened a bit, adjusting the red spectacles. "Yes, I can tell you that he will."

"So you can understand that she was very distressed to hear of your experience. She has written you a note saying how sorry she is that your writing was disturbed." Alice lifted the pink envelope partly out of her pocket, then slid it back in.

He nodded, focused on her pocket. "Very kind."

"And of course she wants to get to the bottom of this. She's very disturbed to hear the property was—what? Invaded?"

He took his elbow off the mantel and stood straight up. "Exactly! I woke in the night to hear voices! I pulled back the curtains to see two men clanking around near that whatever-it-is, sheep pen. They'd set a lantern on the ground."

"What did they look like?"

"One big, with a light coat. The other—I can't remember details. He was burly, with a dark jacket."

"How many times were those men at Gran's—Mrs. Greer's farm?"

"Oh, at least three times! The first time, it was around eleven at night. The moon was bright and I couldn't sleep. I heard their car, then I saw them walking down toward the coast. They were carrying something over their shoulders. I thought maybe they were going fishing at the cove. So I went back to bed. I just assumed Mrs. Greer would have let them come. That was the first. Then the next time was two nights before I left. At two a.m. I woke up, very suddenly. I'm sure you know how alarming that is. I looked out the window and there they were, going round and round the sheep pen, and then through it, with shovels or metal detection devices. At least I think that's what they had."

"You didn't think she'd permit that, did you?"

"Well, what did I know? Besides, I didn't like their looks. And something interrupted them and they left. I think they got a message on the phone, saw one looking at it anyway."

"You have good eyes."

"I do." He took off the red glasses, gave them a little wave. "These are only for close work."

"Ah," said Alice. "And quite unusual."

He smirked.

"Was it always the same two men, when you saw them?"

"I think so."

"And you must be very sensitive to voices. What kind of men were they? Could you tell where they were from?"

"Scots, but . . ."

"Educated?"

He snorted. "Very coarse language. Taking pleasure in exaggerating their accents, do you know what I mean?"

She nodded. "Could you hear anything they said?"

"Yes. The window was open, of course. I have to have fresh air. It was a very still night, the last night they came. And so I could hear quite well when they spoke. The tall one stopped to smoke—disgusting, I could smell the odor instantly—and the other one said, 'Let's get on with this. We've got to find the stuff before he gets back.' And the tall one said, 'But will he know?' And the other one said, 'If we find it, we'll leave. Tonight. And go where that bastard won't find us.' 'Hope you got a good idea on where that might be?' The other one just grunted. And then they were digging again."

"You have the writer's ear for dialogue." Honestly, Alice told herself, you are engaging in deplorable flattery. "You say the blocky one said, 'Before he gets back.' Definitely 'he,' not 'she,' then?"

"Definitely 'he.'"

"Didn't they know someone was staying at the farm?"

"Perhaps not. Mrs. Greer was gone, of course. The main house was dark. She'd said I could put my car in the shed so it wouldn't get dusty. Of course I'd closed the shed door."

Alice scanned the flat. No dust. Not even stray dust motes in the air. In contrast to the mild disorder he'd left at the tenant cottage, here order reigned: no half-read newspaper, no coffee cup on the table, no magazines scattered by the couch. Books stood stiffly in the bookcases. He'd lined up his pencils on the desk. An old British Empire typewriter, black paint gleaming, sat on the desk, no paper on the roller. What sort of vision did Clyde Pendennis Creighton present? Breton red pants, white linen shirt, impeccable Italian loafers—perfection itself. And the red spectacles. But no paper in the typewriter. Odd that this man wanted to write on a real farm, with its odorous history of sheep. "What drew you to the country, Mr. Creighton? Here you are in Leith, with galleries and shops and cafés at your doorstep. Why come to a rural cottage with sheep for company?"

"I wanted a bit of landscape for the book," he said. "Part of it takes place on the coast. I'd hoped a small village would offer beauty and peace. That was not the case."

"So, the third night you saw them, you got fed up? The next morning you wrote your note to Mrs. Greer and dropped it at the pub?"

He lifted his head high. "I did."

"But why? They didn't scare you the first two nights, did they?"

He snorted. "Maybe you're used to renting property that has been presented as a peaceful retreat for writing, and then finding yourself waking at all hours to find strange men stalking the property, but I am not. And the third time I didn't like their language. 'Fookin' this' and 'fookin' that' and some vicious-sounding threats. Limited vocabulary, but violent. I didn't like the tone."

"Threatening? You didn't want to meet them at, say, the pub."

"Too right."

"But had you seen them in town, at all?"

"No. That is—I did see them, the morning I left. They were on Harbour Road, coming out of the grocery store. They were waiting to cross to the seafront."

"What did you do when you saw them?"

He actually blushed. "I turned off Harbour Road and went up-hill, toward the church, and then circled back down. When I got back they were gone and I headed straight back to Leith. I'll have to say, I didn't particularly want them to see me. Now, if you don't mind, I'd like to get back to my manuscript." He glanced at his desk.

"You still use a typewriter, I see."

"Um, no. Actually, I write in longhand. Occasionally I use the typewriter for letters. It's antique, of course."

So, just another accessory. Alice stood up, pulling the pink envelope from her pocket. "I wonder if you saw, when you were leaving Broadview, where those men went from the grocery store. You didn't see them anywhere else, either in town or out on the road?"

"I did not."

"Thank you for letting me know all this. Mrs. Greer will be very grateful that you spent the time. She wants to keep the farm a peaceful retreat. For herself, too, of course."

He clearly hadn't given thought to the alarm an owner would also feel. "Oh, of course. And, um, I promise not to put a bad review online. The cottage is quite comfortable. And those butter things she makes . . ."

"The butteries?"

"Yes. With the homemade jam. She'd left me some. Quite nice, actually."

Alice delivered the envelope, thanked him again, and marched out the door, his barely suppressed sigh of relief fading behind her. Arthur's heir, returning to his solitary desk, having graciously suffered the uncouth, importunate commoner. But her thoughts churned: Who was "he"? Where was "he" coming "back" to? Edinburgh? Broadview? And what was the "stuff"?

C h a p t e r   T e n

"Great Times"

till a few hours before Ann could leave the shop and join her. Plenty of time.

She moved the car closer to Ann's, in a grocery parking lot north of Holyroodhouse, and headed back up the Royal Mile and down to Princes Street. She was on a mission—and there it was—Penhaligon's. Alice sidled in, admiring the beautiful bottles, listening to a graceful salesman divine a customer's preferences, murmuring interrogatively, "Orris . . . bergamot . . . leather . . . ?" She found the men's testers. She sniffed. Gran was right; this was a memorable fragrance. Alice considered herself picky (who wasn't?) about scents. On Kinsear she preferred his fragrance from the shop on Boulevard Saint-Germain: basil, bay, elegant but not cloying, not loud. She told a hovering salesman what she wanted and left with a refill for Ann and a tiny sample of Hammam Bouquet. "A true classic, madam," said the salesman, handing over the small package. "If we can be of further help . . ."

Perfume, single malt, wine. So hard to convey a specific fragrance and its olfactory impact on the brain. Just look at wine: "jammy" or "flinty," with a nose of "leather" or "fig" or something else. The effort to describe went on and on but still could not replicate the experience itself, the feel on the tongue, the joy expressed by the nasal passages, the brain's quick calculation and assessment.

She strode along in the slanting sun of late August, enjoying the bustle. No, she didn't need any sweaters or kilts, nor did she need more cashmere gloves, not even purple ones. She turned into the National Museum of Scotland, dutifully checked her bag after a pointed stare from the clerk, and headed straight for the Scottish history and archeology displays, curious about what might draw a trespassing detectorist to Hardie Farm. And she remembered once seeing stunning gold ornaments here. EARLY PEOPLE, read a sign. She examined the diorama of Early People, with little figures fishing, hunting, celebrating around a fire. "Great times!" said the explanatory card. "Great times!" Alice felt that "great times" should involve hot baths, preferably bubbled. She stared at the miniature shelters. No bathtub included. How warm were Early People in the winter? How long were the nights, without books? Was there music, and the singing of long sagas?

Okay. On to her next goal: the gold torcs. And there they were, drawing her near, shimmering in their display case, with the sheer beauty of handworked gold. Her favorites were the twisted ribbon torcs, neck ornaments whose design seemed so modern, so spare, so perfect. These torcs were simply a wide, flat ribbon of gold, twisted into a spiral, bright and shadowy, with an elegantly simple catch at the nape of the neck. Alice's face drew nearer and nearer to the display. She was imagining the gold spiral around her own neck. She wanted to put it on, to feel it around her throat. To look in a mirror and be made—powerful. Bracelets, rings, and earrings felt fun, felt decorative. But the gold torc held magic. Pure gold, warm, never tarnishing. Her nose was almost on the case. She looked suddenly at her own eyes in the glass. Lust for gold. She tore herself away from the ribbon torcs and examined the more ornate braided gold torc, reportedly from France. Who had brought this to Scotland? Who had worn it? She hoped it had been worn in beauty and excitement, then put away safely. Alice squinted at the explanatory card. Ah, these were treasure: a metal detectorist had found these, she read, buried inside the remnants of an ancient wooden building sunk in a boggy area. She gave one more longing look at the ribbon torcs and moved to the case holding the Lewis chessmen, stubby, wide eyed, carved of walrus teeth, holding their secrets. So, games by firelight in the long winter. Great times.

Next, weapons. Bronze. Swords, daggers. Spearpoints. If Kinsear did drive up from Cambridge, she would bring him here. He could perhaps tell her how, four thousand years ago, someone could collect the right proportions of copper and tin, and build a hot enough fire to make these bronze weapons. And explain how they were sharpened. She heard the raised voice of a docent and the shuffle and scatter of children's feet, heading for her display case. Alice listened. "So people have reconstructed the bronze foundry process that was used. The mixture had to be right so the sword was not too soft, but not brittle, and could be honed until it was sharp."

"How could you sharpen a sword?" asked a boy.

"Stones?" said a girl.

"Sharpening was laborious. Much slower than just pouring the molten bronze into a mold. Sharpening took hours, we think, and yes, the right sort of stones were useful."

"How sharp could they be, the swords?" asked the boy.

"Very sharp indeed, based on our reconstructions. But again, hours of work were required to sharpen the blade evenly."

Alice moved around to the next case. Behind her, the docent herded her group to a hunting display, and then on to the next room. Alice examined the daggers. One caught her eye: the blade looked about seven inches long, with remnants of a grippable-looking handle she felt would fit her own hand. The polished bronze blade glinted in the fluorescent light. Small, but not toyish. Small, but lethal. "Believed to be a grave good. Found at Welby. Early Bronze Age." Whose grave? And nearby, a smaller dagger with a carved ivory handle. "Grave good, possibly a child's." She puckered her brow, imagining the sadness behind the "grave good." What happened to that child? Nothing could make up for such loss. And nothing, not even the lovely small dagger, was sufficient to keep a child company on the journey into darkness.

She went back to the Early People display to take a picture of the "Great times!" card, thinking John and Ann would love it, then belatedly realized her phone was in her checked bag. Behind her, voices at the dagger display. I've heard those before, she thought. Where? Suddenly she was back in the mist, hearing the same voices. She stood frozen, peering at the "Great times!" display. What were they looking at?

"That's what you wanted to see?"

"That's one thing. He said the one we found, the one we gave him, was just a worthless version of the one in this museum. But I wonder what it's really worth."

"Yeah, but our handle was partly broken off, above those rivet holes. He sneered, didn't he. But then if it's not worth much, why is there one nearly like it right here in the effing museum?"

"Would *he* tell us the truth? Not likely."

"Of course not."

"So how are we going to get paid? And when? I'm sick of hiding in that dump. I'm ready to finish it and get out of there. We don't have much time."

"We can leave when we get the stuff. If the stuff's there."

"You know it is. We got a good signal out there."

"Couldn't it be old horseshoes?"

"Sheep don't wear horseshoes. That's sheep turf. No, something's there."

"He did say he'd zeroed in on the likeliest place, didn't he."

Silence. Alice lowered her head and edged to a point where she could peer at them through the glass case. No question. Both men, the tall and the blocky, were staring moodily at the daggers. Lord God. Blocky Man, a rooster-tail cowlick of black hair erupting above his forehead from under his hood, spoke. "If that bastard's shorting us on our share, then what?" He stared, eyes intense, at the daggers. More silence. He answered his own question: "We could sell it all ourselves."

"He's the one with the connections, though."

"So he says. I'm guessing there are other connections."

"He wouldn't like that."

"Tough. Now for the gold stuff," Blocky Man said. The men had moved to the torcs, standing sideways to Alice, voices reflecting off the glass case. "I'm beginning to think this is what he's after. I'm telling you, if we find something like this, I'm not so sure I'd let it out of my hands. We could get rid of him, easy. Find our own buyer." He looked sideways at Tall Man.

Tall Man, pale, with a beaky nose, shifted nervously. "I'm not so sure."

"I'm sure. Remember the guy in Stirling who found four gold neckpieces like this? He got 650,000 pounds! I'd want every bit of that."

"Yeah, but he was legal. Getting it legal takes time."

Blocky Man grunted. "Think about it. We're doing all the work, for a bullshit share, with crap equipment. Plus taking all the risk. We ought to have camo and night-vision goggles."

"Yeah. But he did pay us right the first time, didn't he? And we can't go back to Glasgow yet." No one else was in the gallery. She and the Early People were alone with these two men, as frightening as the long daggers they'd admired. She willed them to leave.

Then a crocodile of children jostled into the room, the docent walking backward in front of them. "And now"—the cheerful Scottish voice rang out—"we'll step back hundreds of years, when your great-great-great-great . . ." And on she went.

"Hell's bells." As the crocodile disintegrated and children swarmed around the display, Tall Man headed for the entry arch. Blocky Man didn't budge, still staring at the torcs. Then he turned and was gone.

She blew out her breath. Why were they here, right at this moment? Just coincidence?

Sudden need to pee. She remembered the toilets were next to the stairs. She exited into a group of schoolchildren and got to the women's restroom just ahead of a gaggle of girls. When she came back out, the two men were nowhere to be seen. Good. She retrieved her bag. Now what about the museum shop?

She bought a book with pictures of the museum's collections, plus a reproduction gold bracelet for Ann and stone chessmen for John. Then she bought earrings for Gran and Robbie. Finally, she pointed to a reproduction gold torc. For herself. "Ah, you'll look quite stunning in that. It'll make you feel like a queen!" said the saleswoman, wrapping tissue around Alice's treasure.

She was about to pull out her credit card when she spotted the daggers. Reproduction daggers, the edges safely blunt, cast in heavy, tactile bronze. And there were her two, the seven-inch Bronze Age dagger, and the child's. Wooden handles were riveted to the blades and wrapped with an intricate pattern of leather thongs. She had to have them. For—Kinsear? Yes, and she would keep the small one. For some reason.

"Oh, lovely," said the saleswoman, sliding the larger dagger into a slim box. "I just sold another of these. People do love the old bronze work. There's just something about it, isn't there." She handed the ticket to Alice to sign. "Just remember to put them in checked luggage!"

"Oh, right," said Alice. Really, what was she doing with these daggers? And a reproduction gold torc?

And even after hearing those men talk, she was no further along. Were they Angus's murderers? Or just thieving trespassers? The unnamed "he" had the "connections"—who was "he"?

* * * * *

Purchases stashed in her shoulder bag, she headed for the echoing museum entrance hall, and felt eyes. Where? She looked around, scanning faces, but saw no one familiar. Outside she headed east down the Royal Mile. Suddenly starving, she opted for coffee and a sandwich at a coffee shop with chairs outside.

She would soon see Ann: time to call the other baby.

"Mama, it's barely morning here!" groaned John.

"Just checking in. How the job's going?"

"It's okay." John had landed a summer job developing conservation plans at a wildlife management outfit outside Austin. "Actually, I got to help on a bird survey yesterday."

"Bet that was early."

"Yup, very."

"Where?"

"Down Ranch Road 12, on a creek north of Wimberley. I heard some painted buntings and golden-cheeked warblers."

"The owner may not be pleased about the latter." Golden-cheeked warblers, an endangered species, could limit development on hill country property. "Any other projects?"

"Coming up with strategies for property, like riparian management, native grasses, erosion control. You know, Mama!"

She did, too. "Everything okay at our place?"

"Yup. The donkeys are happy. And another donkey has come to call."

"What?"

"I saw three, not two, yesterday. For a minute I thought I needed my eyes tested. Mama, there's a little guy burro out there. Very friendly. Knock-kneed and chipmunk-cheeked. He doesn't look elegant, but he has great ears."

"Huh! Should we put up a sign? How'd he get through the fence?"

"No idea. I'll walk the fences today and see if we can figure out whose he is. How's Gran doing?"

Alice reported on Gran and the Difficult Tenant, all the time thinking of the toddler now turned grown man on the other end of the phone. "You're still coming next week, right?"

"Yes. I leave Thursday at four on British Air."

"Love you, darling."

"Call me back anytime. Well, almost anytime. Love you, Mama."

Alice sometimes worried about John, how he was faring without his father's presence. How hard it must be, suddenly to lose the solid shelter of a man as formidable as his father, the big Scot. Jordie had loved John's quietness, his fiddle playing, his deep academic interest in matters economic. "My man," he called John. Well, Alice thought, all the world's before him.

Then she remembered how blind she'd felt in law school—as if everyone else knew the right paths, the right gates, the right courses, the right answers . . . and knew, of course, not to make faces in moot court during opposing counsel's presentation. Would John feel the same kinds of uncertainties? But that she'd never know. He wouldn't show it. And neither did you, she told herself. She always tried to look like she knew what she was doing, just the way her pastor had instructed when she worried about the order of worship for her wedding service. "Just act like you know what you're doing, and everyone will assume you do."

That became her mantra, in client meetings, probate hearings, emergencies. I'll handle it. Got it. Done. Lately she'd begun to suspect she'd carried that mantra too far, or that it had morphed into pretending not to need help. And that was a hard way to live. But wasn't it good training? Your parents died, removing the protective awning above your head. Your husband died, requiring you to feed and clothe and love the children, by yourself. And someday, she thought, you, Alice, must go through the parted curtain, by yourself, hoping to meet the voices on the other side, softly murmuring a greeting. Recently Kinsear had pointed out that her DIY mantra wasn't universally admired. "Alice, a Japanese person might feel insulted by someone who says he or she doesn't need help. People are supposed to accomplish things together." She'd stared at him, astonished. Well, maybe she could try an alternative method for the second half of her life. On occasion.

What was it to be a man, these days? Alice wondered. The ones who always let women enter the elevator first . . . the younger ones who didn't . . . What was the burden, the freight of being a man, now? The burden of chivalry, still, but without ever getting knighted? The burden of loving the children, trying to plan for school, braces, cars, crises . . .

Well, what was it to be a woman now? A woman in a man's world, still; look at the Middle East, look at India. And other places. Sometimes Coffee Creek. And how does a woman function, living by herself, at the end of a gravel road, defended only by curious burros? Trying to run a business, make a living, support two children? Same way as a man, Alice thought, but perhaps with more caution around the edges. And yet, how could she live trammeled up by caution? Just, sometimes, remember to lock the door and reload the flare gun.

She made a quick call to Silla. Silla listed the new items on her Coffee Creek docket and ended with "Enjoy your vacation!" Right, only one dead body so far, Alice thought.

One more call to make. Would Ben Kinsear answer or be in class? He'd signed up for Bronze Age Discoveries in a Cambridge summer program for visitors. She thought back to the conversation when she'd asked, "Why the Bronze Age?"

He'd answered, "Mass-produced weapons, that's why. Bronze made humans into readily armed warrior bands. Have you seen pictures of the weapons found off the cliffs of Dover and elsewhere on the channel? Shipwrecks with bundles of axe-heads, bundles of daggers. Not single polished stone axes of great beauty and value, like the Neolithic axes in chiefs' graves, but bundles of them. Like bundles of muskets or Colt 45s in the nineteenth century, and now Kalashnikovs in shipping containers. Mass production! The difference between chipping stone and casting metal."

"Why are you so interested?" Alice had asked.

"The warrior culture that you see in the *Iliad* and *Odyssey*, which some writers think reflects the arrival possibly as early as eighteen hundred BC of the Greeks in Attica—where they adopted ships and chariots—depends on bronze. Swords, bronze spearheads, daggers: those require shields and greaves and helmets. So, now we have armed armies, instead of hunter-gatherer bands with stone axes. A new warrior culture. What does that say about us as humans?"

Into her mind had flashed images—a distinguished political consultant falling through the air before a horrified public. A beloved folksinger's drowned face, staring from the bottom of the pool. The slow revelation of another singer-songwriter's crushed skull as Kinsear gingerly pushed dirt aside. Dry bones, hidden for a decade in rocks above a ranch. And she'd never seen the dead body of the ranch owner, pushed from a cliff.

Now, waiting for Kinsear to answer his phone, her mouth tightened, thinking of the rancher and the others. "Stone axes probably worked just fine. Advanced weapons aren't always needed," she muttered.

"Alice! I thought you'd forgotten all about me, lost down here in the Bronze Age."

She thought, I do like his voice.

"Alice! I can't hear you. Are you there?"

"Hi!" she said, after a moment. "How's Cambridge?"

"Ridiculously pretty. Hey, I'm thinking the professor's going to announce a break this Friday. I've got a proposition for you: let's take a walk."

"A walk?"

"Yep, a walk in the parks. What if you meet me for the first few days of the Coast to Coast? We could start at St. Bees, on the Irish Sea, and walk across the Lake District into Grasmere. Wordsworth and Coleridge country."

"What's that part of the walk like?"

"Lots of up and down. Great views if there's no fog. What do you say?"

"It's a little fraught right now—Jorgé and Birnbach are here checking out the malt whisky scene." Kinsear had met the Beer Barons. "Also, something's going on with Gran's farm. An agent keeps calling but Gran doesn't want to sell. And the ghillie for the big landowner, who owns the land uphill from Gran's, is dead. Head wound."

"Did he fall?"

"Yes, and was he pushed?"

"Alice. Not again."

She described her fleeting vision from the Sisters, but decided not to mention how Blocky Man came up looking for her. Maybe later.

"Here's hoping you can stay out of it. For God's sake, Alice, can't you go anywhere without falling over a dead body?"

She ignored that. "Gran had a couple of unpleasant incidents herself, last fall." Alice told him about the last All Hallows Eve. But she didn't mention the anonymous phone call to Gran about the "little Texas lawyer." "And I promised I'd help Gran figure out who's been digging in her old sheepfold and scaring off her tenant."

"What does it look like, the sheepfold where the digging happened?"

Huh? "Like a muddy stone-walled falling-down sheep pen. Very sheep-y smelling."

"Send me a picture. And think about the weekend. Can we meet somewhere? I don't want to invade your Scottish home."

"It's not my home, you wouldn't be invading, and Gran would love to meet you," Alice said. "But I'd like to be somewhere else for a few days."

"Where can we walk that lets us stretch our legs and see some real countryside? And talk?"

Alice thought. "What if we walked part of the Great Glen Way? It starts at Fort William and heads north to Inverness. We could do a few days of that if we can work out how to take the bus back down to Fort William. Part of the route is above Loch Ness. Does that sound appealing? Some height and a big fierce loch?"

"Done," said Kinsear. "If class gets cancelled Friday as I'm expecting it will, I can be in Fort William on Thursday night."

She felt liberated, like a balloon let go.

"I'll get us reservations along the way," he said. "We'll hire some Sherpas to move the bags every day and you'll only need to carry a backpack. And of course, bring your 'proofs. No serious British walker leaves home without waterproof jacket and pants."

'Proofs? That meant going to an outdoor store. She turned back uphill toward the castle and the detour back into New Town. But she had time.

It would feel good to get away from events in Broadview. Tell the truth, Alice. It would also feel very good to be with Kinsear.

* * * * *

Alice smiled as she walked down to Holyrood and the green relief of Arthur's Seat came into view, with the surprise of its lion-shaped head. She loved Edinburgh's distinctive silhouette: the volcanic plug topped by Edinburgh Castle on one end, and the green turf and sudden cliffs of Arthur's Seat on the other. Alice had climbed Arthur's Seat one blustery Christmas morning with John, Ann, Jordie, Gran, and thousands of other Edinburghers, all looking out at the city from the castle to Princes Street and New Town and the port at Leith, the wind nearly blowing them off the path. Edinburgh stimulated her mind, with its intellectual history as the home of Adam Smith, David Hume, with its university and medical center. And then there was the breeze off the firth, blowing the cobwebs out of her brain, making her think in new ways.

So, couldn't she solve this little problem? Alice mulled the reasons she was here: loyalty to Jordie's mother and her own atavistic family ties to Scotland—a homeland whose merciless religious strife and perpetual battles with England her family had fled with relief several hundred years earlier, trading the eternal warfare of Scotland for the unknown perils of the American frontier.

Still, the shapes of the hills called to her. Standing on Precambrian stone, hearing the ridiculous but irresistible opening bleat of the bagpipes, Alice always felt the tug. But the place couldn't feed, couldn't hold, couldn't satisfy the Scots who'd left in earlier diasporas. Sometimes she wondered what it was like for those left behind.

"Left behind," she said to herself. No, they chose to stay. Either way, how did they now see their still scenic, still dangerous world? Scottish independence . . . They'd voted no, but would it happen one of these days? Or were they still so bound by mingled ties of loyalty and resentment to the rest of the island that they couldn't give up the connection? Nursing grievances, but triumphing by conquering every aspect of culture? She thought the latter.

Chapter Eleven

Fiddle *and* Harp

"**M**ama!" Ann bounced down the steps from her third-floor flat, in a small building north of Holyrood. "Excitement!"

"What?"

"Lori Watson and Rachel Newton are playing! We're going!"

"Where?"

"The Royal Oak. The bartender's a buddy. Come on, if we hustle he promised spots where we can see. I've got a tiny picnic in my bag in case pub snacks don't appeal." Ann led the way, cutting over to Holyrood and then taking a shortcut to Infirmary Street, talking all the way. "Mama, they play harp and fiddle, and they both have amazing voices. You'll like it." Alice was too out of breath to manage anything but a nod.

The Royal Oak was buzzing. Alice squeezed behind Ann, thinking how delightful it was to have an independent daughter who knew precisely how they should spend the evening. Alice ordered her Talisker, and Ann ordered a pint and a packet of crisps ("That's our vegetable") and, frugal child, produced from her bag slices of cheese and apple. The harp reverberated, the fiddle zoomed, the voices braided into unearthly harmony. Bliss, thought Alice. Nothing to remind her of midnight skulkers, threatening phone calls, someone swerving at Gran. She let the music work its magic.

During a break Ann asked Alice what she'd done today in Edinburgh. Alice hesitated, then thought, Ann's an heir. And a grown woman. Or almost. So she told Ann about the hastily departing tenant, then about what she'd seen in the mist. And why she'd decided she had to know more about the midnight skulkers, and about Angus's death.

"Not Angus? Angus is dead?"

"You knew him?"

"Yes! Of course I knew Angus! When Robbie took us to Gran's, John and me, Angus gave us fishing lessons. Casting for salmon, down on Gran's farm. He fixed my cast, Mama. He showed me how to make the line just float. How can he be dead? What happened?"

"I'm not sure. He had head injuries."

"And you saw him in a shouting match with two men above the

Hardie?"

"I never met Angus, but the man I saw carried a stick as I understand Angus did."

Ann sighed. "He could be pretty protective, in an aggressive sort of way. We all went to the pub after the fishing lesson. Some guy hassled John at the darts board, and Angus read him the riot act." She paused. "He and Robbie—they seemed close. But distant. Does that make sense? I couldn't quite figure it out."

Alice shook her head. "Gran thinks Robbie had a crush on Angus, but maybe she, or he, thought she was too young. Or that they didn't have enough in common. And later on—well, maybe Robbie will tell you. But I've got to find out about the midnight skulkers, because they're still around. Robbie and I saw them the other night. And chased them."

"Chased them? Tell!"

Alice shook her head. "We never got the license tag and got stopped by the constable to boot. But I need to figure out who they are because someone is worrying Gran to make her sell the farm."

"Sell the farm?" Ann's mouth dropped open. "Mama, no! It's the place Daddy loved! It's where if we ever—if we ever—you know, where he'd be, if we could ever find him." Jordie's body had never been found. So hard on a child.

The harp and the fiddle again silenced the crowd. This time a haunting duet mourned shipwreck, lost life, the unrelenting sea. The harp rippled, the violin challenged, the voices rose and fell together, until the lament, the unending grief of a sea-girdled island, filled the minds of all the listeners.

Another pint for Ann, and for Alice a last sip of Talisker, but no more. "Nearly time to go," Ann said. "I've got to be at the shop by nine tomorrow." She'd picked up where she'd left off in June, funding her year abroad by working part-time at a shop selling original women's designs in the Cowgate.

"You're lucky they'd take you back just for a few weeks," Alice said.

"Everyone in Europe's on vacation during August and they're all here for the Tattoo and the Edinburgh Festival," Ann said. "They needed me."

The music stopped, crowd noise swelled, and Ann and Alice squeezed through the patrons and out the door. It was dark now: the long summer twilight was beginning to shorten as the northern autumn approached. This time Ann led Alice back up Clerk Street all the way to the Royal Mile, turning downhill toward Holyrood. "I don't take shortcuts at night," Ann said. "My roomies drummed that into me. Edinburgh's pretty safe, but at night, take the big streets whenever you can."

"Good to know."

"And Mama, don't you want to spend the night with me, instead of driving back at night? We can share my bed. Or you can sleep on the couch!"

"No, I should head on back, see what's up with Gran. You were right to tell me to come, Ann. She's worried. I want to get this straightened out. You're still coming down next weekend, right? Before I leave?"

"Yes. Hey, are you going to see Kinsear while you're here?"

"Yes, we're doing a bit of the Great Glen Way this weekend."

They'd reached the turnoff where Ann would turn right toward her flat and Alice would turn left, under the bridge and the train trestle toward the carpark at the shopping center.

"Text me and let me know you got home all right."

"You'll be asleep!" said Alice.

"Nope. We stay up late. Sure you don't want to stay over?"

They hugged. "Thanks for the pub picnic and the fiddle and harp!" said Alice.

Under the bridge her footsteps echoed, and echoed again. Were those her own footsteps? She glanced back. Someone had turned and was following on the sidewalk beneath the bridge. She walked faster. The orange sodium lights did not comfort. They turned everything unreal. She sped up, now walking in the road. Not a car in sight. Silence, except for echoing steps. Almost to the carpark. She glanced over her shoulder. Two men, one taller, one blockier, now only fifty yards behind, moving with purpose. A few dim lights glimmered in the closed grocery store. She darted across the street and into the carpark, rooting in her handbag for keys. Headlights swept her: a security car, moving slowly around the parked cars. She reached her little rental, got in and locked it, and started it as fast as she could. How to get out of here?

She headed back up the Royal Mile, dodged down to Cowgate, got lost but eventually found the A70 and started back. Little traffic tonight; a few trucks, a few cars. She checked the rearview mirror. Odd to have to look left to see in the rearview. She pulled her phone out of her bag, put it in her lap. So far, so good. She passed through Currie, then Balerno, then cut down to the A702, rolling toward Dumfries. Why hadn't she stayed with Ann? She thought about it, scanning the darkness ahead, glancing in the mirror at the darkness behind. She was just jumpy. How else, except by ridiculous coincidence, could she suddenly be trailed to the parking lot? Come on, Alice.

To stay awake she worked through what she'd learned. She'd learned the two were looking for "stuff" at Gran's. She'd learned they felt quite free to invade, at least when no cars were visible at Gran's. She wondered if they'd left the blue van somewhere or were walking to Gran's when she'd seen them in the mist. She'd learned they needed to find the "stuff" before "he" got "back" to wherever "back" was. Who was "he"? If "he" was in Broadview, who else knew his connection with the two men? And how had two such noticeable men—tough, aggressive—escaped notice in Broadview? Neil said he knew nothing of the two men in the mist. Nor had she seen any indication that the inspector, or Robbie or Gran, knew anything. The Arthurian scribbler, Mr. Clyde Pendennis Creighton, said he didn't see them again after he scuttled around the corner on his way out of town. How was that possible, in a town the size of Broadview? Someone must have seen them. She'd check the grocery store, find out who'd been working when Creighton left, just days before she'd climbed up to the Sisters and seen them below. Didn't groceries mean the men were staying in Broadview, or somewhere close by?

So where had they gone? Vanished like Pictish fairies into thin air? She giggled at the thought of fluttering wings on the back of the big guy's light jacket. Tinkerbelly. Automatically she glanced back at the mirror. A van. Was it blue? She sped up, glanced back in the rearview mirror. It was passing the car to her rear, moving in behind her. They passed under a light standard. Yes, it was blue. Her heart thumped erratically. She tapped the brakes, began slowing. The blue van suddenly turned on a blinker and moved into the passing lane. As it moved past her car the driver didn't even glance at her. Bald, bespectacled, he was leaning forward and squinting at the road ahead. On the side of the van: "Dumfries Best Bakery Supplies." Oh, good grief.

Alice settled in for the rest of the drive. Now she was really sleepy. She sang, fiddled with the radio, rolled down the window, feeling the rush of chilly night air. She roared over a hill. Ahead was an exit for an all-night café and fueling stop. Tea? Coffee? Without signaling she quickly exited and skirted the café, looking for the entrance side. Whoops, too far. She parked in the back and got out. Just as she reached the rear corner of the building she looked through the glass and saw two men entering the front door. A tall man in a light jacket; a blocky man in a dark hooded jacket, eyes scanning the café. She recoiled, backing away from their line of sight, then turning and striding back to her car. Heart thumping, she started the engine, and, lights out, drove slowly toward the fuel pump island on the front apron by the café entrance. Ah. A blue van was parked in front of the café. Lord, she thought, if they'd circled the building the way I did, they might have parked right next to me. Now she could get the digits on the license plate. She noted a dent on the van's rear. Just then a big delivery truck rumbled up the entrance ramp toward her and stopped right behind the blue van, engine idling, waiting to make the turn to the fuel pump island. Through the café windows she could see the two men turning away from the cash register, heading for the doorway. Too risky. She floored the accelerator and headed out the exit onto the highway, heading for the cutoff to Newton Stewart, repeating to herself, "Remember the dent, remember the dent." Nearly one in the morning . . . hopefully Robbie wouldn't brain her with the broom when she crept in the house.

No one followed her home. The gate creaked. The door creaked. The stone flags in the hallway were silent. Only the moon followed her into the little guestroom, peering at her through the window. And only the grandfather clock in the hall made any remark, sounding a deprecatory three-quarter hour quietly in the darkness. She lay there thinking of missed opportunities. Could have hidden at the edge of the roadside café and followed the blue van to its lair, turning the tables on the two who might be—were they?—stalking the "little Texas lawyer." Then what? Could have gotten the whole license plate. Could have confronted the two men in front of the café owner and asked what the hell they were doing, following her. Could have taken a picture of the van. Of the men. Damn it all. The moon disappeared behind a cloud. She heard a lamb bleat for its mother, then stop, presumably burying its face in its mother's woolly underside. Alice buried her own head in the pillowcase, ironed by Gran, and thought of Ann, thought of John, thought of Kinsear.

C h a p t e r   T w e l v e

The Specter *of Death* Had Joined *the* Party

Alice woke Wednesday morning with a sour feeling of failure. She still hadn't identified the nocturnal invaders or defused the inspector's undue interest in Robbie as a possible suspect in Angus's death. She hated feeling as helpless as she did here. In Coffee Creek at least she had a decent relationship with detective George Files of the Coffee County Sheriff's Department, and could offer, and receive, needed information. And she held a license to practice law, allowing her to crank up the weighty machinery of court to protect her clients. Here she had nothing— no friendly police connection, and no authority whatsoever to ask questions and demand answers. Frustrated, she tugged on her bathrobe and stalked into the kitchen. At the kitchen table sat Gran, who read her face like a book.

"Woke up disgruntled, did we?"

Alice nodded. "Your renter is a piece of work. Cowardy custard. He did promise not to say tacky things online about your cottage. He also heard the two marauders say they had to get the 'stuff' before 'he' got 'back.'" Then she plunged into the tale of her encounter with the two men at the museum. "Gran. How can we figure out who these guys are, why they're roaming your property, and whether they did in Angus? I don't know where to start, here in Broadview."

Gran raised her eyebrows and lifted her head. "I'd say you have at least one superb tool, and that's me. Didn't you say my friend Walter McAfee found Angus's body?"

Alice nodded.

"I've been thinking. Those men Monday night had a shovel and maybe a metal detector?"

"I think so."

"Well, I haven't mentioned the hoary old tale of the old hidden hoard." Gran grinned.

Alice pricked up her ears.

"The tale is that longer ago than anyone remembers, the Norse invaded the cove and settled around the headland. At some point they left, supposedly burying a hoard of weapons and gold somewhere between the cove and the top of Ben Cathair. So far as I know, the Hardies never found a thing, but we should go see Walter McAfee.

He's been here for over a quarter century, he collects those old stories, and he'll know if there's been any talk about the farm. Shall we invite ourselves up to the manse for morning tea?"

"Sounds good," Alice said. "So long as we get back by late morning. The Texas boys have a second tour at the distillery around lunchtime."

"Walter will be delighted. Nothing makes him happier than being needed. This gives him a chance to help his aged parishioner, that's me, and say hello to you." She moved to the telephone.

* * * * *

The manse sat next to the Presbyterian Church of Scotland on Upper Road, looking down across town to the harbor. Low granite walls surrounded the church and graveyard, with the violet of late asters and clematis breaking the severity of stone. "Over there's where you'll please bury me, next to the far wall," said Gran cheerfully, pointing. "Under those rowan trees. Just there." She walked Alice to the far end of the graveyard, looking south and west.

From that point in the churchyard a panorama opened—Luce Bay, sparkling today, and far to the west, the gray smudge of Ireland.

"It's beautiful," Alice said, wondering where she herself would want to be buried. Or sprinkled.

"Easy to see how St. Columba could get himself here from Ireland, on a good day, even in a coracle," Gran remarked.

"But also the Vikings, and faster."

"Yes. Imagine the terror you'd feel, seeing those carved prows heading your way, swords and axes glinting! You'd be grabbing the children, tugging the cow, running back up the burn to hide behind Ben Cathair—or even further—if you could get away in time."

"Losing everything you left."

"Watching smoke rise from your house."

"Hearing the sheep and lambs bleating."

"And your dog, left tied so he couldn't betray your hiding place by his barking. The children sobbing silently over leaving him. And you'd have to keep them from making even a peep," added Gran.

"War all the time? Never peace?"

"A long, peaceful winter, but getting hungrier and hungrier—and knowing that spring, with lambs and green growth, brought peril. Maybe the summer transhumance, taking the cattle up the mountains, was designed to get them away from the tempting foreshore. Maybe tending sheep was safer in summer, far up a mountain pass," Gran said.

Alice shook her head, her imagination momentarily transforming her into a fleeing mother clutching a baby and a toddler, racing for safety.

"Ah, here's Walter." Gran headed back through the churchyard gate and into the manse lawn. A white-haired man holding a dog on a leash waved at her from the porch. Alice followed, admiring late roses by his door.

"Ah, Kathy! Knoxie and I just got back from our first morning walk." Gran and Alice both patted the spaniel. "And you are Jordie's Alice. So good to see you. Those are Souvenirs de la Malmaison, those roses," said Walter, noticing Alice's admiration of the old-fashioned shell-pink fragrant roses, with their tightly furled rosette and central green eye. "Aren't they something? Come in, come in. It's a treat to have a visit."

The manse smelled of books, old wood, and baking.

"Let me put the kettle on. Find a seat if you can! The books keep invading!"

Gran scooped up several volumes scattered across an elderly chintz-covered sofa and stacked them on an end table, then settled herself on the sofa. Alice roamed the shelves. Mysteries in one corner; an entire bookcase holding Scottish history; sermon collections; MacCulloch on the Reformation. And the books Gran had moved? Cunliffe on British archeology and Broodbank on the Bronze Age.

"Oh, my guest was looking at those." Walter entered with the tea tray. "Kathy, will you pour while I grab our scones? Mrs. Whitley heard you were coming."

"She cleans for Walter," whispered Gran.

The smell of tea and scones rose in the cool air. Alice took a bite. Perfect anticipatory crunch, followed by tender crumb and an uprush of fragrance. The scone was delicious.

"Not to forget the clotted cream!" Walter admonished Alice, who wondered how many treks up and down Ben Cathair it would take to justify her scones.

When all three teacups held fresh tea, Walter fixed his attention on Alice, who endured a thorough cross-examination on her education, law practice, children, and church options in Coffee Creek. Finally Gran intervened.

"Walter, we're here to ask you about my tenant! My former tenant."

"Fled the scene, didn't he? I heard he left before he should."

"Walter, what did you hear? He told Neil at the Sisters that there were lights and men roaming the property at night."

"Probably just lads."

"He said they were in the sheepfold, with lights," said Alice. "So he told Neil."

He frowned. "Might be some of those metal detectorist folks. But they shouldn't be trespassing."

"And why on Hardie Farm? You haven't heard of any reason for that, have you?"

His brow knotted. "I did hear there was someone waltzing about, here and there," he said. "From Angus McBride, poor man. A terrible thing."

"What did Angus say?" asked Gran.

"He said he'd told them right smartly to stay off the Flemings' land. But he didn't mention yours to me." The bristly eyebrows turned to Alice. "What else did Neil report about the tenant?"

"He was scared." Alice heard footsteps in the hall. The steps paused, then seemed to go back toward the kitchen. She raised her eyebrows at Walter.

"Oh, that's my houseguest, Philip Ansley. He and I have corresponded for years. He stopped by in June and I prevailed on him to visit, and now he has finally made his trip to Broadview. He's writing a book on the Bronze Age."

That pricked Alice's interest.

"But back to your tenant being frightened. Are you sure he wasn't just looking for a reason to skip?"

"Could be," Gran said. "Now, Walter, what about poor Angus? It must have been horrible for you to find him."

"Yes. My Knox found him, actually." Hearing his name, the spaniel perked up. "We were late going for our walk and didn't go out until about six. There'd been dense fog before that. Knoxie always runs down to the river when we get to the bridge. He started barking, running back and forth, so I went down. And there was poor Angus." He closed his eyes, shook his head. "I always try to get these pictures out of my head, but it's hard this time. Angus, that muscular man, always the strongest, the quickest, the most decisive. But there he lay, sprawled down the bank, his face in the water. I turned him over, of course. Maybe I shouldn't have, but I had to hope he'd just fallen a few minutes before, that something could be done. But he—I couldn't feel a breath, couldn't feel a pulse. So I called the ambulance."

Alice felt that the specter of death had joined the tea party and was sitting on the couch next to her. She shivered.

"And could you see—had he hit his head somehow?" Gran asked.

"Yes. Very badly, across one temple. He'd damaged, um, the bone around one eye, I believe." Alice imagined splintered bone, the wounded eye. The pastor's cleaned-up language somehow made her imagination produce worse images. "Funny, though, it was a regular-looking blow, not jagged, not like he'd fallen on a rock."

She'd misidentified the guest. The specter of murder, instead, had joined the party.

Gran said briskly, "What can we do, Walter?"

His face sobered. "I've been to see the family. You know, Jennie and little Jamie."

"Jennie's Angus's wife," Gran clarified for Alice. "Jamie's the son."

"Jennie's completely at a loss," Walter said. "She can't imagine he just fell into the burn. I mean the stream, Alice, but you'll know that. Like a mountain goat, Angus was. But getting older, of course."

"She must feel a chasm has opened up before her," Gran said. "It's hard to imagine Broadview with Angus gone. He straightened out many a lad, just being the man he was."

Walter's eyes sharpened. "He might have been a little too hard on a few of them. *Nil nisi*, though."

Gran nodded. "Walter, I thought perhaps Alice should tell you what she saw on Sunday afternoon up by the Sisters."

Alice felt reluctant. She'd already told the inspector, hadn't she? She glanced at Gran but could see no reason not to tell. Briefly she described the three men she'd seen in the mist. She didn't tell the rest.

"If he said 'Stay away from Hardie Farm,' that man would certainly sound like Angus, medium height and all," Walter agreed. "I don't know who the other two could be. They don't seem local. Except—" He paused, then shook his head.

"We thought you might have heard of someone else who's found them digging or looking," Gran said. "With a little blue van."

"Blue van. That rings a bell, but I can't quite—Oh, Ansley! Good morning!"

At the door, smiling slightly, stood a middle-aged man, bald, round-shouldered, spectacled. "I hope I'm not interrupting?"

"No, no. Alice, Kathy, this is my Cambridge friend and houseguest, Philip Ansley. Ansley, meet my very dear friend Kathy Greer and her—um—daughter-in-law, Alice. From Texas. Alice, that is."

Alice stood up and extended her hand. Ansley took the fingers only, his blue eyes speculative as he glanced quickly at her. Alice detested fingers-only handshakes, which hurt her fingers and left her with a negative impression of the person. Ansley installed himself on the other end of the sofa. "So, Mrs. Greer—" He looked at Gran, then Alice. "Oh, you are both Mrs. Greer."

"We were just talking about Angus McBride," said Walter. "You heard about his death at the pub Sunday night, didn't you, Philip?"

"I did," he said. "Very sad."

"Kathy owns Hardie Farm," Walter went on. "You know, Ansley, on the headland below the Flemings, with the little Hardie running through it. Kathy, you and the Flemings share the fishing?"

Gran straightened her shoulders. "I'm not sure what you mean by 'share.' I own the fishing rights in my stretch of the river. I've allowed the Flemings themselves to follow a fish down from the glen, and I suppose Robbie or Jordie may have followed a fish up. But in any case a long time ago we both agreed never to lease out the fishing rights to others."

"What about houseguests?" asked Alice.

"Oh, of course you can have a go, Alice—you're family! And I might let your charming clients see if they like our fishing better than links golf."

"Your clients?" asked Ansley.

"Alice's law clients from Texas are investigating the possibility of building their own distillery," Gran said. "Apparently distilleries even for malt whisky are popping up in their part of Texas, right, Alice?"

"Right!" she said. "On Monday we visited Uisge Dorain, and we're going back today so the guys can take a second look at a couple of steps."

"When?" asked Ansley.

"Just before lunch," said Alice, surprised.

"What did your people think?" Walter asked Alice.

"They seemed fascinated by the process, and particularly the role of the stillman."

"Who took you around? Fiona?"

"No," said Alice. "A young man named Davie Dockery. He seems young to me, anyway. Very hospitable, though."

"You've met him, Philip," said Walter, turning to Ansley. "He's the young man we spoke to at the pub when you first arrived."

"Ah. I'd forgotten his name." Ansley settled back into the couch, then leaned forward, facing Alice. "So your clients—how soon will they build a distillery?"

"I'm not sure, and if I knew I couldn't tell you." Alice smiled.

"But with all the competition,'twere well it were done quickly."

"Surely Macbeth referred to a grimmer task than building a distillery! Here they're conducting research—due diligence, we call it—in a lighthearted manner." She wanted a new topic. "So, you're working on a book?" she asked.

"Oh, not a book, necessarily, but perhaps a monograph. I'm just an amateur," Ansley replied. "I'm quite interested in the Bronze Age in England and Scotland."

"Oh, Ansley, you're overmodest." Walter leaned forward, his

eager face toward Alice. "Ansley's really looking at possible Bronze Age structures here in the southwest. This part of Scotland had more Bronze Age activity than scholars have thought, isn't that right, Ansley?"

A trace of emotion—irritation? arrogance? anger?—crossed Ansley's face, then vanished. "You make me sound too expert, Walter. This is my hobbyhorse, merely."

"What do you do when you're not working on your hobby?" Alice pressed (then thought, Right, that rude American question, "What do you do?").

"Oh, I'm a retired former schoolmaster. History."

"And you live in Cambridge?"

"Yes. You've visited?"

"Not yet, but a friend is there for a summer course."

"Ah, the summer program is quite well regarded."

"Did you study archeology at Cambridge, then?" Alice surprised herself, pursuing these questions. But she was irritated by Ansley's reluctance to talk—his lack of forthcomingness. Surely it wasn't only visiting Americans who should be quizzed.

"I have not. As I said, I'm just an amateur, Ms. Greer."

"But you've been drawn to this area by your research?"

"Oh, I've just begun, really."

"Come now, Ansley! You've been with me for six weeks! Give us a hint of what you've learned on all those long walks," Walter said.

"I just like tramping about. I always have. And of course I'm always bird-watching on my walks, too. But I do enjoy the views from the tops of the hills. You can see—can imagine—what the landscape was like."

"Three thousand years ago?" Alice asked. "Is that what we're talking about?"

"Or more." He warmed to his topic. "You'd be surprised what you can see. I've seen photos of causewayed camps, likely Neolithic, and then halls and sometimes hill forts that support the Bronze Age communities that followed."

"You've seen them this far north?"

Ansley didn't answer directly. "Do you not know about the Ness of Brodgar? That's Neolithic and five thousand years old. It's up in the Orkney Islands, and not really discovered or excavated until the last two decades. The site was in use for a thousand years. The standing stones there are five hundred years earlier than Stonehenge. That's not a Bronze Age site, but as the Bronze Age cultures moved into Scotland, in the second millennium BC, some of these sites continued to be used through the Bronze Age and into the Iron Age and later."

"And I believe that's where the Fleming boy, Reid, has done summer studies for his archeology program at Cambridge," Walter said. "But then this summer he, um, came back to Broadview to give Angus some help. Ansley, I thought perhaps you'd discovered something intriguing from up on Ben Cathair."

"Oh, I hoped to, but it's a no-go, I'm afraid."

"What sort of something?" Gran asked sharply. "You said halls and hill forts, didn't you? Do we have anything like that around here? And what did you say—causewayed camps?"

"As it turned out, all I've seen is just fence lines, not a hall or hill fort," Ansley replied easily. "But I did get some good bird-watching."

The pastor furrowed his brows, puzzled. He glanced at Ansley, then leaned back in his chair.

Ansley cocked his head. "That's a lovely bracelet, Mrs. Greer. It almost looks Bronze Age. Is it an antique?"

Gran looked down at her arm. Around the thin wrist, old gold shimmered. The bracelet was a single twisted piece of gold, with a small dome at each end, carved with a curved knot. Beautiful, thought Alice.

"My father gave it to me."

"Very charming," Ansley said. "He was from here, was he not?"

"Oh, the Hardies have been from here for—how long, Kathy?" put in the pastor.

"Quite a while," Gran said. "Well, we'll be off. Lovely tea. Thank you, Walter." She stood. "Good to meet you, Mr. Ansley."

The pastor rose to walk them to the door. Ansley stood and nodded at Gran, then at Alice. His lips smiled slightly but his eyes were watchful. Alice felt something still hanging unsaid in the air.

Chapter Thirteen

The Queen's
Remembrancer

On the flagstone walk back to the street both women were silent.

"Odd little man, that Philip Ansley," said Gran, finally. "Most amateurs can't wait to tell you all about their hobbyhorse. Or maybe he's another stuck-up Cantabrigian who thinks we women aren't worth his words. Cambridge was dreadfully slow to admit women as full members, you know. Ridiculous."

"Mmm," Alice said. But she would ask Kinsear what else Ansley could see besides birds, up on Ben Cathair.

At the farm Alice took her phone to the sheepfold and took pictures for Kinsear of the two corners where the dirt was disturbed. "If this were Texas, I'd say an armadillo had been rooting around," she told Gran. "Or a skunk." Maybe a human skunk, she thought. On impulse she borrowed a spade from Gran's garden toolshed.

"I'm just curious how deep they dug," she said, to Gran's inquiring look. Alice surveyed the sheepfold and chose the corner closest to the house. She planted her foot atop the spade and leaned in. The soil was set, but loose. She dug deeper and deeper. Now her shoes were covered with dirt and her hands and temples were sweaty. She stepped heavily on the spade, expanding the width of the hole. Gran came over to watch. Alice planted the spade again and heard a clink, then saw metal glinting in the dirt. A coin. "Gran!" She lifted the spadeful of dirt onto the grass.

Gran was already there. She wiped the coin's face clean with her gardening glove, and laughed, holding it out to Alice. "British sixpence, dated 1963." She bent over the clods with her trowel and prised them apart. "But look," she said, holding out a small blue bead.

"So there could be more in here."

"You know, you might try just under the corner stones," Gran said. "The old saying was, 'Bury it under the corner stone, find it again when the blades have gone.'"

Quite an image. Shining blades.

Alice heaved at the spade. A speck of blue lay quietly in the hole. Gran bent over. "Oh, look," she whispered. "Another bead." Then Alice felt Gran grab her arm, still holding the spade. Gran turned her head toward Ben Cathair. Abruptly she said, "Cover it quick, Alice. Hurry."

Startled, Alice began shoveling the dirt back in. It was just as hard as digging the hole in the first place.

"Don't look up," said Gran. "Just look normal." Gran walked over to the clothesline and felt the laundry. "Nearly dry," she said.

Alice finished and stomped on the dirt. Gran returned toting a black rubber water tub for the sheep. She plopped it over the disturbed soil and walked back for the hose. While the tub filled, Alice said, "What's your thought here?"

"This corner's been dug already, right?"

"Yes. But I got down below that part."

"So someone already knows about the sheepfold. For some reason I looked up at the mountain—I saw a flash of light, probably binoculars catching the sun. Anyone can see us from up there. "

Alice lifted her head as casually as she could and let her eyes sweep Ben Cathair. She could just see the Sisters, and a speck of blue—a blue-jacketed hiker, just climbing over the ridge into the stone circle. Alice walked toward the clothesline and glanced up again. The hiker turned, binoculars toward the sea.

"Can you help me carry this?" Gran pointed to a fresh salt block inside her toolshed. Alice rolled it over to the sheepfold. Gran pushed it into place by the water tub. "Otherwise, the tub looks a little foolish," said Gran. "This will draw the sheep. A great deterrent, except they aren't brave."

Alice evaluated the minatory signals from her brain. "You don't suppose we have to report two beads?" she said.

"I'm not worried about the beads," said Gran. They scraped the soil off their shoes and, in their socks, sat at the big kitchen table. "Alice."

Alice looked up. "Yes'm?"

Gran slowly held out her arm, with old gold shimmering around her thin wrist.

"Gran, it really is lovely. I've wondered how old it is. But I didn't want to ask you in front of Ansley!"

"That's what I want to talk to you about. What if it's treasure

117

trove? Shouldn't I offer it to the Queen?"

Alice thought that British law might require antiquities to be handed over to the Crown. "Where did you get it?"

"My father gave it to me. And he never would tell me where he got it. He just said, 'It's been part of our property for years.' Now I'm wondering—what if he dug it up here?"

"But you don't know that, do you?"

"No. I did see one that looked very much like it once, in the British Museum. The label said 'Bronze Age.' It was from the hoard found at Sadwen."

"This has been bothering you, hasn't it."

"It has."

"You don't know where this came from, and there's no telling where he got it. So I don't think you need to worry, Gran."

But Gran showed signs of distress.

Alice pulled over her computer and rooted around the Internet. "Scottish law of treasure." Hmm. Scotland didn't have a statute like the one that applied to England, Wales, and Northern Ireland. That statute, the Treasure Act 1996, said that any "treasure" found, regardless of how it was buried or lost, belonged to the Crown. And to qualify as "treasure" under that act, objects other than coins must be made at least ten percent of silver or gold, and at least three hundred years old.

Okay, that was clear enough, thought Alice. But just across the border in Scotland, the law was different.

Scotland's law of "treasure trove" was part of the ancient common law, and followed the rule that "that which belongs to nobody becomes our Lord the King's or Queen's"—so, even now, the Crown had a right to treasure trove. Treasure trove had to be precious and concealed or hidden when found, without the possibility of tracing ownership to a currently living person or family. It could be "precious," Alice read, even if not made of precious metal: a porpoise bone had been held by a court to be "precious," along with the silver objects found with it.

Aha. Treasure trove was to be reported to the Queen's and Lord Treasurer's Remembrancer. Who came up with these names? "Hey,

Gran," she said. "Listen to this."

"Great heavens," Gran said when Alice had finished reading. "The Queen's and Lord Treasurer's Remembrancer? Who is that?"

Alice pointed at the screen. "It says finders must report their finds to the Crown Office or the Treasure Trove Unit at the National Museums of Scotland in Edinburgh. And after that, finds are to be assessed by the Scottish Archaeological Finds Allocation Panel, which must decide if the find is of national importance. And that panel also recommends a reward for the find, 'when appropriate.'"

"A reward is recommended?"

"The fine print here says that the Crown has no legal obligation to offer rewards for the treasure trove objects it claims. But it usually does so, based on market value."

"So do I need to contact the Queen's and Lord Treasurer's Remembrancer?" asked Gran, fondling the bracelet on her arm.

"About your bracelet? I don't think so," Alice said. "It was given to you by your father. He said it has been part of your family's property, so it does not seem to qualify as treasure trove, since there's a link to an existing family."

"A link?" Gran said. "I wonder. Come look at something."

Gran opened the door to her bedroom. Inside her closet, framed on the wall, was a typewritten document. Alice had never seen it.

"That's my grandfather's will. My father had it framed and told me to keep it always near."

Alice turned on her phone flashlight and squinted at the will. His name . . . last will and testament . . . and there was the granting clause: "To my son, the Hardie farm and buildings, the Hardie and its waters, the land, the house, and all that lies within."

"And all that lies within." Alice had no idea whether that represented normal Scottish testamentary language.

"I have always wondered what that meant," said Gran. "The fish in the river? The dirt beneath our feet, all the way to China? The swallow nests in the eaves? All the apples in the root cellar? But I do know my father read that line to me a number of times, and said we were never to sell this place."

"Well, if you were looking for another link in the chain of ownership of your bracelet, perhaps there it is."

Gran looked down at the bracelet, gleaming in the dim light of the bedroom, and turned it slowly on her wrist. "I do love it so."

"Gran, I honestly don't think there's anything to worry about." She saw the doubt on Gran's furrowed brow. "As you saw, I have done my extensive legal research, both online in the kitchen and here in the closet, just in the past five minutes. However, that may not be convincing and I know almost nothing about Scottish law. Do you want to talk to your solicitor in Edinburgh? You could."

Gran shook her head, a small smile beginning. "The cloud of guilt is lifting from my head. Thanks, Alice."

Chapter Fourteen

Malting Floor *and Pagoda* Tower

Davie Dockery had agreed they could come back to see the malting floor and pagoda tower again at eleven, just before the communal lunch hour at Uisge Dorain. When Alice called to ask for a second visit, Maggie Smith had said, "All the employees lunch together in the canteen at noon, most days, unless we have errands. That's our tradition. So let's make your visit at eleven. Sounds like it shouldn't take too long." After this visit Alice planned to hunt down the inspector to tell him what Creighton said and to report her museum sighting of Tall Man and Blocky Man. And once again she'd be asked, "Did you get the license? Did you get a picture?" And she would have to say, "No . . ."

With the sun playing hide-and-seek with towering clouds, casting light and shadow on Ben Cathair, the four of them walked along Harbour Road, crossed the Dorain as it ran into the harbor, and swung up Distillery Road toward Uisge Dorain.

Davie Dockery stood by the entrance to the tasting room. His face was pale—almost green, Alice thought. His eyes stared like an owl's, with dark half moons underneath. Alice stopped, uncertain what was wrong, but imagining that it involved Angus.

Birnbach stuck his hand out and Davie automatically reciprocated, but his face didn't change. "Thanks, Davie, for letting us come back. We're awfully sorry to hear about Mr. McBride." Davie nodded mechanically. Birnbach went on. "We've been talking about the malting. We've got some ideas as to how we could manage it. Can you show us again? And we'd like a closer look at the kiln and the tower."

Jorgé added, "We're used to barbecuing in Texas not over, but near, a small fire of aromatic wood, like hickory, pecan, mesquite, or oak. We're thinking that even though you may think we're very presumptuous to try to make malt whisky, we might be able to add our own flavor, judiciously. It could be distinctive."

"Could be distinctively horrible," said Birnbach. "But—we may give it a shot."

Alice noticed that Davie had not mustered an answer. Following Davie, they retraced their steps, first walking back to the malting floor in the main building, the men peppering Davie with questions about timing, moisture, germination status. Davie waved briefly at the same two men in blue Uisge Dorain pullovers, now on the far side of the malting floor, next to the back door of the building, still turning and inspecting shovel scoops of malted barley. Four blue Uisge Dorain shirts still hung neatly on the wall by the back door. Davie walked the visitors over to the alcove where the conveyor belt left the malting floor for its trip to the pagoda tower, pointing out the old Bakelite control knobs for adjusting speed. "Like I said, adjusting the speed of the conveyor and heat of the kiln, that lets you control the toasting process. This is an old conveyor but still works like a charm," he said.

"One more thing, Davie, do you mind if we see the pot stills again?" asked Birnbach. So they all revisited the still room, where Birnbach and Jorgé had thought of twenty questions more apiece. Birnbach was taking pictures and making notes on his phone.

Then Davie shepherded them back outside the main building and past the tasting room to the walk leading directly across the yard to the tower stairs. Alice trailed behind, stopping to sniff the roses blooming at the corner of the main building. She thought it must be an old rose variety, deeply crimson, richly fragrant. Furtively she snapped off a rose hip and slipped it into her pocket. Alice! she chastised herself. But too late, she'd already done it, as she always did. Out of the corner of her eye she saw a man in a tan cap and blue jacket move out of the shadow of the malt conveyor where it emerged from the main building and walk quickly toward the rear of the property.

She caught up with her group and climbed the metal stairs past a landing with one locked door, then up a short flight to the top landing. Davie stood at the top with the others, looking through a window in the door into the toasting chamber just below the pagoda roof. To their left, the long, covered conveyor belt, supported by metal poles, clanked its way from the main building's malting floor up into the toasting chamber and back. Alice peered through the window at the conveyor belt of malted grain, which moved very slowly from left to right, then curved its way into a small opening in the far wall for its return to the main building. Flames showed through the grated floor, glowing from the firebed beneath the conveyor. They could dimly see a wall thermometer, the red needle pointing straight up.

"Could you let us in, let us see the fire?" asked Birnbach.

Davie hesitated, put a key in the lock and held it for a moment, then pulled it out. "I really can't. It'd be worth my job. First, it could mess up the temperature. Second, it's dangerous. Look, there are no railings between you and the conveyor. But I can take you down these stairs to see the room where we tend the fire, very briefly. If you'll just peek in?" They agreed. He led them back down the metal stairs to the landing below and unlocked the door. "Just you two, if you don't mind, and I can close the door so the fire isn't disturbed and we don't mess with the heat." He opened the door for Jorgé and Birnbach, who slipped in. Davie shut the door, then opened it and urged them out.

"How does it smell?" Alice asked.

"A little like peat," Birnbach said. "One peat block was on the firebed, right, Davie? With more peat stacked by the wall. There's a sort of golden smell, like morning toast, but I can't really describe it."

"The stillman can choose to add a bit of peat. Or, and I like this, we can alter the speed of the conveyor. I'm not telling you when or why, though," Davie added.

"It's all art," Robbie commented. "How hot, how fast, what fuel."

"Right," said Davie. He glanced at his phone. "Um, seen enough? Looks like I have another appointment."

"We understand," Birnbach said. "Remember, any time you decide to take off and see the world, just catch the BA flight to Austin; we'll pick you up at the airport and put you to work!"

Yesterday's smile was now a small grimace. "Right now I'm trying to get my feet on the ground here." He paused. "But if I should call, change my mind, are you serious?" He looked back and forth from Jorgé to Birnbach.

"Of course we are," Jorgé said. "We'd help with a work visa. We were thinking fifty thousand in salary to start. Dollars. That's negotiable."

Davie's eyes were fixed on the window into the fire room.

"If you want, you could live in my garage apartment," Jorgé said. "Bank your money."

Davie glanced again at his phone. "Sorry, I've got to go. I've had a text from Maggie about a germination question on the malting floor." He ushered them down the echoing metal steps.

The afternoon air was still and cool. The plume from the pagoda roof rose straight into the air.

Birnbach held out his hand. "Davie, we really thank you, and I just wondered if I could see—"

But Davie's face was set. "I must deal with this text. Please feel free to have another taste in the tasting room. On us, no charge. I'll let Fiona know."

He hurried across the yard, stuck his head in the tasting room door for a moment, then disappeared down the walk and up the stairs into the main building.

"What's that about?" asked Robbie. "He must've checked his phone three times just on the stairs!"

"Do you want any more tastes, Jorgé?" asked Birnbach.

"Yes, of the sixteen-year-old. And let's grab a bottle of the unfiltered."

Fiona greeted them with a broad smile when Alice pushed open the door. "Welcome! Davie said you'd be back. Now don't be trying to steal him away!"

"Oh, no," Birnbach said. "But what about you? We'll need a tasting room. You'd add Scottish flavor! Do you have any desire to see Texas?"

Fiona smiled. "No, I'm well settled here. Now what can I serve you?"

The unfiltered single malt felt warm and smooth in the mouth, but more aromatic in the nose and back of the throat. I like this one, Alice thought. She wondered if the Beer Barons could even come close to it in Coffee Creek. No peat tincture in the water . . . and instead of soft water from ancient granite, artesian water bubbled by carbonate from the limestone. Would it work?

Fiona sold them two more bottles and placed them carefully in brown bags.

"But before we go back I want to take one more look at the pot still room," Birnbach said. "Is that okay?"

Fiona said, "Not a problem. I'll just call and tell them you're coming." She reached under the counter for her purse, retrieved her phone, and made the call. "I'll be joining the others for a quick lunch now, over in the canteen," she said, glancing at them. "Unless you folks would like another taste? Or need to buy another bottle?"

They demurred. Fiona stepped briskly down the walk.

"I'll wait for you here," Alice said. She thought she'd just sit on the bench outside, looking up at Ben Cathair. Jet lag had crept over her.

"Robbie, what about you?" asked Jorgé.

"Do you want to walk with me in a minute or two down to see the Dorain? We just go past the main building and down the hill. There might be ducks."

Yes, he did.

"I'll be back," Birnbach said. "I just want to look one more time at the way the pot stills are set up." He set down his glass and headed out the door. Robbie and Jorgé were still sipping, looking into their heavy little glasses, then looking at each other. Alice thought they spent more time gazing at each other than at the single malt.

Alice left her glass on the counter and wandered out to the empty courtyard to sit on a bench. Smoke rose steadily from the pagoda tower. A little breeze came up and dispersed the smoke toward Ben Cathair. Slowly a cloud covered the sun. Alice shivered. Was starting a distillery a good idea? Alice wasn't sure. How good could a central Texas malt be? Would the Beer Barons be satisfied with the quality? Certainly her clients demonstrated broad capabilities, managing a popular music venue and a microbrewery, but whisky? What if they got into disagreements? Well, she represented the entity; the individuals had waived conflicts. But what if this caused a split?

She glanced back as the tasting room door opened and Robbie and Jorgé emerged, walking away toward the main building.

I won't think about it, she decided. The noon Westminster chime was ringing from the Church of Scotland far up the hill. The last note sounded a little flat. Always is, thought Alice, counting the twelve bells, or maybe the breeze carried part of the tone away. The warm sun came out again, touching her hands, her face. She closed her eyes and thought how nice it would be not to be dealing with Broadview, and instead, to be alone with Kinsear. A long walk in the countryside, and a romantic inn by a river, and . . . ? The sun soothed her. Out of gas after her midnight drive, Alice closed her eyes and slept.

Voices. She woke. The Church of Scotland rang the half-hour Westminster chime. Jorgé, Robbie, and Birnbach had converged on her bench. "Shouldn't we say good-bye to Davie?" she asked, pretending to be awake.

"Jorgé and I didn't see him," said Robbie.

"Me either," said Birnbach.

They stuck their heads in the tasting room door. Fiona was back. "Again, would you thank Davie for us?" Birnbach asked Fiona.

"Of course."

Outside the tasting room the wind now blew smoke every which way above the pagoda tower. Confused Scottish weather, she thought.

"Still trying to get Davie to Texas?" asked Alice.

"Well, I'd have tried harder," Birnbach said. "But he didn't seem very enthusiastic today. Still, we're going to need help if we try to make our own malt."

"Where will you get the barley?"

"I want brewing-type winter barley," he said. "Here in Scotland, maybe, or France. Have to get special whisky yeast too."

"Yikes," said Alice, thinking of shipping issues, customs, cost, quality.

"Air freight may be worth it, sometimes," Birnbach mused.

"What about the copper still?" Robbie asked.

"We'll have it built by an outfit in Kentucky. Specialists." He stopped on the path and looked at his phone. "Oh, wait. Alice, do you mind taking a picture of the kiln? I meant to but the damn phone says it's out of storage. I guess I took too many pictures of the pot stills."

Client service, it's all about client service. Alice walked across the yard to the pagoda-roofed tower and slowly climbed the clanking metal stairs again. At the top she pulled out her phone and pressed it to the glass window of the door. How to block the sun's glare? She hunched her shoulders and peered at the phone screen. Orange light from the fire below, with tiny tongues of flame, flickered beneath the metal conveyor belt, making it look like it was moving. It took a moment before she realized the rivets on the conveyor section in front of her had not moved. Thinking of toasting spices on an iron skillet at home, Alice suddenly thought, The malt's going to burn! Where was Davie? She had to tell him! She looked to the left, where the conveyor entered the kiln. Was it truly stopped? She saw crepe soles sticking up, crepe soles slowly melting onto the conveyor. Olive-green shoes, with white trim, and crepe soles, melting and dripping down into the embers below.

Alice couldn't breathe, couldn't talk, grabbed the door handle, shook it frantically. Locked. "Bill! Jorgé!"

They looked up.

"It's Davie! Davie Dockery!"

Fiona burst out the door of the tasting room. "What?"

"Call someone! It's Davie! He's on the conveyor!"

Alice yanked again on the steel door. She couldn't budge it. Birnbach and Jorgé pounded up the stairs, but couldn't open the door. Down below Robbie was yelling at Fiona: "Get the keys, dammit! And call an ambulance and police!" An interminable time, just minutes, but endless.

Maggie Smith, fat legs flying, hurried out of the office door, followed by a white-shirted manager. Alice heard a siren in the distance. White Shirt hurried up the steps, fumbling with the keys. The inspector's car hurtled to a stop at the edge of the driveway.

Alice called to him down the stairs. "It's Davie Dockery. At least his shoes. On the conveyor!"

"Stop! Wait!" the inspector yelled at White Shirt. He ran up the stairs, two at a time, the constable following. "Okay, man. Open it." Hot air billowed out the door. "Look at the needle," Alice gasped. The red needle pointed hard right.

The inspector shoved past the manager to the conveyor belt, to the feet. "Come in here! Is the fire at normal level? Tell me quick, we need to turn it off." The manager, voice trembling: "Old Will would know."

"Go get him," commanded the inspector. He ordered the constable, "Quick, pictures of the dial for the gas, and all the settings on that wall over there. Quick, man! And turn them off."

"But is it Davie? Is he alive?" called Alice.

"Doubtful."

Old Will came around from the main building, white hair blowing in the wind, face screwed up behind thick glasses. He stopped four steps from the top, catching his breath, holding the rails with both hands. "Is what I hear true?" he asked Alice. "Is young Davie in there?"

"I'm afraid so."

The inspector appeared at the door. "Sir, we need your help. We've got the fire off. Now we need to move the conveyor so we can get—so we can reach him. Does the belt only run one way?"

"Yes. It's an old one."

"Are the controls up here?"

"Two sets. One on the malting floor, where it starts. One set up here, so you can adjust the rate."

"All right. I need you to come in. It's not pleasant. Can you do it?"

"Yes." The old man was trembling.

The inspector remembered Alice. "You can go downstairs. But don't leave." She nodded, and stumbled down the iron stairs, still gripping her phone. Birnbach put an arm around her shoulders and walked her to the bench by the tasting room.

Now a doctor, in scrubs, was toiling up the stairs, bag in hand.

She shuddered. Time stopped. Silent, the four watched the tower stairs.

Chapter Fifteen

Left
Facedown

The ambulance had left.

Will Galloway, inconsolable, had stumbled back to the manager's office. Alice, Birnbach, Jorgé, and Robbie were instructed to sit on the bench outside with the constable while the inspector took their statements, one by one, in the tasting room.

He did not smile when Alice came in. He just pointed to a chair. "Ms. Greer."

"Inspector."

"Tell me what happened here. At this point we're just talking to everyone who met with Davie, or talked to him, today or earlier."

"Earlier? Well, he looked very frightened on Monday when he heard about Angus," Alice said. "Shocked. His face went white. But he didn't give the impression he was going straight to the police. He didn't seem to know what to do, I thought. And then this morning, he seemed silent, grim, preoccupied. And frightened." She sat thinking of the pleasant young man, who'd escaped bad connections in Glasgow to come home . . . where something lethal had followed him. Then she described the visit to the malting floor, pot still room, and the pagoda tower.

"And he showed you the conveyor controls? All four of you?" asked the inspector, pen poised.

"Yes."

"Did you see anyone who wasn't an employee, out on the grounds? Other than the four of you, of course."

"I'm not sure." She described the man in the blue jacket and tan hat. "I don't know if anyone else saw him; they were ahead, climbing up the stairs to the tower."

He grunted. "You saw no one else who wasn't connected to the distillery?"

"No."

"You didn't see anyone else in the malting room or the kiln tower?"

"The same two men we saw Monday were in the malting room. Otherwise, no."

He tapped his teeth with a pen, shook his head.

"And you sat outside and went to sleep. Again."

"Yes." She'd hoped he wouldn't say that. Alice, have you slept through two murders? "Still jet-lagging, I guess."

"How long did you sleep?"

She thought. The Church of Scotland . . . "I heard the noon chimes, before I dropped off. When I woke up the half-hour was chiming." She took a deep breath. "Poor Davie. You know, he was so different today from the way he was on Monday. On Monday he was so full of life, so thrilled about working here." She thought back. "Until he heard about Angus."

"Tell me again about that. Precisely what happened when he heard about Angus."

She nodded. Once again she was standing in the tasting room, remembering Davie's face. "He went pale, grabbed the counter. Then he said he thought he'd seen three men near the bridge the day before. 'But—not Angus!' he said."

"Tell me again who was there."

"Robbie Greer. Bill Birnbach. Jorgé Benavides. Me. Davie. And Fiona."

"No one asked Davie anything more about what he saw?"

"No. I don't know why not, except that he seemed shocked and was in a hurry to leave."

"You're sure he said three men."

"Oh, yes." Was there any doubt?

"And today, your clients wanted to see what again?"

"The malting floor, the pot still room, the kiln arrangement in the pagoda tower."

"And he took you to see them?"

"Yes. In that order."

"And then?"

"We came back to the tasting room. We said good-bye to Davie." No need to tell him Birnbach was recruiting Davie, was there? "Davie said he had a text about a germination issue from Maggie and had to meet someone about that. We four stayed in the tasting room."

"The whole time?"

Tell it all. "No. Bill Birnbach wanted to see the pot still room again and Fiona arranged for that. She made a phone call. Jorgé and Robbie said they were going to walk down to the Dorain to see the ducks."

He stood up. She was excused again.

* * * * *

"Quite a visit to Scotland we're having," Birnbach said. The four of them were walking back through Broadview toward Gran's. "Two deaths in four days. I knew the UK was murderous, what with all those BBC murder series, but apparently they're reality shows."

"But poor Davie," said Alice. "Poor Davie! He was so happy when we first met him Monday."

"Then he heard about Angus," said Robbie, grim-faced. "So how does that fit in?"

"I'm just glad I'd taken all those pictures of the pot stills," Birnbach said, holding up his phone. "Otherwise the inspector probably would have put me in the jail or whatever you Scots call it. Those guys working the pot stills may be my alibi."

"Let's do something to take our minds off this," Jorgé said.

Robbie stopped in the middle of the walk and faced them. "I propose a fishing lesson in the Hardie and then tea and, if she's willing, a tasting seminar with Gran."

The men nodded, unsmiling.

Alice was aching for solitude. "You three go ahead. I'll call Gran and let her know."

When she broke the news of Davie's death, Gran was silent on the phone for a long moment. "Well. He deserved much better. We'll lift a glass to the young man." But her voice was strained. Then she gave Alice an errand to run—pick up smoked salmon, down at the pier. "When you reach the harbor, go out on the pier to the east. John Dougal's smokehouse is at the end," Gran instructed. "He's an interesting person. He took a first at Oxford in Greats and came back here to start this business, a few years ago. You can buy his lovely salmon vacuum-sealed. Take it home to Texas."

Georgie Porgie.

The bell over the door rang when she walked in. "Coming!" someone yelled from the back room. Alice looked around. Spotless white counter. Three bar tables with stools. Music playing. Scottish? Fiddle, guitar. Price list on the wall: "We ship everywhere." Menu: Salmon salad. Spicy salmon salad. Smoked salmon. Whisky-cured gravlax. Yum.

She hadn't heard any footsteps but felt eyes on her back. A man stood watching behind the counter, black hair, blue eyes, white apron. "Lovely day," he said. "What may I get you?"

"It all looks wonderful."

"It is. First you should have some tastes, then you can pick. How about that? Where are you from?"

Alice told him, watching the quick hands assemble little plastic cups.

"This is the spicy salad. This is the gravlax. This one's the smoked. This is plain salad. Try them in reverse order."

She complied. Plain salmon salad: the sea itself. Smoked: delicious. Gravlax: intriguing, sophisticated. Spicy salmon salad: an explosion of flavor. "I want it all," she said. "For tonight, enough for five people or so to taste before dinner."

"What about to take back to Texas?"

"Oh, I'll come back for that. I'm not leaving for a few days."

While he wrapped, he peppered her with questions, expertly extracting information about Coffee Creek, Alice's practice, the hill country. Alice learned that he knew of Jordie's death. Gran was a favorite customer. He was sometimes bored in Broadview but would head to Glasgow or Edinburgh for more music, more ideas. His brother lived nearby. He lived above the shop and kept a sailboat. He and his brother sometimes sailed up to Mull and Arran. "Stay longer and I'll take you sailing. Here, try my newest. Not yet named and not yet on the market."

Alice tasted. Olive, salmon, thyme. "That could be really nice on good bread," she said.

"Come back tomorrow." He grinned.

She left with her purchases, walking down the pier, listening to the gulls calling and swooping overhead. Broadview looked so quiet, so peaceful . . . not a place where one man could be hit on the head and left facedown in a stream to die, and another left on a conveyor belt to bake. Stop. Stop. She wouldn't think of that.

At Gran's, she walked out past the house and looked up the creek, the little burn. Robbie had Jorgé and Birnbach practicing their casting. What was Robbie telling them? Both men were laughing.

"One more way to look ridiculous," Jorgé said. His eyebrow bore a stick-on bandage. "First you Scots get us to try links golf, and tip us into pot bunkers. Then you put us in waders and have us hook our own faces with a trout fly."

"That hook barely touched you," scoffed Robbie. "If the barb had bitten we'd be having more fun getting it out. I thought Texans were supposed to be tough!"

Birnbach pulled Alice aside as she turned to go back to the house. "Hey, Alice. Are you okay? I felt terrible, that you had to find Davie. I'm so sorry I asked you to go up those stairs." His face was so distressed Alice had to hug him.

"Don't worry. I'm fine. But I've been worried about you two, setting out for a little Scottish vacation and finding yourself in the middle of two murders."

He put his hands on her shoulders, looked over the tops of his spectacles into her face. "I hate seeing you dealing with this, Alice. And it's selfish, because we can't do without you! I know you too well to think you'll quit trying to figure out how to protect Gran. But for the Lord's sake, be careful."

She nodded.

Chapter Sixteen

The Bones *of* *the* Land

Birnbach and Jorgé cruised back into the kitchen with Robbie at teatime, clutching bottles from their visits to the Auchentoshan and Glengoyne distilleries, as well as Uisge Dorain.

"Mrs. Greer!" said Jorgé, presenting the bottles with a small bow to Gran. "We need to replenish your cabinet and make you a proposition."

"Oh, really?" Gran smiled, head back, the smile that gave Alice a pang, remembering Jordie. "I am always willing to entertain a proposition."

"Well, Robbie says you used to host single malt tastings in Edinburgh, for parties. She said you have the nose of all noses. She said distilleries begged for you to come work for them."

He stared expectantly at her.

"That's quite true. I studied in Paris to be a perfumer. My nose was admired. And that same nose was also handy for single malts when I came back to Edinburgh to marry."

"We wanted you to give us your thoughts during a taste test, after tea, if you're willing," Jorgé said. "We thought maybe we could learn how to articulate what we like, and what we might want to make, if we can bring off this distillery idea. We brought some comparison bottles. Would you consider that?"

"Absolutely I will," said Gran.

Alice smiled to herself. She'd seen Gran do this only once, for Jordie and Robbie and their friends, producing as lucid and comprehensive a taste trip as she'd ever seen, across the Highland, Lowland, and Island malts, from the lightest and sweetest to the deepest and peatiest. Alice had learned a great deal. On that occasion she'd watched with interest as Gran morphed from the familiar materfamilias, with her light and welcoming touch, into the subtle and severe instructor, rigorously challenging her students to discover and articulate distinctions. Despite the spit cup, by the time her small class reached the Island malts, they were merry indeed.

Now, with Jorgé and Birnbach, Gran was all business. "You have something in mind already. You've narrowed your putative single malt to a quality within hailing distance of the sea, but not so peaty as the Islands. So we don't need to waltz all up and down Scotland, right?"

"You've got it. That's the kind of malt we're after, exactly. We think we can use artesian water from the hill country, and maybe make our own malt at some point, though not at the beginning," Jorgé said.

"Well, let's consider." She set out small glasses and put the bottles in order, including a range of single malts from her own cabinet. She poured small sips from the first bottle. "What do you taste in this one?"

Birnbach: "I like the finish."

Jorgé: "And the way it feels in my mouth. But its initial aroma is not quite what we're after. Wouldn't you like a little more herb with that caramel smell?"

Birnbach nodded.

And so they proceeded, through the range of single malts on Gran's tea table. Then they returned to the Uisge Dorain and retasted it. Jorgé nodded, tilted his head, eyes narrowed, and looked at Gran.

"So we want the aroma of the Dorain, and its mouthfeel, with the initial taste of the Macallan and a long aromatic finish like the Talisker?"

"Is that all?" Gran said.

"Well, a little faint floweriness supported by a honeyed underpinning," said Birnbach. "And lots of character in the finish, like Jorgé said."

"All right," said Gran. "Let's discuss again."

And she and Jorgé and Birnbach were off into the arcane realm of malt toasting and local water. Walking out into the hall, Alice heard Robbie upstairs. "May I come up?" Alice called.

Robbie's studio, Jordie's old bedroom, opened to the right off the landing at the top of the hall stairs, taking up the back half of the second floor. Robbie's bedroom and bath took up the front half. The studio windows looked up at Ben Cathair and out across Gran's pastures to the sea. The stone chimney of the hall fireplace jutted out from the interior wall.

The studio smelled of oil and turpentine. Robbie's worktable, in the center of the room, bore neat groups of brushes, charcoal, oil paint, and acrylics in wooden containers. Robbie stood by her easel, paintbrush in hand, staring out the window toward the sheepfold, then back at her canvas. "I'd never finished this, Alice. It was for Jordie, to remind him of home. Now it's done. I'm wanting you to have it. You and John and Ann."

Alice stepped around, standing next to Robbie, and peered at the canvas. Green rolling pasture, sky, sea. You could feel shadow and sunlight changing by the minute—clouds scudding overhead, shadows suddenly revealing the shapes of the long slopes to the sea, then bright light. In one corner stood the stone walls of the sheepfold.

"It's wonderful, Robbie." She had caught the rolling turf, without overmuch detail. "Like a green ocean."

Robbie nodded, assessing her own work. "We'll let it dry and you can carry down to your room."

But there were more paintings, faces hidden, leaned on the chimney and above and below the counter that ran around two walls.

"Robbie, may I look at these?"

Alice tilted a large canvas away from the wall. Huge bare hills. The next canvas: purple curves, gold, red. The next: the same curves, but green, gorse yellow. Alice pulled out painting after painting. She looked back at Robbie, who was watching her, unblinking.

"I'm painting the bones," Robbie said. "The bones of the land." She started cleaning her brushes. Her voice changed. "Alice, tell me about your Jorgé."

"He's not mine!"

"You know, your friend, your client."

"He's all of that. A good man. Private, though. He's not married, I don't know why. I've heard him talk about his two sisters in San Antonio, both with kids."

Robbie blinked. "I like him."

"How much?" Alice dared ask.

"I'm taken aback, actually. He's—I feel like I have always known him, after just thirty-six hours." She paused. "We stayed up last night until three, talking." She shook her head. "It's been a very long time since I did that for anyone."

Alice grinned. Well, well. A new development. She'd never felt she knew the whole story of Robbie's abrupt first marriage, just as abruptly ended, or her life in the decade since. She remembered how

Jordie would hang up from a call to his sister, shake his head and say, "That's a forceful woman, still searching—watch out!"

After Jordie died and the family endured the awful week culminating in the memorial service in Edinburgh, Alice didn't call Robbie, didn't reach out. She felt, she knew wrongly, that Robbie somehow blamed her for Jordie's loss. Silly, thought Alice. Unkind of me. Immature. She was grieving for her only brother.

One day she'd applied Kinsear's latest maxim: "Don't believe everything you think." She'd called Robbie, and a week later, Robbie had called her, to say she was painting again. When John and Ann arrived in Edinburgh for a college year abroad, Robbie had scooped them up and whisked them off to inspect their Scottish heritage: to Aberdeen to see the North Sea oil industry; to Glasgow for architecture and design, including the bridge their grandfather had worked on; to Rosslyn Chapel to see the green man grinning down in exquisitely carved stone atop a column; to Dumfriesshire to see the Ruthwell Cross standing at a slight angle, sunk into the floor of an out-of-the-way church, its eighth-century carvings protected now from Viking raids and iconoclast depredations. Steel, stone, sea—Scotland, Robbie would tell John and Ann. She'd taken them up to walk part of the Great Glen Way, high above the long rift valley containing the deep waters of Loch Ness locked in Precambrian stone, so old. John and Ann were intimidated by Robbie, with her brusque wit, her habit of pushing their ambitions. And they loved her.

Gran was collecting glasses when Robbie and Alice returned. Alice watched Jorgé watching Robbie.

"So you lads are heading home this weekend?" asked Gran.

"Yes, assuming the inspector agrees we can make our flight," Birnbach said. "So far he hasn't decided we're suspects for Davie Dockery's death." He shook his head, grimmer than Alice had ever seen him. "That poor young man."

"And you've learned enough to start your distillery? Or learned enough not to?" asked Gran.

"Well, we've lined up our barley source, and some sherry barrels from Spain," Birnbach said. "I think we're going to give it a try."

"It may be hubris," Jorgé said, looking at Robbie. "So we'll want your support."

"But you surely aren't thinking you'll export your malt whisky to Scotland?" said Robbie.

"Not right away, but when we enter our whisky in the international competitions—"

"That's going to take a while," Robbie snorted. "You have to age it!"

"Right, some things improve with age! Me, for instance!" said Jorgé.

Robbie raised one eyebrow. Alice grinned.

Birnbach said, "Look, Robbie, I've got a stockpile of stories on this guy. A lot of stories. You have only to ask."

Robbie didn't rise to the bait.

"Have you thought of a name for your distillery?" Gran inquired.

"Not yet," said Birnbach.

"Alice, you fly back not this weekend but next, right?" asked Jorgé.

"First I have to figure out who's trying to make Gran sell the farm, who scared off her tenant, and who's digging on her property. The last two might be the same, but not necessarily the first."

"Do you have any idea who's involved?" asked Birnbach.

"I thought it was the two men I saw in the mist the day Angus was killed, which I think are the same two that Robbie and I chased way past Whithorn," Alice said. "But we lost them."

Jorgé shook his head. "You women know how to have fun. We hate to miss out. You need us to chase anyone?"

* * * * *

Robbie strode off to answer the phone, then returned. "Alice?" Her voice sounded strained warning. "Alice, the inspector asked to talk to you again."

"What about?"

"Davie Dockery. Now, if you don't mind."

142

It *Was* Wiped

Once again she found herself stalking up the steps of the whitewashed police station on Harbour Road, feeling it had been a very long day already. The inspector pulled out a chair for her. He rubbed his eyes, then sighed.

"Ms. Greer. Just one more time, can you tell us about the person you saw walking away on the sidewalk under the conveyor running from the main building to the pagoda tower?"

She nodded. "Medium tall, not fat, dark navy windbreaker or anorak, wearing a tan cap. The sort of wool cap you call a driving cap. About the color of a graham cracker."

"A what?"

"An American cookie or cracker, a bit like a Scottish oatcake."

"You could not see the person's hair?"

"No, nor his face."

"Any other impressions? Age? Race? Anything? You're sure of the sex?"

"Sex? I assumed it was a man." But was she sure? Alice stared at the ceiling, trying to reroll the tape of mental memory. "He—I'm pretty sure it was a he, but not positive—was scurrying. Hurrying in that way that I thought meant he does not want to be stopped or interrupted. He has no time to chat. He was heading straight out that pathway."

"But how far did he go?"

She couldn't quite remember. She'd stolen a rose hip, she'd been watching her group climb the pagoda tower stairs . . . then she went to join them.

"I'm sorry," she said. "I wish I could be more help."

He nodded.

"But I do have a question."

"Yes?"

"What—how was Davie killed?"

"He was stabbed in the back. We're waiting to hear details on the blade."

"And that's what killed him? Oh, I'm so glad it wasn't the—the—you know."

"He was dead before he got up to the toasting floor, we think."

She closed her eyes in relief.

She realized she'd forgotten, in the horror of finding Davie, to tell the inspector about her wild chase with Robbie. "Inspector, the two men I think I saw with Angus McBride, in the fog on Sunday"—he looked up at her sharply—"I don't think I've told you I think I saw them again, at Gran's—Mrs. Greer's house, on Monday night. And tried unsuccessfully to catch them."

"I am sure you mean the man you *assume* was Angus McBride. Do you mean you literally tried to catch them?"

"Yes. They were in a blue van, and Robbie and I tried to catch them on the road south of here, and lost them. And I've looked but I can't seem to find that van anywhere in town."

He made her describe the van.

"Not too big. Medium blue, not navy." No, she did not know the automaker or plate number, except that the last digit was zero. She went on. "Then I believe I saw the same two men again yesterday in Edinburgh, at the National Museum of Scotland, and again on the way back to Broadview."

Now he was taking notes. "What makes you think it was the same men?"

"At the museum I was trying to get close enough to hear what they said without alerting them. What I overheard makes me think they're our trespassers. Then last night I saw them at a roadside café but I was alone on the road, I didn't want a road race with them."

"Why didn't you mention this earlier?"

Sense of outrage. "You mean today when Davie was killed?" Her mind had been on the locked door, on the embers, on the melting shoes. "I guess I could ask whether anyone has found the two men I saw Sunday."

"We haven't detained them in connection with investigating Angus's murder because we haven't seen them and can't find them. And, frankly, no one has seen them . . . but you."

Alice felt fury push up in her chest, tried to damp it down so she could speak calmly. "You don't believe me?"

"No one has seen these two men but you. That's a problem.

And you're telling me the same men were at Mrs. Greer's farm. At midnight. In the dark. How can you possibly confirm they're the same people you saw in the mist . . . much less describe them? As I recall, you couldn't give us a description from your brief glimpse in the mist either."

"Robbie also got a glimpse, as you call it, Monday night. And what about Davie? He said he'd seen three men by the bridge, the afternoon Angus died!"

"But unfortunately he didn't get a chance to expand on that, did he?"

"Surely you would know better than I," Alice said, indignant at any implication that she or her friends had prevented Davie from talking to the inspector. Then, curious, she asked, "Didn't he try to talk to you?"

"Yes," admitted the inspector, shifting in his chair. "I got a phone message from him earlier that day but I was out. I called him back but no one could find him."

Well. She gave the inspector her best long stare. "I have a couple of questions."

"Yes?" The inspector straightened the tablet on his desk and looked back up at her.

"Were there fingerprints on Angus's stick?"

"No."

"It was wiped?"

He didn't answer.

"Was he still alive when he went in the water?"

"I'm afraid so."

Alice shut her eyes. "But he couldn't get himself out?"

"Apparently not. It's not clear yet whether he couldn't move or was just unconscious and drowned. But his eyes were open."

Alice felt sick. Who could put anyone in the water to drown with his eyes open? Surely not Robbie. She thought some more.

"Angus was a big man. You don't think Robbie carried him down there by herself."

"She's a strong lady. A rower and all."

"Be realistic. It's a long way down there from the road."

"Not if she just bashed him while they were both standing there!"

"There's no proof she did!"

"There's no proof she didn't. She and he have been seen down there before."

Well, damn. Alice pushed ahead. "Surely Scottish law requires more than that. What time did he die?"

"Time's not going to be exact, you know."

"Walter McAfee says he found Angus at six."

"And?"

"My mother-in-law says she dropped Robbie off to go for a run right at six fifteen, as they drove into town."

"She's Robbie's mother, and hardly disinterested."

"Inspector, you know they're telling the truth. No one's going to believe Robbie Greer's a murderer. What does the pathologist say about Angus's wound? What made it? It wasn't his stick, was it?"

The inspector let out a sigh. "I have no obligation to tell you any of this and I don't know why I should."

"Because I'm trying to help you solve these deaths."

That brought a disbelieving look from the inspector, but after a moment he answered. "The pathologist believes Angus was hit with something metal. There are traces of rust in the wound, and also the way the bone shattered looks like metal was involved. It's possible he was also kicked."

Kicked! Alice felt sick. But she pressed on. "And since no metal weapon was found by the river, but someone did leave his stick there—because someone wants you to think Angus met his death there instead of elsewhere—it's not unreasonable to think he was somewhere else when he got that blow to the head. And then he was dumped in the river."

"That is one possibility."

"Which makes it very unlikely that it was Robbie. And very important to find the two men."

The inspector didn't reply.

"I assume that's all?" she said.

He nodded brusquely. Alice walked out into the dark street,

realizing only then she'd forgotten to tell him what Creighton reported hearing. But the inspector wasn't going to listen, and she wasn't in a mood to beg. Indeed not.

Chapter Eighteen

Pot Bunkers

G ran hugged her good morning. And did she want sugar for her oatmeal? Or salt? Oh, just coffee? And when could she and Alice have a good talk and figure things out? "What's the 'stuff'?" asked Gran. "Whatever's buried in the sheepfold? And who is 'he'? And where is 'back'? Is it here in Broadview?"

Alice shook her head, clutching her coffee cup. "No clue."

Gran's face brightened. "Well, nothing to do but go after it ourselves, Alice. Let's have another digging party! Shovels by moonlight!" Her face sobered. "But this morning I'd like to pay my respects to Angus's wife Jennie and I'd like you to come with me."

I could ask Jennie about what I saw in the mist, Alice thought. And I could ask why her husband would have then gone over to the distillery. Then she thought, Is that tacky? Is it too soon? She's mourning him! Or maybe not. Her law practice had made her cautious about attributing conventional emotions to heirs of the departed.

"I'll come with you, just as soon as we get back from this damned golf game."

* * * * *

Robbie had insisted that Birnbach and Jorgé join her for a round of golf at the local course, with an appallingly early tee time. She'd dragooned Alice into playing too: "I need to see if these lads learned anything about links golf, Alice! Besides, I want you to see our town course. We're quite proud of it. And we'll only play the last nine holes. Plus, I'm taking your clients touring today."

North of and abutting Gran's farm lay the Dorain Refuge, dedicated to otters. Along its northern boundary lay the Broadview Links Course, which ran from the sea back toward the shoulder of Ben Cathair, ending at the coast road that meandered back behind Ben Cathair and then bent around toward Broadview. An overnight cold front had brought low clouds and chilly wind. The four shivered as they entered the small clubhouse, with its smell of wool carpet and pipe smoke. A twinkle-eyed man greeted Robbie: "You're back! Our

Robbie!" He gazed speculatively at the men's clubs, brought from Texas, and outfitted Alice with clubs. "You're only doin' the back nine, I hear. You should be okay. Bit windy, though," he said. Outside, the wind whipped yellow leaves against the windows. Understatement, thought Alice, zipping her jacket against the wind and pulling her hood tight.

The first six holes at Broadview extended from the clubhouse back to the entrance at the road, then turned northwest and ran back to the sea. The thirteenth lay along the sea cove. Fourteen through eighteen—famous challenges, according to Robbie—ran back along the otter refuge boundary and over two low hills, to end at the famous eighteenth, below the porch of the clubhouse. The foursome started on the tenth hole, heading back toward the sea and into the wind.

Robbie teed up on the tenth hole and hit her drive straight out, nearly to the green.

"Whoa," said Birnbach. "Nice shot!"

His own drive soared up and sliced right. Alice winced in sympathy, dreading her own trip to the tee box.

And that's how the nine holes went. Robbie played golf the way she talked: directly, efficiently, forcefully. "Your motto must be 'Take dead aim!'" said Jorgé.

"Of course! Isn't yours?" she shot back.

Manfully the Beer Barons fought the wind, shook their heads at crafty greens, and stalked through the rough looking for lost balls.

On twelve, Alice encountered her first pot bunker. There, down in the bottom, sat her ball.

"How do you get in and out?" she demanded, looking at the sheer sides.

"No idea. But don't forget to use your 'weepon'!" called Jorgé, grinning at her.

He wasn't grinning on the seventeenth hole, almost back at the clubhouse. As they pulled their carts up to the tee box Robbie warned, "Be cautious. There's a pot bunker lying in wait for you, ahead of the green."

And they all watched as Jorgé's perfectly straight drive disappeared into the ground.

"That's so low, Robbie," he complained, clambering back up from the bunker. "I thought I'd birdied this one, with my drive! I kept it down and straight, like you said!"

"But look," called Birnbach, horrified, from the back side of the green. "There's a second one back here! You're screwed either way on this hole!"

The groundskeeper waved from the cart path, driving down toward the beach. "These days he has to patrol to keep people from setting up tents and camping on the course," Robbie said. "Yes, people actually do that here. It's a big problem for the links courses on our lovely Scottish beaches. Especially on sunny holidays."

"Aren't those rare?" Jorgé wiped the raindrops off his face.

Robbie took them back to the clubhouse.

Jorgé looked at the dining room. "Closed. And I'm hungry."

"Sorry," Robbie said. "The clubhouse has cut back on hours. There aren't enough customers, even in summer, sometimes."

"Is money an issue?" he asked.

She nodded. "The members would like to rework a couple of holes, and be able to host small tournaments. But we can't afford it. And that's too bad, because the town could use some more tourists, more business. Let's grab some hot soup at the Soup Plate and then I'll take you two tourists to see Whithorn. Alice has things to do."

*****

"Always uphill to Angus's," Gran panted. They'd marched uphill from her house, crossed the Hardie, then climbed the stile onto Hardie Road. At the top of the hill they reached the wide driveway into the Fleming property. "We turn here," Gran said.

Off to the left a short muddy track left the driveway and disappeared downhill into trees along the edge of the glen. Ahead, on the driveway, iron gates stood open. "The ghillie's cottage is inside, just there." Gran pointed. A short drive led back to a white plastered cottage with a thatched roof. Gran did not approve. "The Flemings thought it looked quaint for their ghillie to have a thatched cottage. It's quite impractical up here," she said with finality. "Now, Alice, Jennie's younger than Angus, about thirty-eight. I like her fine. She'll be curious about you."

Jennie, an apron tied around her soft waist, opened the door with a sweet smile but sad, red-rimmed eyes. She hugged Gran, shook Alice's hand, bustled back to the kitchen to make the inevitable tea. Alice walked over to the tea table by the front window, looking downhill toward Gran's and the sea. From here, across the deep ravine of the glen, hidden below treetops, Alice could see Gran's house, the sheepfold, and the pasture below. Alice pointed. Gran grinned. "It's why I'm so well behaved, Alice. Any sinning on Hardie Farm must occur indoors."

Jennie set down the tea tray, whipped off her apron, and sat down. "So glad to see you, Kathy," she said to Gran. "Everyone's been so kind and attentive I can't stand it. So if you don't mind, let's just talk honestly. I miss him, yes I do, and I always will. And I'm shocked to the core. But I find I'm just so angry!" She burst into tears, then sat up straight, fumbling for a tissue. "You see? I'm angry at the man, for leaving me like this! What was he thinking? But he always had to be right, didn't he."

"Do you mean," Gran said cautiously, "that he was reading the Law of Angus to someone? Are you talking about how he died?"

"Yes, of course I am. The police say he was hit in the head. Of course I wonder about his stick, that infernal cudgel of his. I always considered it was just an incitement to violence for him to carry it around all the time. Oh, he loved it though. But if someone hit him on the head, I'm afraid it's because he was chewing on them for something."

"You know, Jennie, I think Alice may have been one of the last people to see him."

Jennie looked straight at Alice. "Please tell me. Every bit."

So Alice recounted again the vision in the mist. Jennie wanted to know every detail: What did the man who might have been Angus look like? What did he say? What about the other two men?

"I'm ashamed to tell you how scared I was," Alice admitted. "When I saw that man start up the ridge to the Sisters, it scared me, and I hid in the rocks. Still can't believe I did that."

"He must really have been scary, then," Jennie said, "because, Alice, you don't look like you scare easily."

"She doesn't," Gran said with satisfaction.

"But Jennie, I have a couple of questions too," Alice said. "When I first heard a body was found in the Dorain, not in the glen down below here, I just assumed it couldn't have been the man I saw in the mist. But if it was Angus, and if he was hurt in the skirmish in the mist, and that's two if's, how did Angus get from above the glen on this property, on this end of town, over to the Dorain? And assuming he took himself over there, as opposed to being carried by someone, what would have taken him to the distillery?"

Jennie poured more tea. "I'm sorry I didn't make anything of my own for you, Kathy," Jennie said, passing the cookies. "Please have these biscuits, though. The pastor brought them along." She set down the plate. She's being deliberate, Alice thought. "Now, about your questions. I do not know the answer. He did say recently he'd caught some men trespassing. 'Damned detectorists,' he said. Of course I assume he meant they were here on the estate. And then he said, 'That Dockery lad's got a lot to answer for, if he's why they're here.'"

"So did he mean Davie Dockery?" asked Alice.

"I assume so, but he wouldn't say more, or why." She looked at Gran. "You knew him, Gran. I always thought Angus would be a great spy, because if he didn't want to tell you something, you couldn't torture it out of him. Though I was sometimes tempted."

Alice wanted to hear more. "How did he know Davie Dockery? If he meant Davie, what would he have been thinking Davie had to answer for?"

"Davie—well, after Angus and I married, I knew Angus worried about some of the Broadview boys, and Davie was one. He coached Davie on the town football team. I remember he tried to help him find a job after school. Then when Davie moved to Glasgow to work, he got in some trouble and Angus drove up there to try to talk sense into him. Angus said he was running with a bad crowd. If I remember, one of Davie's friends who also worked in that fancy kitchen got arrested for theft, and Davie nearly got arrested himself. He had to give testimony in court. After that's when Angus helped him get the job at the distillery, to get him away from Glasgow."

"And now Davie's dead too," Gran said. "What's the link?"

Jennie shook her head. "You're assuming there is one. If so, I don't know. I never really knew Davie's family. Davie had a rough go of it. His dad flew the coop right after he was born. His mom moved back near Newton Stewart after Davie finished school. Davie told me once that Angus was the only father he really had." Her nose turned pink and she wiped it. "Sorry."

"Did Davie have a girlfriend?"

"Hmm. You might ask the people at the distillery. Fiona Smith would know. Or her nosy mother, Maggie. She'd make it her business if anyone would."

Gran put down her cup. "Now, this is enough, Jennie. Let's talk about you. What are you going to do? Will you stay here?"

Her eyes filled but no tears spilled. "No, there's no way. The Flemings are desperate to sell the property. They had an offer last fall, but it fell through."

Alice wondered if Jennie had heard anything about Gran refusing to sell.

Jennie went on. "The Flemings don't think they can make their land pay under that proposed Scottish Land Reform Bill. They're afraid of what the new taxes may be on deer stalking. This summer I know they got a new offer from a man named Zhou, from Shanghai. Apparently it had conditions in it. The buyer wanted a package deal, with Angus to stay on as ghillie, so the buyer could bring his London clients up to shoot, or fish. With Angus dead—I don't know whether he'll still buy or not, but any way it turns out, I'll likely be turned out."

"Where will you go?"

"There's insurance money. I may try to find a small place here. Jamie's happy in his school. My sister's in Newton Stewart so I have family close enough. I'm not ready to try a new town."

"Well, if you decide you do want to try something new, talk to Alice here. She lost her husband—our Jordie, you know—and moved her law practice to Coffee Creek, Texas. That took some getting used to, didn't it, Alice? But was it good, ultimately?"

"It was good. I was down to wearing all brown, if you know what I mean."

A weak smile. "I do."

"I was completely in a rut. Moving to Coffee Creek—I met new people." The Beer Barons. Her friends Red and Miranda. Clients like Ollie West and Muddy Mackin. And Kinsear. "And I encountered a new set of problems to occupy my mind." Maybe it would be tactless to mention to this widowed woman that the new problems involved solving murders, like who killed her client.

"So, change helped?" asked Jennie.

"Yes. But I didn't make that move until sometime . . . after Jordie died." She always had trouble saying "after Jordie died," since his body was never found. When had he died? Instantly? Or had he floated in the North Sea for hours? She shut her mind to the thought. "But you will make your own decisions and they'll be right for you."

They heard a quick knock, then the sound of the back door opening. Jennie got to her feet. "I'll just be a moment." She returned quickly, with an apologetic smile. "Sorry. That was Reid Fleming."

"He's Mr. Robert Fleming's grandson. Robert Junior's son," Gran explained to Alice. Ah. The archeologist.

"He was helping Angus this summer, getting ready for the grouse," Jennie added.

"Yes, the Glorious Twelfth," Gran said, exaggerating *glorious.* "You just missed it, Alice, the day we open season on our red grouse." Alice knew that Gran despised the mass slaughter of toothsome birds across Scotland on that date, but she also knew that Gran liked to cook red grouse.

"I remember," Alice said. Personally she liked red grouse with a reduction of cream and port wine and a few juniper berries. "So the Flemings have lots of hunters?"

"Well," Jennie said, "they used to, but not so many booked this year as last. The lodge got a bad review online."

"A bad review? I thought it was all private parties!" Gran said.

"Old Mr. Robert Fleming's son, Robert Junior, thought it would increase bookings to put the lodge online. A miserable group arrived in August last year and wrote some really unkind things."

"But surely not about your cooking!" Gran exclaimed. She turned to Alice. "Jennie's dinners are very well known."

"I wasn't cooking," Jennie said, stone-faced. "They thought it would go better with a London chef."

"Sounds a bit like Samantha Fleming's thinking?" asked Gran.

Jennie nodded. "No harm in saying yes to that, with Angus dead. Yes, Samantha. She wanted fancy dinners for fancy groups. Not my usual menus any longer."

Gran put down her teacup. "What was Reid doing for Angus? I thought he was spending the summer working up north at that Orkney site, for his degree."

"Yes, he was. But I think funding was down. And he says the weather is horrid in the Orkneys even in summer."

"Was he working at the Ness of Brodgar?" asked Alice. "Big Stone Age excavation?"

"Yes, but he'd tell you many times it's 'Neolithic,'" said Jennie.

Gran persisted. "Wasn't he to finish his degree this year, in bones or archeology or anthropology?"

"Oh, you know kids these days. They all seem to take a gap year."

"Did you ever get one?" Alice asked, smiling, meaning to be funny. "A gap year?"

"Right now I feel my whole life's a gap. In a different way. No Angus . . . and finding a new job, and a new place to live."

Gran said with asperity, "It's very difficult for me to believe the Flemings would ask you to go."

"Well, this is the ghillie's cottage. And they'll need a new ghillie. Or the new owner will."

"Who told you that?"

"Miss Samantha."

Alice shuddered at the "Miss Samantha" and the idea of living with such class-burdened mores.

"Taking over, isn't she." Alice had never heard Gran so acerbic.

A shadow passed the front window and again Alice heard steps in the back entry. An athletic-looking ginger-haired youth, over six feet tall, appeared from the kitchen and walked over to the tea table. Alice recognized him from Sunday night at the pub.

"Oh, Reid!" said Jennie.

"Sorry to interrupt," he said, "but I wanted to mention we're fixing the lock on your gate today. Hello, Mrs. Greer. What an unexpected pleasure." He extended his hand.

Alice saw a speculative look, then certainty, in Gran's face. "Surely not unexpected that I'd call on our dear friend Jennie, after this awful news about Angus," said Gran. "So what are you doing at home messing with locks on gates, Reid? What about your studies in the Orkneys?"

A slow flush colored his neck, then his jaw. "I came home to help Angus with the grouse."

"But isn't this the best excavating season at the Ness of Brodgar?" asked Gran. "Will you be back at Cambridge this fall? As I recall, your degree is nearly finished."

The flush rose further. "I've told the department I'm taking a short break."

"Ah."

"Well, I'll say good-bye, ladies." And he walked out.

Gran turned to Jennie. "Does he always just walk in, Jennie? Seems a bit 'lord of the manor,' not even to knock."

"He—well, he's been coming around a good bit," said Jennie. "Likely to see if I need help, with Angus gone."

"He didn't do that when Angus was here, did he?"

Jennie shook her head. "Of course not! Angus would've—" But she teared up, grabbed for a tissue and blew her nose.

"Was he working a good bit with Angus?" asked Gran.

"No. Not that much. Angus said he couldn't always find him. But you know what boys can be like."

Gran shifted subjects, asking about Jennie's little boy and school. Alice wondered when Gran would send the "time to go" signal.

"There is one thing bothering me, Kathy," said Jennie. "One of Angus's guns is missing. It's not in the locked cabinet at his office, where he always kept it. The Flemings asked me to come get his belongings. I've looked everywhere for that gun. Do you suppose he had it when he fell, and the police haven't told me?"

"Perhaps it's in one of the Land Rovers?"

"I've glanced in, but maybe I didn't look hard enough."

"It'll turn up." As an afterthought Gran said, "It's his gun, right? Not the Flemings'?"

"Oh, it's Angus's father's shotgun. Angus was fond of it. There were still two rifles in the cabinet and I brought them home."

"But this one was not a rifle?"

"Right."

They all stood up. "Thank you for a lovely visit," said Gran. "If you think of anything else about Angus or Davie, will you let us know? Those men who were trespassing on my farm—we're pretty sure they are the same ones Angus was chewing out in the mist."

"I will," said Jennie McBride.

"And keep me posted about the Flemings. Did you have a lease? I mean, were you a tenant? Would you have any rights under the new land reform law?"

"I don't know. I don't think so. There wasn't any lease—the ghillie just always lived in this house."

"If you have to make a sudden move, let me know." Gran was thinking Jennie could stay awhile in the tenant cottage at the farm, Alice was sure.

Jennie nodded. Her face was stark. She closed the front door.

Chapter Nineteen

Who'd *Gotten More* Answers?

"**W**ell, that is odd," Gran said, as they walked downhill from Jennie's. A lark sang off to their right, high above the barley field that reached the edge of the glen. The air smelled of water running over granite, of earth, and faintly of the sea. Alice took a deep breath and held it before she let it out.

"Gran, you sounded like Sherlock Holmes back there. I felt dumb and Watsonian. What's odd?"

"Odd that Reid Fleming thinks he can come and go in Angus's cottage. Odd that the Flemings would turn out Jennie when Angus worked for them thirty years."

"But won't they need her cottage?"

Gran sniffed. "They have other cottages. And it's odd that Reid Fleming isn't finishing his degree in bones or whatever. Maybe he's decided he doesn't have to work."

"Or maybe he's having trouble finding a job in anthropology. These kids"—Alice thought of her own John and Ann—"we tell them to follow their interests, and then they discover they can't find a job, except as a bartender or barista."

"Was that true for you, Alice?"

"I was lucky. Went to law school, found it was like solving moving crossword puzzles for real people. Then I met Jordie."

"And found a job, did well, and raised your children," Gran said.

"So I'm very lucky, even if Jordie had the poor taste to take that helicopter ride."

"I'm lucky too," said Gran. "Jordie brought you here." She smiled. Alice smiled back at the suntanned, wrinkled face, the thoughtful eyes, the faint and faintly worrisome fragility of her mother-in-law.

"So, was that everything that seemed odd?"

"Angus's death is very odd," Gran said. "The world seems upside down without him."

"And Davie Dockery?"

"I don't understand that boy's death at all. Poor Davie. Why did he have to die?"

Alice shook her head. She had no answer.

"I'll tell you one more thing that was odd," Gran said.

"And that is?"

"Reid Fleming was wearing Hammam Bouquet just now. I'm positive."

Aha. That was why Gran's face had changed when she was talking to Reid.

"So was he the one who held you down? At the apple bobbing?"

"Seems so."

"And then ran his car into you?"

"I'm thinking so."

"But that was last fall, when maybe he was hoping to make you sell. What's the story now?"

They had almost reached Harbour Road. "Let's stop and get smoked salmon for tea again," said Gran. "Do you mind walking over to John Dougal's? I'll stop at the grocer's for biscuits and cheese. And brown bread at the baker's."

Alice didn't mind. She was curious about Georgie Porgie. The wind swooped down from the Sisters, ruffling her hair, as she crossed Harbour Road and walked out onto the long pier, made of massive wooden beams. Two men fished off the far end. She passed an art gallery, a knitting store, a pizza shop, an ice cream store, and a fly-fishing shop and entered Dougal Fish Merchants. No other customers were there. She pressed the counter bell.

"Ah! Mrs. Greer the Younger! I'm awfully glad to see you again," he said, popping through the door behind the counter. Lord, thought Alice, he is ridiculously handsome. Criminally handsome.

The criminally handsome one fixed her with an appraising eye. "What'll it be, madam?"

"Some plain peat-smoked salmon please, for Gran's tea today."

"And what about adding my quite spicy salmon spread?" He emphasized the spicy. Good grief, thought Alice. "Mrs. Greer the Elder is fond of it, she tells me."

"All right."

He bustled about, carefully filling a container with rosy-orange salmon pâté and laying perfectly smoked salmon slices on a sheet of brown paper. Alice salivated, staring at the salmon.

She pulled out her wallet.

John Dougal said, "When are you going to let me take you sailing? Show you the coast? Have a picnic?"

"This is a bit sudden. I've only made a small salmon purchase."

"You've been here a week so you're already a citizen."

The awareness of Kinsear popped into her head. No, he'd been there already, before she pulled open John Dougal's door. Like a reminder, a caution. Still—Robbie had taken Birnbach and Jorgé to Whithorn today, and she hadn't gone. She felt the pull of the sea, wanted to get out in a boat, look at the shore from afar. "Where do you keep your boat?"

"Right there where I can see it. *The Catch*." He pointed. She was black and sleek, though small, rocking gently in the sunny water fifty yards away. "I'll bring the picnic," he offered. "I close at noon today. Just a picnic for a couple of hours? I'll have you home for tea."

Alice looked at him for a long five seconds. Why was he so insistent?

"You can crew, I assume? You've sailed *Lark Arising?*" He nodded at Gran's boat, moored just beyond *The Catch*.

"A few times," Alice agreed.

"Well, take these to Mrs. Greer the Elder and come back and we'll go for a sail."

* * * * *

Carrying her purchases, she met Gran outside the Harbour Road bakery. Gran raised an eyebrow and grinned upon hearing of her plans. "John Dougal invited you, hmm?" Then she narrowed her eyes. "Maybe, Alice, you can find out why he and Angus were so cool to each other."

"Ah. Okay." Two tomcats, perhaps?

* * * * *

Once on the water Alice felt her mood lighten. The rush of water along the side of *The Catch*, the sparkle on the waves, the wind tugging at her clothes, and the familiar thrill when the sail flapped, then filled, and the boat responded and was cutting across the harbor toward the bay—it's like champagne, she thought, like someone just popped the cork. She lifted her face to the sun.

She found that her scanty nautical vocabulary was returning. Dougal, at the tiller, said little as they worked their way out into the bay. "Heading in the direction of Cairngaan," he called. "We'll stop in the lee of the peninsula for our picnic." Cairngaan lay on the tip of the little peninsula that pointed south, toward the Isle of Man, across the bay from Broadview.

Late summer sun stayed with them all the way. Nearing the peninsula, they dropped sail and let the boat rock. Alice unpacked the hamper and passed salmon and butter sandwiches on brown bread to Dougal, who had made them. He unscrewed the cap on some New Zealand sauvignon blanc. Alice liked that wine. She liked New Zealand pinot noir even better, but was keeping her preferences private from this overeager salmon smoker. She planned to query him, per Gran's instructions, but he beat her to the punch.

"So, how is it being daughter-in-law to the saintly Kathy Greer?"

"Saintly?"

"Oh, everyone loves her. The perfect parishioner."

"Parishioner? How would you know her status? Are you active in her church?"

"Clearly I've gotten off on the wrong foot. How is it that even after Jordie Greer's death you're here?"

"You think I should've dropped the acquaintance? Of my children's grandmother?"

"Ah. I hadn't heard about the children."

"Son and daughter."

"Back in America, of course?"

"My daughter"—she started to tell about Ann's job in Edinburgh, then suddenly felt cautious. "My daughter will be a junior in college. My son will be a senior. And you? Married? Children?"

"No, and no."

"Why not? No one in Oxford appealing enough?"

"Broadview had its own charms but that didn't work out." Before she could pry further, he said, "Mrs. Greer must have mentioned

Oxford."

"She said, a first in Greats. That sounds impressive, but doesn't explain how you became the artisanal salmon smoker here."

"I learned from a master who died and I wanted the art to live."

"Was he from Broadview?"

"She. My mother."

"Oh."

"She'd always wanted her own business. She knew how to smoke salmon to perfection. But she died."

"I'm so sorry. After Oxford?"

"No, just before I finished."

They bent to their wine, their salmon, their apples.

"So, back to Mrs. Greer the Senior," he said.

"You don't seem to like her."

"Oh, of course I do. Just curious what she's like."

"She's lovely." Alice considered. "Very farsighted. Very strong."

"And she'll always keep her farm?"

"Of course! It's part of her heritage."

"Must be lonely for her."

"Not really. She has friends here."

"But isn't her main home Edinburgh? Isn't most of her acquaintance there?"

"Why are you so interested?"

"Just making conversation. So, you just came over to see her?"

"Yes." Awkward silence. Alice thought, I'm not explaining that someone's been frightening her, maybe you, for all I know. "How'd you know about the offer?"

"Probably at the pub." He poured more wine into their plastic cups. "Isn't it hard, getting loose from a law practice?"

"Yes. And I'll bet your customers grouse when their favorite salmon-smoker's out of town, right?"

He nodded. "They do fuss."

"Is it easy starting an enterprise in Broadview? Do you sell to Newton Stewart?"

"Oh, yes. I deliver to Glasgow and Edinburgh too."

"Refrigerated van?"

He frowned at the question. "Big coolers."

"How can you smoke salmon and deliver it too?"

He grinned. "Marketing. I find delivering it myself is the best way to get feedback and repeat orders. So I organize the workweek that way. I make my deliveries to Edinburgh and Glasgow on Sunday afternoon and late Thursday."

"And is that blue van yours?"

"What blue van?" He squinted at her, brows drawn together.

"Oh, I've seen it around town."

He shrugged.

"What's it like living in Broadview, after Oxford?"

"Do you mean, is there anyone here to talk to about the Second Punic War?" Laugh lines by his eyes.

"Small towns," Alice mused. "I live in one too. I've made good friends there. Really, I'm there because of those friends." She wondered who his friends were in this little Scottish town.

"Broadview's a bit small," he said finally. "It would be nice if we had a few more real chefs here. My products get lots of appreciation in Edinburgh and Glasgow . . . not so much here."

"'A prophet is not without honor, save in his own country'?"

"Something like that. And it's true that Broadview sometimes feels a bit short on interesting new people. Why don't you stay longer?" He moved closer. The boat rocked. He leaned forward and kissed her cheek, holding her shoulder with one hand, then began to slide his mouth toward hers. Alice turned her head, leaned back and looked at him.

"I seem to be rushing my campaign." He poured more sauvignon blanc.

"I thought we were having a friendly sail into the bay, back in time for tea." She took one more sip of the wine, and looked south. "The wind's coming up." A gray wet cloud was moving fast, out over the bay, coming their way.

He looked back. "We'll have to run for it. Get your proofs on—it'll be wet." He stowed the picnic in less than a minute.

Alice pulled on her rain jacket and held tight.

"Coming about!" She ducked. Ropes rattled. "Hold the tiller for a sec!" They swapped places, Alice grabbing the tiller and trying to hold the point. "Jib!" he called, pulling up the jib. The bow plunged and bucked and suddenly they were flying down the bay on a reach taking them toward Broadview. "We'll come about again when we get far enough south, and head in to Broadview!" he shouted. She blinked to clear the sea spray from her eyes. Now they were passing Gran's small cove, with its white curve of sand and stack of gray boulders.

She pointed. "Viking landing spot?"

Dougal looked where she pointed and shook his head. "I don't think so!"

"Why not?" It was hard yelling into the wind. "Gentle slope to land your boat and rush uphill, right?"

He shook his head. "They'd simply make for the bigger harbor next door."

Alice frowned, the strong images of her imagined Viking foray still vivid. She thought he might be wrong. And why so adamant on such a small point?

The boat skittered and bounced, wet cold air rushing past Alice's eyes, spray stinging her face. The far side of the harbor was coming up fast. Dougal crawled back and took the tiller. "Hold the line! Ready? Coming about!"

Alice ducked, holding the line, and they came about, heading straight into the harbor. "Take the tiller!" He scrambled up, dropped the jib, then the mainsail. They were almost to his buoy. The wind noise lessened. Dougal grinned a piratical grin at her. "Good sail," he said.

"I surprised two metal detectorists on Gran's farm," she said. "You know anything about that?"

"Of course not." He gave her an annoyed look. "What'd you do?" he asked.

"Chased them away. Literally. In their van."

"Ah. Their blue van?"

"Mmm."

He leaned over the water, reaching for the mooring buoy, attaching the line. He waved at the boy at the harbormaster's office, who set out running down the pier to the harbormaster's Zodiac. "Did you get a good look at them?"

She recited, "Big guy, light jacket; shorter blocky guy with fierce black hair. Know anyone in town like that?"

"You think they're locals?"

"No, but."

"Why do you think I know anything about it? I'm hurt! We just met and you think I'm a villain!"

She laughed. One more question to ask. "Someone said you didn't care much for Angus McBride."

"Who's talking about me?"

She shrugged.

His face tightened. "Angus was a fine man."

"But?"

Silence. They heard the motor on the Zodiac start. Alice slung her backpack over her shoulder. She felt exhilarated. Was it the race home against the wind and rain, beating the storm? Or that cheeky exploratory kiss? Or their sparring—he answered questions with questions, and hadn't she done the same? The Zodiac was fifty yards away and closing fast. Dougal took her chin in his fingers. Alice raised an eyebrow and pulled her head back. "My campaign continues," he said. "Next time, try for Arran and hike up to the stone circle over there? Day after tomorrow?"

She dodged. "That's way too far. And I'm heading out of town for the weekend." She and Dougal clambered into the Zodiac. "You just made it," said the boy, nodding at the onrushing gray cloud, rain beginning to shatter the waves. The motor roared.

At the dock she thanked Dougal.

"Tell the sainted Mrs. Greer I hope she stays, even if Mr. Zhou buys the Fleming place. He buys my fish when he's in town. And you didn't say my campaign is futile, so expect my invitation to crew to Arran. Or at least the Isle of Man."

Alice smiled and tipped her head sideways. Maybe yes, maybe no. And Mr. Zhou?

Walking back down the pier, she thought, Alice, Alice. Just tell the man no. But Gran said to find out. The rain renewed its efforts, raindrops bouncing off the wooden pier. She pulled up her hood, dashing through the noisy rain to Harbour Road and on to Gran's, still wondering why an Oxford graduate had come back to a small town like Broadview. But Alice, what about you? asked her inner critic. You chose Coffee Creek, Texas. Yes, but after marriage and children and building a career. Well, but he's building a business based on artisanal local salmon. You tasted it, it's excellent. Why so suspicious? Because . . . because he wanted to take me sailing. So? Maybe he really did want to take you sailing. Maybe . . . but . . . and at this point she wondered who'd gotten more answers, he or she? It had been a mutual interrogation.

She felt better about Georgie Porgie, though. At least if he made deliveries to Edinburgh and Glasgow every Sunday, he wasn't the third man Davie saw upstream from the distillery, which not only narrowed the field, but came as a relief. She wouldn't want to have gone sailing with a murderer.

C h a p t e r   T w e n t y

Lassie, *Lie Near* Me

171

On the way home to Gran's, partly fueled by faint guilt over her picnic sail, Alice called Kinsear. "How are things looking? Are we on for the Great Glen Way? What are you doing right now?"

"Thinking about you," he said, "because our prof did indeed cancel class for tomorrow, so he can travel to Orkney to examine a new find. We have Friday and Monday off, in fact. And Alice, you didn't answer your phone. I confess I'm already over halfway to Fort William. Can you leave now and meet me there? Late dinner?"

Yes. She could.

She told Gran where she was going. "Will you be all right for four days?" Alice asked her. "We still haven't found the invading detectorists. We still don't know who killed Angus and Davie."

"Of course you should go. It'll be lovely," Gran said. "I'll be fine with Robbie here."

Jorgé and Birnbach had driven north to taste Speyside malts near Inverness, and would fly home from Edinburgh on Sunday. Alice had the impression Robbie hadn't spent the night in her room, and allowed herself to imagine how Jorgé and Robbie might be feeling about each other. She found Robbie upstairs and got assurances that yes, she would watch Gran like a hawk, would lock the doors every night, and would bash any invaders with the winning oar that still hung over her bed upstairs.

Alice was packing. A road trip!

And she was ready for fall. Fall had been sneaking up in Texas when she left for Scotland. Oh, sure, the infernal August heat hadn't abated, but when she took her coffee out on the deck in the early morning, she could hear the marching band of Coffee Creek High School practicing miles away; she could practically feel the vibration of the big bass drum, ready to be unleashed on the football field. When she got back home, if there'd been a couple of good rains and the county lifted the burn ban, plumes of blue smoke would rise across the hills, perfuming the air with the aroma of cedar from the burn piles cut and stacked on neighboring ranches. But Scotland, further north on the planet, offered a different fall. The air felt chilly and damp, with odors of green turf and real dirt, deep dirt, and, instead of cedar smoke, the old-fashioned and penetrating whiff of the first coal fires in iron stoves. In Scotland fall color meant purple heather blanketing the hills, punctuated by pockets of bright yellow gorse, with the green bracken beginning to turn to bronze.

"What is it about fall?" she asked Robbie who'd come in to watch and, unusually, had perched companionably on Alice's bed. "Is it all those years of going back to school? I feel some vague regrets for the past—not sure why—and nostalgia, for smells and sights I can't describe, and a desire for new ventures . . ."

"First day of rowing practice," Robbie said. "Watching the trees change color on the bank, watching the geese fly south above you, while you're rowing hard, knowing that next week you'll need another layer of wool . . ." She looked at Alice's open suitcase. "You'd better take a couple of those woolly layers with you. And for God's sake don't forget your proofs! Show me your proofs!" Alice dutifully lifted the folded hiking pants and pointed at the guaranteed waterproof pants and jacket, still bearing store tags. "Very sexy," Robbie said, grinning. "And they'll make a lovely swish-swish noise when you walk in them."

* * * * *

Alice met Kinsear at the Loch Inn in Fort William on Thursday evening. Her heart thumped when she saw him waiting outside, a tall man, rangy, in jeans, his dark curly hair showing some gray. Alice, Alice, she thought. Admit you are extremely glad to see him. Extremely glad. Not just because of the way he appreciates your neck, your— but he was opening her door now. She climbed out of the car into a serious kiss. Guilt surged; no, she would not think of Dougal. She kissed Kinsear back, banishing the salmon smoker. This was Kinsear. She had not underestimated the appeal. Here he was, the intelligent eyes, the bristling eyebrows, the certainty of his warmth, his strength. And his enthusiasm. "You're here! The place looks great. And so do you." Alice was a sucker for that blue chambray shirt of his and suspected he knew it.

He took charge of her sticks and bag and headed up the stairs of their B&B. "You'll like it."

Alice let out a low whistle at the room. Somehow they'd lucked into a former living room, now rearranged as bedroom with bath. The four-poster bed stood next to a fireplace, glowing with welcome heat.

"You could drown in the tub," Kinsear said. "Or swim laps."

She peeked into the bathroom. Victorian fixtures, a wavery antique mirror, a stack of generous towels. A most inviting long tub encased in dark polished wood. "What about a bath, before dinner?" she said.

"You're talking about a communal bath, I trust? Let me just help you with those clothes."

Hooks. Zippers. The bath had to wait.

At one blissful point, Alice's eyes popped open at an intruding thought about the men in the mist. Then she dismissed it, but set aside for later consideration how very *comforted* she felt with Kinsear. An odd word, for this mix of passion and hilarity, hiking and book talk. Yet she always felt herself pulling back a bit. She resolved to think later about her suspicion that her resistance partly arose from her effort to dodge future pain—pain like losing Jordie.

Kinsear looked at his watch. "Oh no! We still need to buy maps!" After a dash to the outdoor store, fortunately still open, where they bought hiking maps and the highly recommended map case ("something no Central Texas hiker has ever dreamed of," Kinsear said), they searched out a pub on the main street of Fort William. "Classic," said Kinsear, after reconnoitering. "Is pub grub okay? It will fortify us for the hills ahead."

They settled into their corner booth. "Here's to the Great Glen Way." He lifted his glass. "And a little uninterrupted time together."

She clinked his glass with hers. In her head rang the sweet voice of the Seaheart guitarist, singing "Lassie, Lie Near Me." And she thought, yes, I will.

* * * * *

The proprietor of the B&B announced he could be happy for a wee fee to watch their cars for a couple of days. He shook his head, smiling, as they stalked out after breakfast Friday morning, clutching maps and backpacks and hiking sticks. Kinsear and Alice, scanning each other, agreed they did look comical, trotting down the sidewalk with their hiking sticks akimbo, while trying to pinpoint their starting place on the partly unfolded and flapping map. "We can't walk side by side with these sticks on this sidewalk!"

Kinsear collapsed the sticks and she tied them to his pack.

"The map's getting wet!" Alice said, as a few raindrops began to speckle their jackets. "Where's that map thing?"

The map case that had been heartily recommended at the outdoor shop consisted of a clear plastic envelope worn around the neck, so that a doughty Scottish hiker could squint through the rain at the route without getting the map soggy.

"I'll flip you for who has to wear it," Kinsear said. "Ridiculous. Looks like a baby's bib." He lost. Resigned, he let Alice drop the new encumbrance over his head and around his neck. "Oh well, since I have the map, I get power over the route," he remarked. "And I say the route requires that we have some real coffee before we cross that bridge and start the trail."

Clouds were settling down atop Ben Nevis, looming over Fort William, when they finally escaped the town and crossed onto the bridge over the River Lochy. The rain pelted harder. Alice peeked out from under her hood. Ben Nevis had completely disappeared. The rain rattled on her hood.

"That's not rain. That's sleet!" said Kinsear, holding out his hand, looking in disbelief at the wet crystals. "Sleet in August!"

"Scotland forever!" cried Alice, wiping her nose with a wet tissue. They took selfies on the bridge. "Is my nose really that pink?"

"Yep." And they were off the bridge and on a wooded trail, watching for the way markers.

That day they tramped up the river and then along the Caledonian Canal, always heading north. They'd doubled up on distance for their first day, deciding to make it all the way to Laggan. It was nearly dark when they found their B&B. Their hostess welcomed them with hot tea and pointed them down the road to the Eagle Barge restaurant at Laggan Locks. The barge rocked slightly as they walked up the gangway and into the warm fug of a combined bar and restaurant. "This is a 1926 Dutch barge that carried troops in World War II," Alice read on the framed photograph inside the entrance.

"Bar first," said Kinsear. "I want to taste some single malts."

The bartender, a non-smiling no-nonsense hefty-armed woman, gave them small tastes of local malts, showed Kinsear how to add only a teaspoon of very pure water to his whisky, and finally warmed up enough to his questions to give suggestions as to what to try next. They sighed, contented: they'd finished their long first day, and their feet, their legs, and their minds felt pleasantly tired. They collapsed into a booth and lifted a toast as Alice's poached trout and Kinsear's peat-smoked salmon arrived. The barge was full of low laughter, hustling waiters, memorabilia, varied faces. Alice made up stories about the raffish characters at the table by the bar. Kinsear invented a backstory for the bartender.

Flashlights in hand, they made their way through mist and rain to the B&B. "It'll still be wet tomorrow," promised their hostess cheerfully. "Now what time would you like breakfast?"

And they did need their proofs again as they set off on Saturday morning toward Fort Augustus, but had to stop to take them off and stow them in their packs by eleven. The sun sparkled on the canal. In the woods, leaves were turning gold and red. "Fall here, already!" Alice said.

On the second day they hit their stride, walking, talking, stopping to watch a barge move through the locks, eating lunch in watery sun by the famous swing bridge. They talked about their children. They talked about the Scots. They talked about books. Kinsear told her what fascinated him about archeology. "We always underestimate our ancestors, Alice," he said. "We think we're so special because— we're alive! Right now! And they're dead! So we must be smarter! But when you look at the beauty of the jade axes, when you look at the efficiency of the bronze weapon casting, when you look at the far reach of trading—farther than you'd think—well, we shouldn't underestimate their thoughts, their imaginations, their creativity. It's an exercise in humility, studying recent findings, because we're having to swallow prior assumptions that didn't credit the ambition, the navigation, the exploration, that drove our ancestors at least as much as it drives us. The migration! The distances! The sophistication!"

"And the bloodthirstiness, the slavery, the kidnapping?"

"Not much different from today, with armed piracy off the Horn of Africa and in the Straits, drug wars in Central and South America, sex slaves worldwide, religious warfare . . . You know what they say. Humans are far more murderous than most mammals, and certainly as murderous as most primates."

"Does your professor offer any hope for our murderous species?" she asked.

"That's not his job," Kinsear answered. "Maybe that's a question for physicists attempting to explain the universe, or for those who study meditation and its ability to expand empathy in humans. Or for Schweitzer, Mother Teresa, the Dalai Lama. Not archeologists."

Alice had felt her own murderous rage when trapped on a cliff by a killer. And without it, would she even be here walking with Kinsear? No. Had it scarred her? It certainly scared her. And, yes, scarred her some.

"Survival," she said. "What about the human drive to survive?"

"It's a conundrum. Our species has those who save, those who sacrifice—"

"—and those who murder," she answered.

"Okay, let's hear it. I've been waiting. Every detail, please."

She told him about Angus, the "arbiter of the village," dead, with a head wound that was not from his own silver-headed stick and, apparently, still alive when he hit the water in the Dorain. And why the Dorain, far from where she'd seen him? She told him about Davie, young, ambitious, saved by Angus from criminal connections in Glasgow, embarked on a promising career, but killed and stuffed onto a malt conveyor where—well, more than malt had been toasted. "Some toasting exposure occurred," the inspector had said euphemistically. She told him about Gran, frightened by a big SUV, harassed by phone calls, invaded by metal detectorists, dunked and held down at a children's party. She told him about digging up the blue beads. She told him about the two men at the museum and their blue van at the highway stop.

"But who are they and where are they?" he asked.

"It's weird. Robbie and I lost them. I looked all over Broadview for them. We can't find that van."

"It's got to be there. Unless they're keeping it in a mine, or quarry, or cave!"

"Or castle! But there's not one."

They walked on.

"If we didn't have to go back we could take the ferry to Orkney and see the Ness of Brodgar," Kinsear said. "My professor was up there when the season opened this summer. He knows the folks that run the program. They take in random guests every summer. I might do that next year."

Ahead of them Fort Augustus suddenly appeared, a village built along the locks of the river that poured into Loch Ness. And glimmering in the distance, blue in the afternoon sun, lay Loch Ness itself.

A would-be gypsy had decorated their rented bedroom ("all mod cons, en suite, charming décor") in the exotic "Kandahar B&B" style of Fort Augustus. Multicolored lengths of tulle fabric fluttered from the bedposts and rose into a canopy; a patchouli candle perfumed the room; gold stars were stenciled on the blue ceiling. More tulle made up the turban of their landlady, heavily made up, who fluttered her mascaraed lashes at Kinsear, then Alice, then Kinsear again, and glanced at their left hands. "I so hope you'll enjoy this little refuge!" she breathed. "See you at—breakfast!"

"Never has anyone made 'See you at—breakfast' sound so improper!" Kinsear said once she had left.

Alice was dousing the patchouli candle and opening windows, which looked out onto the locks. She peered into the en suite facilities. "A tub! Not just a shower, a tub!" Hot water. Bubble bath, even. "And it's a big tub. Left over from the Raj and shipped home in a huge steamer. Come look!"

Later, quite a bit later, they toweled off and remembered dinner.

Alice had reserved at the Boathouse Lochside, reached by a pretty garden of lavender that overlooked the loch. "I'm starving," Kinsear said. Walking all day, even with their substantial and comforting lunch, had made them wildly hungry.

And they were already hungry again at breakfast. Day three, Sunday, would take them up and along a multi-peaked ridge, hooded with clouds, on the west side of Loch Ness, to the little town of Invermoriston. "I'm puzzled by toast racks," Kinsear said, looking up from his guidebook, which he had leaned against the toast rack. "Why do you want your toast to cool? Why don't you want it hot so the butter melts? Anyway, did you know Loch Ness is a rift valley dividing the Grampian Mountains from the Northwest Highlands? It's the Great Glen Fault!"

"I knew that," said Alice. "Did you know that the deepest point of Loch Ness lies over seven hundred and eighty feet deep?"

"I knew that," said Kinsear. "More or less. I understand that's where Nessie lives. Did you know that the Great Glen was full of a glacier ten thousand years ago?"

"Great times!" said Alice, reminded of the museum display in Edinburgh. "Did you know how cold the water is? Only forty-two degrees Fahrenheit but it never freezes!"

"So, let's don't fall in," said Kinsear. "Ready?"

And they were off.

They stopped to eat granola bars at a stone bench high above the loch. Pine forest lay below them. Above, clouds flirted with the bare rounded knobs of the ridge. They hadn't seen a soul all day. In the silence, Alice heard delicate single notes, like a violin playing pizzicato. She tugged Kinsear's sleeve and pointed at a small yellowish bird darging from tree to tree. "Gran calls that a chiff-chaff," she said. They sat side by side, listening to the birdsong.

"Here's a question," Kinsear said. "What about the guy who's staying with the minister? Ansley, you said. An archeologist of sorts?"

"Apparently. But I don't know any connection with Angus or Davie."

"Have you looked into whether he is who he says? I mean, who just wanders around looking at birds and archeological sites?"

"Maybe hundreds of retired Brits?" But Alice remembered seeing the binoculars glinting out from the Sisters, and remembered Gran's hasty concealment of the pit inside the sheepfold. "What could you see, archeologically speaking, from up on Ben Cathair?"

"Perhaps a good bit, depending on how much modern land disturbance there's been."

"Well, how would you look into someone like that?"

"You said he went to Cambridge, didn't you?"

"He said that."

"I'll check the alumni records. They're online."

"But he wasn't around last fall when Gran was getting those harassing calls, when she got dunked and her car was hit by that big SUV."

"Tell me about those calls."

"He said he was the agent for the Flemings. He told her she was holding up a valuable deal that would protect jobs for people like Angus McBride. Gran worries that her property's not contributing to the Broadview economy."

"Surely Gran wouldn't believe that's her duty?"

"The agent suggested that if she didn't sell, the village might organize to buy her out for more 'sustainable' development under a proposed land reform bill." Alice shook her head. "I don't think that has any teeth yet but who knows what will happen. The Fleming agent called back this week to say he's got another offer for the Flemings, suggesting she should sell too. And she got another call, an anonymous one, last Monday, telling her she'd better 'sell the farm fast.'" Once again she omitted any mention of the threat to the "little Texas lawyer." The thought made her stomach knot with anxiety, not for herself, safe above Loch Ness with Kinsear, but for Gran, at the farm. Well, Robbie was there.

"Two different callers, huh," Kinsear said. "That seems like overkill. Or are they even related?"

On the last switchback up they stood on top of the ridge, looking down into the leafy valley, where they could see a whitewashed, open-armed building. "Looks like a pub to me," said Kinsear. "A cold cider, a cold ale, a packet of crisps . . ." Down they went, and across the stone bridge to a small square. A wide-horned Highland bull, ruddy-gold, stood placidly on the lawn before the Glenmoriston Arms. "Stay put—you're fine where you are," Kinsear told him.

They sat on a bench in the sun, licking salt off their fingers from the crisps, sipping cider (Kinsear) and ale (Alice). No noise, other than birdsong, the snuffling of the bull, wind in the trees. "I don't want this to end," Alice said. "It's so peaceful."

But there was only one night left. At Drumnadrochit, their final destination, they would catch the bus back to Fort William, not going all the way to Inverness. One more night together, one more walk in the hills. Alice looked at Kinsear, who was staring at the bull. The bull stared back.

"I like his life," Kinsear said. "Standing on the town green, above Loch Ness. Lord of all he sees."

"Bet it's wet and cold in the winter," Alice said.

"He won't care. Look at that coat. And his bangs."

That night, after a mediocre but merry dinner, they curled up in bed at the B&B. Their room opened onto the upstairs hallway. The stairs creaked, the floors creaked, and they could hear other guests walking, laughing, talking, opening and shutting drawers and armoires and doors. "I'm not confident about the acoustic privacy here," whispered Kinsear. "How quiet can we be? Potentially?"

"Hmm," Alice whispered back. "I, personally, could be very quiet. I think."

* * * * *

The trail to Drumnadrochit ("I like to say that," said Kinsear, rolling the r's with gusto) split into the "High Route" and "Low Route." "Oh, we'll take the High Route," he sang, and up they went, up to the high bare slopes above the forest, stopping for pictures at the splendid views of the loch. But gray clouds moved in. They hurried through their lunch sandwiches and the inevitable crisps as rain began, and scrambled back downhill through partly logged pine forests to the Low Route.

It was nearly three when they reached Drumnadrochit. The rain stopped and low afternoon sun lit the water as they walked into town. "I need a Snickers bar and I'm going to have it this instant," Alice announced, pulling a squashed bar from her pocket. "But I'll share." They stashed their packs with the service which had moved their bags and headed down to the harbor pier, where a sign offered "Boat tour! Views of Urquhart Castle!"

They were the only takers for the afternoon tour. From water level Loch Ness felt even vaster than it looked from the ridgetops. Big, dark, deep. Full of secrets, she felt. Like all of Scotland. Including Broadview. Thinking of the cold depths below she was relieved when the boat returned to the pier.

The romantic interlude ended abruptly after their late-afternoon bus trip back along the loch to Fort William, retracing in just a few hours their four long days of walking. Once they arrived at their two separate cars, they kissed. They kissed again. "Tell me again why we brought two cars?" Alice asked.

"You wanted to," Kinsear reminded her. "I've noticed you always like to have your own wheels. In case you need to escape."

It was true. Alice felt in control only when she had her own car, her own keys. "Not very environmentally responsible," she thought. But.

They kissed again, retreated to their separate cars, started their separate engines, got on the motorway. At Glasgow he waved as she exited southwest. What was Kinsear thinking, on his long way back to Cambridge? wondered Alice. And she let herself think about him, about how easy a companion he was on this long walk, how solid he felt, how much fun it was to plop down with him for the post-walk cider and ale. How she wanted to sit longer at dinner with him, hear his comments about the Bronze Age, why he'd signed up for the Cambridge course, what he planned next for his Fredericksburg bookshop. He was interesting. And not alarming. She thought about his light hand with her. Never did he say "Here's what you need to do"—words that made her bow up, squint her eyes, resist. And without permission her mind went back to last night. He wasn't just interesting. Did she love him?

Love. Alice thought it required skin, fragrance, being fond of someone's hands, and also deep respect, comfort in someone's reliability, and the certainty she would not be bored. A tall order. The miles whirled by. She headed southwest through the night toward Broadview. She did love him. Could she just quit being skittish about saying so? She shook her head at herself.

Chapter Twenty-One

What Could *You Possibly* Do Next?

lice was dreaming the dogs were barking, but woke to
silence. Then what woke her? She shuffled into slippers
and down the narrow hall into the entry hall. A whimpering, on the porch. She unbolted the tall front door
and pulled it open. At her feet, a whimper, a quivering black-and-
white form: Sue, Gran's border collie. The dog crouched at the door,
unable to lift her head. Where was her boon companion, Queenie,
Gran's fat corgi? In the moonlight, motionless, by the hedge, Alice
saw the comical form. Not moving. She turned on the porch light,
listened to Sue's rapid breathing. She tiptoed through wet grass to
the still corgi. Queenie's eyes were open. She was still warm but Alice felt no warm breath.

She ran for the phone, found the vet's number in the list taped to
the back door. "Bring them here," said a sleepy voice. "I'll meet you
at the door."

Maybe he could save them. She threw on her bathrobe, ran to
the shed for the car, loaded both dogs, and found her way to the vet's
office. A yellow light burned above the door.

He didn't even glance at her robe and slippers, just helped carry
the dogs into the examining room.

"Bad luck." He looked up from Queenie's still form. "She's gone.
But Sue—let's see what we can do with you, my girl." He gave Alice a
sharp glance. "You'll have to help. She has a little nosebleed. I'm afraid
it's rat poison. We need to make her vomit."

Alice held Sue. To her relief, the dog finally vomited, and Alice
managed not to. "Aha," said the vet. "It looks like she did get hold of
some rat poison. At least we know what to treat for, now. Hold onto
her while I get my medication."

And finally, "Okay. You can go on home. I'll keep an eye on Sue
tonight. She's a determined sort. She may make it."

Alice looked at the still body of Queenie, on the other table.

"Mrs. Greer will want to bury Queenie at the farm, I believe,"
she said.

"Come get her in the morning. If it was rat poison, I may want
to take some sort of sample."

* * * * *

At first light Tuesday, Alice was outside, searching. And there it was—steak, under the hedge: two pieces, one more heavily gnawed. She wrapped them in plastic wrap for the vet and started for the stairs to waken Robbie, wondering how she would tell Gran.

Too late. Gran stood at the foot of the stairs. "Alice? What's wrong?"

Alice told her—told about finding the dogs, about Sue whimpering a warning on the doorstep, about the trip to the vet. And told her about the two pieces of gnawed steak, under the hedge.

Dry-eyed, Gran stared at the floor, hands clenched. "Who would do such a thing?" Then, looking at Alice's tired face, "Oh, Alice, thank you, thank you. You raced them to the vet. My poor dogs. Did they suffer?"

"I don't know," Alice said. "We can go by and see Sue this morning. And take the two pieces of steak to the vet."

Gran nodded, and lifted her chin. "Alice. I can only thank you again for flying across the Atlantic and coming to help. You've had to deal with such dirty work. I should've been the one to find my Queenie out there—I've had her all these years, you know. And the brave Sue."

But then Gran turned away and cried and cried, and Robbie, rubbing her eyes, came downstairs in her flannel pajamas and burst into tears too, patting Gran's back.

Good lord, Alice thought, wondering as usual why she wasn't crying at what seemed like the proper moment. So often, she didn't. And that embarrassed her. But after all, these weren't her dogs, though she had enjoyed Queenie's exuberance and admired Sue's purposeful intelligence. Still, for someone to do this to Gran now—what did it mean? The theft of building materials, disturbance of Gran's tenant, Gran's All Hallows Eve experiences: those were all consistent with pressuring Gran to sell. Poisoning dogs, though?

Gran echoed her thoughts. "Once you've killed someone's dogs, what could you possibly do next?" asked Gran. "How could losing my dogs make me sell? It breaks my heart, but it wouldn't make me sell." She looked at Robbie and Alice. "Maybe it's a warning, like in *The Godfather*. If I'm not scared, kill my dogs? Then once the dogs are gone, what? Kill the sheep? Or you two?"

Maybe it's simpler than that, Alice thought. After all, it was Sue who sounded the alarm when she and Robbie nearly caught the nighthawkers.

* * * * *

Kinsear was on the phone. She told him about the dogs. "Alice. That's sickening. What kind of lowlifes are you dealing with?" She could imagine the expression on his face. "Listen, speaking of lowlifes, I looked up your friend Ansley."

"He's not my friend."

"He's not exactly what he says he is, either. He enrolled at Cambridge, but was asked to leave. I can't quite tell why, but a friend here says it must have been cheating of some sort. It's an academic violation. Anyway, he got no degree and had to leave."

"He told me he had not studied archeology at Cambridge."

"But he did—at least, he enrolled for archeology."

"How'd you find all this out?"

"Oh, Cambridge has its little ways, keeps its little records. Here's something else. Didn't he tell you he taught history somewhere?"

"He did."

"He was asked to leave a boys' school in the Midlands because he'd falsified his resume."

"Whoa. So how is he surviving? How does he make a living?"

"That's a puzzle. I found an address for him and drove by. It's a nice-looking urban apartment building. But here's my big find. Are you ready?"

"Yes!"

"Okay. If you are really devoted to someone, thinking of her and seeking her love, and you look for hours at obscure sites online, you'll find a reference to P. Ansley offering antique jewelry for sale—really antique: 'Pair of Bronze Age earrings.' Also, 'Roman and earlier coins from Middle East.' Those references are a couple of years old, but

188

they made me wonder, especially with the antiquities smuggling these days from war zones in the Middle East. Collectors are still buying, you know."

"Mmm. That's *very* interesting."

"If I could only win her love," sang Kinsear in a hearty baritone, "I'd search the web both night and day . . ."

"I do miss you," she said. "I wish you were here right this minute."

"And how would you reward me for this research?"

Alice, standing in the hall, checked in both directions. No Gran, no Robbie. "I would start with your toes, and . . ."

"My toes?"

"Highly erogenous, if properly treated, which I think in your case would mean . . ."

"I'm hopping on one foot, trying to get my boots off so you can get at my toes."

She giggled.

"But seriously, Alice, you see what this means, right?"

"Not really. All I see is that Philip Ansley sounds like a loser, but we have nothing connecting him to anything that's happened. Whether murders or treasure hunting." But was he bird-watching up at the Sisters, or doing something else? She thought for a moment. "I wonder if Walter knows what you've found out. The minister, I mean. Ansley's been staying with him for six weeks now."

"I wonder too. Meanwhile, be careful of Ansley, will you? And, hey, I talked to my professor again. We're getting to be friends, actually. We've gone out for beers a couple of times."

"Yes?"

"So, about Ness of Brodgar. He said Reid Fleming is no longer welcome on that site."

"Really! Why?"

"He was discovered one night digging in a supposed temple area. Literally under a tarp, by flashlight. The prof had identified that as the site to be excavated the next day, anticipating figurines and other temple offerings. But of all things, the site is guarded by a watchdog, who started barking and raised the alarm. The archeologists and students came running out of their tents and lo and behold, there was your friend, bumping around underneath the tarp. Then he made things worse: he tried to lie, claimed he was just excited, wanted to make a discovery, make his bones as an archeologist. But it turned out he already had stashed a figurine in his pocket. And two students said he'd been asking them how valuable the artifacts were, what the market was. Then he tried to throw his weight around. 'My mother will take legal action,' et cetera. So, he's now persona non grata and not allowed back in the program. Ever."

"Not a believer in academic honor, huh?"

"No. He threatened my friend the professor when he left. My friend doesn't scare easily, but now he's had a security alarm installed at his home. So, that's your report of the day. And, by the way, I will be in your neck of the woods on Friday, at Newton Stewart."

"Really!"

"Yep. My prof is bringing us up for a field trip and talk. It was optional but I jumped on it. So cancel any dates you have. Let's have dinner."

This was it—time for Gran to meet Kinsear.

She agreed to come with him to the talk in Newton Stewart, then said, leaping into space: "Come for dinner here. It's time for Gran to meet you."

Silence. Then, "You're on."

She'd sold the breach, allowed entry to the interloper. He was coming to Jordie's turf.

She found Gran.

"Gran, that was my friend Kinsear. He's here Friday for an archeology event at Newton Stewart. May he spend the night? Or should I try to find him a bed at the pub?"

"Of course he can spend the night. Of course. We're all grown women here. Will he like my butt'ries, do you think? What about dinner? Will you eat out, or come here?"

Alice laughed, then heaved a big sigh. "You're the best. He'll love your butt'ries. I do want you to meet him. Let's eat here. He loves to cook, too."

Chapter Twenty-Two

Graves Speak *to* Us

At the vet's, Gran and Alice delivered the suspect pieces of meat. Then Alice left the keys with Gran, who was cooing over Sue. Once again Alice headed for town, marched up the police station stairs and asked for the inspector. She reported the dog poisoning and Queenie's death.

"But you saw no one, correct?"

"That's true."

"You're assuming the dog poisoners are the same two men you talked about earlier?"

"It's likely, isn't it? They've already trespassed at the farm."

"But there's no evidence here of a connection. The problem, Ms. Greer," said the inspector (she hated the way he drew out the "Ms."), "is that you have been able to give us no description of any help. You don't know their names. You have no photographs. Other people use their phones to take pictures of people they believe are criminals. You jump in your car and drive to the public danger and then cannot even provide a plate number for this supposed blue van!"

Alice felt rage, red rage, rise up to her eyeballs, her eyebrows, her hairline. "And you give no help to an elderly woman who has received threatening calls, been held down in a kettle of water, nearly been hit off the road, and now had her dogs poisoned!"

He leaned forward, eyebrows bristling. "Why didn't she call me? She hasn't asked us for help. She didn't report threatening calls. Mrs. Kathy Greer did not report the so-called kettle incident or that her car was hit. Once again, you are the sole source."

"She was ill and then in the hospital." Alice's voice trembled with rage.

He went on as if she had not spoken. "Only now am I hearing about her dogs."

"And again, I will be the only witness, as to finding the dogs and the poisoned steak, and that's not good enough for you," Alice said bitterly. She stood to leave. "I flew over here at Gran's request, to try to help her deal with these threats, but you don't credit anything I'm saying. Wrong sex, wrong nationality, and wrong profession."

"I don't even know who you are," he said, still planted in his chair.

"Nor do you care," she said. "God help the anonymous citizen who walks in and asks for help."

She was so furious she nearly walked into the doorjamb on the way out, but dodged it at the last second. Then she turned. "I'm glad my people left here in 1715," she said. "You probably wouldn't have liked them either." And she left.

* * * * *

Standing on the rocky verge of Harbour Road in this odd little town, so far from home, Alice angrily kicked a rock. But she kicked it with the soft toe of her running shoe, thereby adding pain to her wrath at herself. Why had she ever thought she could help Gran?

Here she knew no one. She had no resources, no one to call for the inside dope. The inspector thought she was a twit, a lightweight. Her professional status at home? Here, it was worthless. Worse, she was an outsider, a mere tourist with a return ticket, sure to disappear soon. In her Coffee Creek cases, she'd had a framework: she'd been trying to solve legal problems for her clients. Here, Gran's problem seemed to be trespassing metal detectorists, and a vague sort of hooliganism. And yet there were two dead people—what did they have to do with Gran?

She was so far from her comfort zone—so far from *her* town, *her* property, *her* office, *her* friends, *her* clients, *her* contacts. *Her* places— the Beer Barn, Rotary, her pasture, her view over the creek. Over here she literally did not understand the lay of the land—whose was it, and who could do what on it? The law? Weird. Treasure trove and the Queen's Remembrancer, for heaven's sake. Local politics? A mystery. The pub? What did those people talk about, in their soft, smiling, incomprehensible Scottish burrs? If they didn't want you to understand what they said, they could sure make that happen. It was like listening to a beehive, and about as helpful.

She was no further along with the hooligans. The inspector was right. The men in the mist? She'd never seen their faces. She couldn't give a description. The blue van? A chimera, with no license plate. And her own cowardice, her refusal to confront them? Disgraceful.

She kicked the rock again. She should go home. People needed

193

her at home. People counted on her to close sales, probate wills, draft conservation easements, solve problems. Here she floundered, failed, accomplished nothing. Didn't think to protect Gran's dogs.

Well, she countered, really, who would think that Gran's dogs would be poisoned?

Okay, Alice. She could think of nothing to do but run.

She pounded east along the harbor front, counting out the intervals in her head, and passed a surprised cyclist. Then she turned left for the uphill pull. Passing the distillery, on her left, she shivered at the thought of Davie Dockery, stabbed and thrown—no, cold-bloodedly arranged—on the conveyor belt that inexorably carried malted grain to the burning embers of the kiln. She shook her head. Think of something else. Think of the weekend with Kinsear. Think of something beautiful. But again she saw in her mind's eye the conveyor belt through the smudged window at the top of the pagoda tower stairs. Her instructions to her mind were not working. She speeded up, attacking the steep uphill section past the distillery, then turned left onto Upper Road. The sun came out and the view stopped her. Blue ocean. Two fishing boats headed out into the bay. She could almost see Ireland, could imagine St. Columba setting out to sea in his hide-covered coracle. She stopped on the bridge, looking down at the distillery. The pagoda roof puffed above the kiln. Fiona Smith, head down, was trudging from the parking lot back past the main building and toward the tasting room. Alice watched her. She looked a little lonely.

Okay. Pick it up. She headed west along Upper Road. Fields stretched off to the right along the uphill bank of the Dorain: barley, then pasture dotted with sheep, then trees climbing the southeast side of Ben Cathair. On her left, residential streets led down to the harbor. The road rose a bit and now on the right she saw the graveyard, with its wide view out to the bay, then the looming gray stone of the church, its front door ajar. Alice stopped. She always visited churches when traveling. And she'd visited this one often—she'd brought the children to the early Christmas Eve service. Ann had put her doll in the manger during the children's visit to the makeshift stable.

She walked up the gray flagstones, peered in the door, slipped through. The odor of sanctity—hymnals, pew cushions, late flowers. And the faint vibration she sometimes felt in an old church.

"Alice! How nice to see you!"

She jumped. Walter, the pastor. He'd stood up from the last pew, holding a small book.

"Oh, I'm sorry to startle you. I was looking at the text for Sunday."

Greek letters on the cover. "You're reading it in Greek."

He blushed. "It's an old habit of mine. Not important."

"I'm glad to see you." Pink light, blue light, gold light came through the windows. "It's peaceful in here."

"At the moment." He smiled. Suddenly Alice found herself saying, "May I talk to you for a moment?"

"Of course. Let's walk. As St. Augustine said, *solvitur ambulando.* Things come clear when we walk."

Out in the sun, murder seemed impossible. But as they walked into the graveyard she asked, "Did you know someone tried to poison Kathy's dogs? Little Queenie is dead."

He stopped, face horrified. "Are you sure it was poison?"

"Rat poison, the vet says."

He shook his head, eyes closed. "I'm so sorry. And Sue, how is Sue?"

"Recovering. She still has a little tremor. Also, did you know someone tried to run Kathy off the road last Halloween? All Hallows' Eve?"

This time he stopped and turned, scrutinizing her face. "No."

"Did she tell you about the phone calls she got urging her to sell?"

"No . . ." And he looked hurt. "Why didn't she tell me? Of course I'd want to know!"

"It was right after that when she had the first serious problem with her heart and had to go stay put in Edinburgh."

He nodded. "And now she's had this problem with the tenant, and the dog poisoning."

"And Angus is dead, and Davie Dockery."

"Do you think there's some link there?" he asked.

"I don't know yet."

Inside the graveyard, Alice sat on a granite bench by the wall, facing the sun. Walter sat down too. She faced him. "Did you ever hear any stories about the loan that the Flemings made to the Greers, and others, back after World War I, and how the Greers paid their debt off just before the Flemings were going to foreclose on the farm?"

"Such a long time ago! Well, I'm ancient, but of course I've only been here about a quarter century."

"I see," she said, disappointed.

"But I did hear—you know how people talk to the minister, when you come to a new community." Alice nodded. "I expect they're hoping the minister will adopt their prejudices about other people. So you need at least a grain of salt. But I did hear once that the Flemings thought the Greers must have sold off some old jewelry, to make that payment. That's nothing but a rumor, Alice. When I heard it the phrase seemed funny—'sold off some old jewelry.' That's what the person said. Why would she say 'old'?"

"Maybe she meant treasure?" Alice said.

"Oh, I don't know." He settled back, holding his face up to the sun. "There's always been a rumor of treasure in Broadview—Viking hoards, Iron Age hoards, maybe even older. So far as I know, though, nothing significant's been found. I suppose someone could find a treasure and keep it secret—seems unlikely, though, given human nature in a small town. Someone did find a couple of Roman coins when the golf course was built."

"The golf course up the beach from the Greers' land?"

"Yes. And of course there have been finds at Whithorn, down the coast."

"You'd think," Alice mused, "with the Sisters, such an important archeological site, that there would have been digging up there."

"Well, there was," he said. "But nothing has been found underground that I know of. Although there are several rocks that have cup marks. You've seen rocks like that?"

"No."

"They're quite old—five thousand years or so. They look like little hemispheric depressions atop rocks, sometimes with grooves and circles around them. Some think they were part of rituals involving

196

the sun. But, as they say, no one has survived to tell the tale. You can still see some atop some large stones in the pasture on the east side of Ben Cathair. They don't speak to me, those cup marks. They're silent as the grave." He looked out at the headstones of the graveyard. "Well, actually, graves still speak to us. Let's just say that cup marks are silent."

They sat for a moment.

"I can't figure it out," Alice said.

"What?"

"Who killed Angus. Who killed Davie. And why."

"Evil," he said simply. "There's still evil, Alice. Human evil."

"Why Angus? Why Davie?"

"Well, Angus was a powerful man. Yes, 'just the ghillie.' And, I think, fearful he'd lose his job when the Flemings sold. But powerful because he found things out and tried to right wrong. As he apparently was trying to do when you saw him in the mist."

Alice nodded.

"But," he said, "people resented Angus, too. When he was extracting Davie from Glasgow, he told the police what he'd learned about the people who were trying to involve Davie in their schemes. The police told him to watch his back. And of course that was a worry for Jennie—though she was glad Davie was safe, I'm sure."

"People don't like someone—someone without authority—to take on the role of policeman of the world," Alice said. "A frequent criticism of American foreign policy."

"Even, or maybe especially, when it saves someone," agreed the minister.

Alice lifted her face, eyes closed, grateful for the sun.

"I will say, and I don't think it's breaching a confidence, that just before he was killed—I know the timing was merely a coincidence, because surely Philip Ansley would have nothing to do with his death—Angus came to see me. He told me he'd looked up Ansley's credentials at Cambridge and that he hadn't graduated but had been asked to leave. Angus said he'd done more digging, and that my friend was asked to leave the boys' school where he taught."

"What did you think?"

"Typical Angus—wanting to be the one who knew everything. But on that, I felt Angus was out of bounds. I knew Philip had had a disappointing life. I suspected he just wanted a few weeks of free room and board from me. Nothing Angus said made me think it could be harmful to have Philip here, doing his bird-watching and hoping he'd be the one to make a great archeological find, if that's what he's doing."

"Did Philip know what Angus had told you?"

"Not that I know of. Certainly I didn't tell Philip."

So the minister had filed Angus's investigation of Philip away with all the other human peccadilloes that he would never mention, always "holding a good thought" for frail humanity to reform. Or maybe, thought Alice, maybe he was lonely, rattling around in the manse? Maybe Walter found it pleasant to have a Cambridge friend to stay, even one who had not met his admittedly high personal standards.

And then she wondered. Had Angus told Philip Ansley? Did Ansley have a motive for murder? "How long is Ansley staying?"

"Only another few days. Another guest arrives August twenty-first for a visit, so he has to yield up the guestroom. Why?"

"I'm worried about Gran—Kathy."

"Surely you don't suspect Ansley? He seems like a gentle soul. Do you think this trouble's because someone wants her to sell? The Flemings wouldn't have anything to do with that! Robert Fleming was a fine man . . ." His voice trailed off.

"And he's dead," Alice said.

"But you can't think his wife would countenance any such behavior. Betty Fleming wouldn't stoop to that."

"Her children might," said Alice.

"You're thinking of Samantha, I expect." He sat up, energized. "But it wouldn't work, anyway!"

"Why not?" demanded Alice.

"Because if anything happened to Kathy Greer, the estate would have the farm, and it would have to go under her will! That would complicate any sale."

Of course, Alice thought. But did he know? "And you know what her will says?"

"Well, she told me. I haven't read it, of course. She told me when I visited her at the hospital in Edinburgh."

Alice hadn't known he'd driven all the way to Edinburgh to see Gran in the hospital. "What did she say?"

"She said that after Jordie's death, she'd changed her will; the farm would go to Robbie for her lifetime, in trust for any issue of Robbie and Jordie. Then it got complicated, she said."

"Ah."

"Of course that's confidential, but since you're her daughter-in-law, I hope I haven't breached my duty."

Alice was motionless, again grimly aware of risks to those she loved. At least John was safe in Texas.

"What's wrong?" he said, alarmed by her face. "I thought you'd be glad that no one would gain anything by harming Kathy Greer!"

"But if someone knew the will—couldn't they still make her sell by threatening Robbie, or her grandchildren!" She imagined someone stalking Ann on the dark streets near Holyrood. "I suppose someone truly horrible could do that anyway without knowing the will."

She heard him exhale heavily, imagined him thinking of human evil.

"You haven't talked to anyone about this, have you?" she asked.

He looked at her with a small smile, shook his head no. "Of course not." She already knew that. They stared together at the gravestones; then Alice left for Gran's.

* * * * *

Back at the farm, Alice was stalking around the garden, when Gran called her to the phone.

"Inspector Walker here," said a voice when she picked up the receiver.

Stony silence on her part.

"I've called to apologize. My attitude was uncalled for."

"Yes, I agree."

"I've looked you up online. I see you've had to help in some police investigations in—what is it, Coffee Creek?"

She was still too mad to talk.

"I spoke to a gentleman named George Files. He, um, said you had been very helpful in solving some murders. He said you were actually quite courageous."

She just breathed, trying not to speak what she felt at this moment.

"So I would like to apologize. And I wonder if perhaps sometime tomorrow you could come in and we could go over where we are on these matters."

"Which matters?"

"The threats to Mrs. Greer. And possibly the deaths of Angus McBride and Davie Dockery."

"I'll try to come by later in the day tomorrow."

"Thank you. I'll see you then. Meanwhile, you know what you said about being basically the only witness? Since Robbie Greer, after all, didn't get much of a look?"

"Yes?"

"Try to be careful. Because . . . assuming, as I do of course, that your two men exist . . ."

"I'm the main witness." Well, damn.

She hung up and turned to Gran. "We might get more help now, from the inspector."

Gran nodded. "Read him the riot act, did you? He's got an ego, that one. It's why I never called him."

Sneakers

Wednesday morning dawned cold and damp. Robbie and Gran had gone to retrieve a surprisingly chipper Sue from the vet.

Halfheartedly Alice inserted her comments on a set of closing documents Silla had emailed. By the time she finished at eleven, Alice felt stir-crazy and desperate for coffee, and maybe another run. If she stayed much longer in Broadview she'd start thinking about a half marathon. The place was driving her to it.

* * * * *

"Chicken Soup with Rice," read the rain-splattered chalkboard outside the Soup Plate. Alice ducked in, rain dripping from her jacket. The temperature was barely sixty and rain had settled heavily onto the gray roofs of Broadview. Even the waves looked wetter.

Hot coffee.

Robbie's friend Mae smiled at her from behind the counter. "Alice! What can I do you for, on this soggy day?"

"A macchiato, please."

Someone had her seat—her "never aces and eights" back-to-the-wall corner chair, where she could see the whole shop. Occupying her chair was a Chinese man in a Barbour jacket. Could it be? She picked up her coffee and headed for his table.

"Excuse me, I'm Alice Greer. Are you by any chance Mr. Zhou?"

Watchful brown eyes looked up from chicken soup with rice. "I am."

"May I join you for a moment?"

"Please." He moved his chair an inch—a small invitation.

"You may or may not have met my mother-in-law, Kathy Greer. She owns Hardie Farm, just below the Fleming property."

"Ah."

"Her land has been in her family for hundreds of years."

"Mmm?"

He wasn't making this easy.

"She does not want to sell."

"Then she should not sell." His English was unaccented, international.

202

What?

"I thought I'd—" Alice halted.

"What did you think?"

"I understood you were interested in buying the Fleming property that's adjacent to Hardie Farm. I thought I'd confirm there's no condition requiring you to buy Hardie Farm as well."

"I believe that was true of the prior potential buyer, last spring, but not of me."

"No?"

"No. An agent wanted to sell the Fleming property at a higher price to another buyer, but that buyer wanted Hardie Farm as well. I am mildly interested in the Fleming property, but not in Hardie Farm."

"Only mildly interested?"

"I may buy the Fleming estate, but right now the asking price is on the high side. Especially without Angus McBride being available. I liked him very much."

"I never met him."

"He was quite a man. Confidence-inspiring, in many ways. My assessment is that my business connections would have enjoyed him. But . . . he's gone, sad to say. Actually, I'm very distressed about it." And his eyes were somber.

"He was murdered," Alice said.

"Is that what the evidence shows? I'd heard there was some possibility."

"He was alive when he was dumped into the Dorain."

His smooth brow furrowed, and he shook his head slowly.

"Back to my mother-in-law. I just want everyone to understand she's not to be harassed."

"Of course not," he said, raising his eyebrows. "That would be barbaric."

"She does not want to sell."

"Commendable, to care for your ancestors' heritage."

"Her daughter and I will see to it that anyone who threatens her, frightens her, bothers her tenants, or tries to poison her dogs again—"

"Poison her *dogs?*"

"Her corgi was killed."

Mr. Zhou's mouth curled in disgust. "Inexcusable."

"I just want you to know, if anyone else bothers her, they'll answer to me. And I don't give up."

"So I've heard." For the first time a small smile appeared. "Really, Ms. Greer, please sit down. My neck is sore from looking up at you. Though, of course, I do look up to you."

I could get to like this man, she thought, sitting down.

"Tell me," he said, surprising her, "what you like best on the Broadway Diner menu? I have a guest joining me tonight."

The memory of her first dinner there washed over. "If they have the diver scallops, for starters. Unless you love oysters—then oysters. Then, fish. Grilled, I prefer. I always know it just came in. Maybe just a hint of local butter on top. Such imagination, the cooks have, especially with vegetables, but not too much messing about with the fish." She watched his face. "Are you going to buy the Fleming property? Do you like it here?"

"I may. I like to play on that golf course. I like to sail. Are you surprised?"

"No. Just jealous of someone who has learned to sail. What about fishing?"

"I grew up surf casting."

"Where?"

"Connecticut." He was enjoying the surprise on her face. "My parents were there while I was in high school. Dad worked in the city." He meant New York, she knew.

"What would you do here, though?"

"Besides sail, fish, play golf?"

"I meant, on a cold, rainy day. Like today."

"Probably do what I'm doing right now. Then go back home and look at rose catalogues."

"Really! Gran loves roses. She's got a Buff Beauty that has taken over one side of the shed."

"What else does she have?"

"Madame Isaac Pereire. Boscobel. She likes the really fragrant ones. What about you?"

"Historic roses. *Rosa gallica, Rosa damascena.* Centifolia! Moss roses. And of course *Rosa chinensis*, the tea roses, but I'd have to see what they think about chilly weather. Do you have roses?"

"I do, but it's a struggle, in the Texas hill country. It's mostly limestone. I've got Darlow's Enigma, mainly for the name—the flowers are tiny, but smell sweet. Sombreuil, because I like to say it. Souvenir de la Malmaison. Zephirine Drouhin. But Madame Isaac Pereire"—Alice shook her head—"she couldn't stand the heat."

"If I do become your mother-in-law's neighbor, perhaps she'll let me visit her roses."

"Thanks for letting me interrupt your lunch."

Back out into the rain. Well. She was withholding judgment at present, but the balance was tipping in favor of Mr. Zhou. So what about the Flemings? If Mr. Zhou wasn't interested in Gran's property, did that mean the Flemings hadn't been, or at least wouldn't be, harassing Gran, trying to get her to sell? Maybe they'd given up after Gran's solicitor warned them off. Maybe they hadn't instigated the recent tenant harassment. What about Reid and the Hammam Bouquet? The All Hallows' incidents had taken place nearly a year ago.

Then who? And why?

* * * * *

Next stop: the inspector. This time he rose and extended his hand.

"Do you remember saying you heard a rather sharp crack?" he asked her. "Angus McBride's stick has a fracture, and signs it was hit with something metal. We're thinking that might have been that sharp cracking sound you said you heard."

"I wonder if he was defending himself," Alice said. "Do you know yet what was used to cause those head injuries?"

"It was at least partly metal."

"Could it have been a spade?"

"That's a possibility."

She plunged ahead. "Have you gotten the pathology information on Davie? A better description of what he was stabbed with?"

"It was a triangular blade, about seven inches long. It was sharp, but irregular on the borders," he said. "We're still waiting to hear more. The pathologist does not think the blade was steel."

Alice's mind flashed to the two men, talking in front of the display case. She repeated what she'd heard the men say about the broken-hafted dagger they'd given to "him."

"So, could it have been a really old blade?" she asked.

"How old?"

"Bronze Age."

"You're really reaching here, Ms. Greer. For one thing, pathology says there's no sign that the blade Davie was stabbed with had corroded. So how could it be Bronze Age? Also, we still don't know who these men are, or who 'he' might be. And we still haven't identified the man you saw at the distillery. There is one thing—the distillery workers say two of their blue shirts are missing, that were hanging on the back wall of the malting floor. But the man you saw wasn't wearing one of the distillery blue shirts, was he?"

"He had on a blue windbreaker or anorak. And my recollection is that when we went back to the malting floor that morning, there were still four blue shirts hanging on that back wall."

They stared at each other, stumped.

* * * * *

The rain had stopped, the sun was coming out, and the air was warmer. She needed to talk to Walter McAfee again. She trudged back uphill from Harbour Road to Upper Road, heading for the manse. Next door the church tower was chiming the hour. Eleven o'clock. Ask not for whom the bell tolls; it tolls for thee, she thought. And Angus, and Davie. She had to find those men.

At the manse, the clouds had lifted and rays of sunlight speckled the lawn. A few leaves had already fallen, heralds of September. She could hear a lopping sound—hedge clippers?—somewhere behind the house. The front door stood wide open.

Alice rang the bell. The lopping stopped. A pink-faced Walter McAfee, beaming beneath his straw hat, hurried into the entry hall. "Alice again! Come in, come in!" He waved an arm. "I was out in the garden," he added unnecessarily, looking around for a place to stow his hedge loppers. "The hedge has desperately needed clipping. And Philip used a file to sharpen my blades for me. Very clever, that man. They're now stupendously sharp. Come back to the study, where we can sit!" He turned back down the hallway, placing his straw hat on a hook on the coatrack that stood in the corner of the entry hall.

An old pastor's collection of outerwear hung on the coatrack. A venerable hooded blue anorak, a much-used trench coat. A wide-brimmed rain hat. And a wool driving cap, about the color of a graham cracker.

Surely not the pastor! Alice thought. Surely she hadn't seen Walter McAfee hurrying away down the sidewalk between the malting floor building and the pagoda-roofed kiln.

But now she was here. So, she'd ask her questions. He was fussing over the sofa, fluffing a cushion, picking up a stack of handwritten papers. The Sunday sermon?

Alice chose the chair closest to the door. She had on her running shoes. She could outrun him, surely. "Walter," she began. Then stopped.

"I'm so glad you call me Walter," he said. "So many people hem and haw and don't know what to call me. I just say, 'Call me Walter.' I can't stand that 'Pastor Walter' stuff. Makes me sound like a different animal from everyone else. And I'm not. I'm just the same. Older, maybe, and have probably sat at more bedsides, and deathbeds."

"I had a couple of questions about Angus. You said he might have been a little too hard on some of the young people. Was there anyone in particular?"

"Why do you want to know?"

"I just need to understand the landscape, so I can protect Gran. I've got to identify those two men."

"And the inspector's not busy on that? Of course he's understaffed, with only the one constable."

What to say? "I think he suspects they're merely my imagination."

He snorted. "We need to pay attention to our imaginations. Well, Angus acted as our arbiter. Self-appointed. He kept a watchful eye on everyone, as if he were ghillie for the entire town, you know?

Not just the ghillie for the Fleming property, but for everything under Ben Cathair. He acted as if he already knew all the facts, or thought he did. He coached football, the town's team, so he knew most of the lads. But sometimes people groused that he took that a bit far. What stuck in my mind was that he got crossways with John Dougal."

"The salmon smoker."

"Yes. I saw it myself. It was after John Dougal's mother died and John came back to manage her business. John's a good lad, and he missed his mother very much. I'd gone in to say hello and pick up a small bit of salmon—just as a birthday treat for myself, you know."

You don't have to explain a love of good salmon to me, Alice thought. I don't believe the ministry requires people to turn all ascetic.

"When I got there, I heard Angus's voice—you could always hear Angus, he would have been powerful in the pulpit. I was embarrassed, which I suppose is why I remember it so clearly. There I stood opening the door, and there he was, yelling across the counter at John Dougal, 'You stay away from her!'"

"From—who?"

"He did not say. And they both saw me and Angus shut up and walked out, right past me."

"And John Dougal didn't explain?"

"Certainly not."

"But you have your suspicions?" guessed Alice.

"I do, but that's gossip, and moreover, I don't want to throw suspicion anywhere right now. So, what else can I do for you?"

Okay, ask. Alice took a breath. "The day Davie Dockery died."

His face sobered. "Yes?"

"Were you at the distillery that day?"

Now he looked puzzled. "Me?"

She nodded.

"I haven't been there since last Christmas. I go every year to buy some Christmas presents, some bottles, in the tasting room. Why?"

"I saw someone walking there that morning and thought it was you."

"It was not I. It's refreshing to be considered a possible villain, though." He was making the effort to be courteous; his voice sounded more annoyed than refreshed. "Anyway, I didn't hear about Davie until I got back that afternoon from a hospital visit in Newton Stewart. You can check my whereabouts"—said with asperity. No, the pastor didn't like being suspected. Who did?

"I had to ask, Walter," Alice said. "I'm worried about leaving Gran, with all this unsolved."

He nodded. "I worry about everyone, all of the time. Occupational hazard. Apparently you're the same way, but with a different occupation?"

"Yes. We're both the designated worriers, I guess," said Alice, getting up to leave. "Thanks."

But that was another clue gone south—she still couldn't identify graham-cracker-hat man.

"Hullo, Walter. Ms. Greer." She turned. Philip Ansley stood at the door leading to the hallway, binoculars around his neck. How much had he heard? And how had she not heard him? Aha. He wore running shoes, "trainers," the Brits called them. Sneakers. You could indeed sneak up in them.

"Philip, there you are," said Walter. "I didn't know you were back here."

"I saw a lovely red-tailed kite today, up on the shoulder of Ben Cathair."

But how long had he been standing there?

"How's the research going?" Alice asked, walking past him into the hallway.

"It's coming along, thank you."

Alice glanced again at the coatrack. Now another jacket hung there. She looked up at Ansley. "Have you been to visit the distillery yet?"

"The distillery? You mean Uisge Dorain?"

Buying time? "Yes. I thought I saw you there last Wednesday, when we were taking our tour. Just before noon. Was that you, by chance?"

"You know, the distillery's on my list of sights to see in Broadview but I have not yet had the pleasure."

Walter McAfee started to say something, then stopped, for which Alice was grateful.

* * * * *

Alice called Inspector Walker. She described the blue jacket and tan cap on Walter McAfee's coatrack, and the possibility that someone else—possibly his houseguest—had worn them at the distillery the day Davie died. Alice did not tell the inspector she'd already asked Ansley if he'd been there. She'd realized, as soon as she asked him, that it might be a mistake. She had no right to make him tell the truth. He wasn't under oath at a deposition, or on the stand. And now he was warned. Damn it.

"Could you at least find out if Ansley was there?" she asked. "And could you find out if by any chance he has the dagger that I heard those two men discuss? The dagger with the broken haft, that they gave to 'him'?"

"I'll try. Whether that's enough for a warrant seems unlikely. What possible connection is there between Ansley and your two mysterious strangers?"

"He's out there with his binoculars."

"We see hundreds of folks like him around Broadview. Very keen on birds, they are."

"He's out there scanning the countryside, and I don't think he's just looking for birds."

"But he's never been seen on the Hardie property, right?"

"So far as I know. But . . ."

"Your mother-in-law's tenant never mentioned him."

"No, but . . ."

"I'll look into it," the inspector grunted. And hung up.

Chapter Twenty-Four

Let's Go *Get* Them!

"We absolutely must go," Gran announced on Wednesday afternoon.

So they were in Robbie's car, Gran riding shotgun (Do you say that in Scotland? Alice wondered). Alice sat in the back with Sue the border collie. They bounced down a dirt road with hand-lettered signs tied to the fence on either side: "Broadview Festival! Music! Sheep Shearing! Sheepdog Competition! Baking Competition!"

"What's the music?" Alice asked.

"Seaheart! You heard them at the Sisters," said Robbie. "But, Alice, what you're really going to like is the sheep shearing."

"You must be kidding."

Robbie lifted an eyebrow and smiled at Alice in her rearview mirror. "Just wait, my darling. Just wait."

They parked, grabbed their water bottles and extra bags for loot ("I'm looking for raspberry jam and gooseberry jam," said Gran), and joined the throng heading for the various tents.

Robbie grabbed a schedule at the entrance gate. "Okay: sheep shearing at two thirty. Border collie competition at three thirty. Show animals, including chickens, are in the blue tent. I want to see the chickens. Music: Seaheart is playing at the picnic tent. We can have lunch there. All right, ladies! Let's meet in the sheep-shearing tent at two thirty, border collie competition at three thirty, and the picnic tent at four thirty!"

Gran headed for jams and preserves. Robbie disappeared into the art tent. Alice, with Sue on a leash, wandered past tents festooned with hand-dyed wool, then met Gran and Robbie in the herd of people pressing to enter the sheep-shearing tent. It would be hot in there, hot and thirsty, she thought, looking at the draft ale counter. What was a country fair without ale? "One Old Peculier, one Old Mortality, and one cider, please!" she ordered. Thus armed, the three commandeered spots at a picnic table near the front. Alice tightened her grip on Sue's leash, as frantic bleats came from behind the competition platform. The crowd quieted in anticipation.

"Contestants, take your spots!" bawled the announcer. Five men in tank tops walked out, arms muscled and gleaming in the diffuse light inside the tent. Each carried a shearing handpiece. They took their spots. The crowd applauded.

"You each have five sheep to shear!" called the announcer.

The buzzer rang and they were off. The crowd erupted, cheering on their favorites. Alice couldn't take her eyes off Contestant Number One: he upended his sheep, pinned it on its back against his crotch, sheared the belly, maneuvered the sheep sideways, sheared up the back and down the left haunch, sheared the chin, sheared the right shoulder and, turning the sheep, the right foreleg and right haunch—done! The sheep, bare and shorn, dived down the chute while the shearer grabbed his second from the pen behind him. Alice watched the hypnotic movements. Face glistening, he finished the last and threw up his arms. The buzzer buzzed. The crowd huzzahed.

"Manly men, aren't they," Robbie said, grinning at Alice. "Want me to take your picture with Contestant Number One?"

Alice laughed, watching the crowd of bright-eyed young women gathering around him.

They sauntered off to the picnic tent to listen to Seaheart play. Again the music, the passionate rapid runs on the violin, the breathless intensity of the reels, the poignance of the young man loving on his guitar and singing "Will ye go, lassie, go?" to the unattainable lassie. Why unattainable? thought Alice, thinking of Kinsear, thinking of the interloping salmon smoker, then thinking again of Kinsear. Why not go, lassie? She had almost convinced herself when Robbie said, "Okay, ladies, I am off to the border collies."

Sue stood up. Alice stared at the dog. "Does she understand 'border collie'?"

"Do you doubt it?"

Sue tugged at the leash; Alice almost lost her grip.

The border collie competition took place out under the afternoon sky. Clouds were rising fast; the sun was hidden; the wind blew off the ocean. Men and women zipped jackets, turned up their collars, as they pressed close to the rail around the enclosure. Intent men with serious faces, completely deadpan, stood outside the ring with their dogs.

"Biggest event of the day," Robbie said. "There's a little betting going on." She nodded, and Alice's eyes followed.

"That's what they're doing?" She saw small knots of men, coming close, heads together, laughing, then dissolving into the crowd, which had grown large, pressing Gran, Robbie, and Alice against the wooden rail. Sue sat, eyes still fixed on the sheep now milling at the end of the pen. The first dog came in, intent on the sheep, body low, eyeing the flock with an intent unblinking stare, now stalking, and moving to the short, high whistles and terse voice commands of the handler. The border collie efficiently collected and moved the sheep into the pen at the far end of the ring. Sue watched, unmoved. "She knows she's better," Gran said. "Sue won three years running." Alice wondered if Sue would regain enough health to compete. Rat poison! She watched a succession of dogs come into the arena, crouch, move and stare down the milling sheep until the sheep obediently clumped and ran out of the ring into the proper pen.

"I'd be unnerved if Sue stared at me like that," said Alice. "I'd do whatever Sue told me."

"Generally speaking, it's a wise plan to do what Sue wants," Gran said.

"Think about it," Robbie said. "We humans would never have been able to herd sheep and cattle without dogs. We'd still be hunter-gatherers."

"Great times," said Alice. "Lounging around, playing chess in the winter, eating dried fish."

"And if you ran out of the fish? That's why we had to have dogs." She reached over and rubbed Sue's ears. Sue tilted her head but didn't take her eyes off the sheep, back in the enclosure again for the last dog.

"Sue first won this contest when she was six," Robbie said. "With Angus's help."

"Angus? Was he good at everything, even training sheepdogs?"

"Yes, he was. The Flemings had sheep. They sold most of them a few years ago but still have a few. For decorative purposes."

Cold wind ruffled Alice's hair. She shivered.

"Let's get Gran home," Robbie said, taking Gran's elbow.

People pushed behind Robbie and Gran. Alice and Sue strug-

214

gled through the milling crowd as a few raindrops hit. Suddenly Sue stopped, a low growl vibrating up the leash. Alice stopped. "What?"

She looked where Sue's head was pointing: at two men, still staring at the sheep. Yes. The tall one with the beaky nose. The blocky one, the black rooster tail of hair arching out of his hood. Sue growled, deep in her throat. The men, oblivious, moved slowly away. How would Sue know about the men at the Sisters? Well, wrong question: had she seen them, smelled them, growled at them the night Robbie and Alice chased them? Or—actually, and/or—had one of them come into the yard with poisoned meat, deadly neurotoxins for Queenie and Sue? Sue growled again.

"Come on, Sue," whispered Alice. "Let's go get them!" But Sue was already ahead of her, head down, back low, eyeing and stalking intently. Unlike sheep, the men did not sense they were her prey, did not turn and eye her anxiously. They headed into the beer tent instead. Sue, tugging the leash, pulled Alice along. "Excuse me," she breathed, following Sue's black-and-white fur through the crowd. And now she was right behind them, at the bar. This time she would face them, get their pictures. They would not elude her this time. She clutched Sue's leash, pulled her phone from her pocket, and tapped the camera setting. "Excuse me!"

The blocky one turned. She took a picture.

"Hey! What the fook are you doing!"

The tall one with the beaky nose turned. She took another picture.

"Dog poisoners!" she said loudly. "Are you the cowards who tried to poison this dog?"

The crowd backed away from Alice, from the men, shocked.

"Give me that!" yelled the blocky one, grabbing at her hand. But Sue leaped and grabbed his arm in her teeth. He shook her off.

"Down, Sue!" called Alice. Sue lowered her back, eyes fixed on the two men.

"We don't know anything about your fookin' dog, lady," said the tall one. But his eyes betrayed his lie.

"Looks like the dog thinks you do," called a man from behind Alice.

"The other dog died," Alice told the crowd. "Kathy Greer's corgi, Queenie. Chuck steak laced with rat poison. Thrown under the hedge at Hardie Farm."

The crowd murmured, their faces assigning all dog poisoners to the seventh level of hell. Especially poisoners of sheepdogs. And they could tell Sue's profession was sheepdogging.

"You'd better watch out, bitch," hissed Blocky Man. "That's slander, that is." He looked around at the crowd. "Lying bitch. Doesn't know what she's talking about."

"Nope. Sue knows you. She's got your number," Alice said, staring them down. She shoved the camera into her pocket.

"Come on," muttered Tall Man, tugging at his buddy's sleeve. Blocky Man's fists were clenched, eyes burning, face frightening. "Come on, let's get our beer somewhere else." Blocky Man was advancing on Alice.

Alice dug in her heels. "I want your names," she said loudly. "Tell me your names!" The crowd murmured, some still backing away.

"Come on!" the tall guy begged. Blocky Man gave Alice a murderous look, then both men pushed quickly through the crowd, which parted and reformed. She could just see the top of Tall Man's head, disappearing in the distance.

"Let's go, Sue," said Alice. She pushed after the two, knees shaking, then stopped. What the hell was she thinking? Now at least she had pictures. But the men had vanished.

"Alice! For the Lord's sake! What did you do that for?" Robbie was behind her now.

"Sue recognized them."

"And now will they be coming back to finish her off?"

"I've got pictures."

"Ah."

"And I'm sending them to the inspector, who doesn't seem quite convinced about the two men we chased."

Robbie shook her head.

"What's wrong?" asked Alice.

"You've shown those men that Sue's alive. You've put Sue at greater risk. And is Gran any safer?"

"What do you mean?"

"Look, Alice, these can't be the same guys who were harassing Gran last fall, or lifting her building materials. No one around here saw them."

"Maybe no one looked. But I think they're the same ones who scared off her tenant. Maybe now they'll be afraid to show their faces again."

"Funny. Since no one's seen their faces until now."

"Except me. And you too, the other night."

Alice texted the pictures to the inspector. After a bit he texted back. Ping! "Will look into it."

Still, Robbie had a point.

Chapter Twenty-Five

Nice Work
If You Can
Get It

Already Thursday. Alice desperately wanted to be alone, to have some thinking time. She slipped out the kitchen door, feeling a chilly hint of fall in the air. She tied her running shoes and thought—where? At the gate she opted to go left, up the Hardie Road, toward Ben Cathair. The Sisters watched as she panted uphill. What are you looking at, ladies? At the turn, where Upper Road headed east, she looked uphill again. When she woke in the mist, she'd seen three men on the edge of the glen where the Hardie ran down through Fleming land. In the pub, hearing Angus McBride was dead, she'd envisioned him falling down the slope into the glen, into the Hardie. But he'd been found in the Dorain. What happened between her vision of three men and his death? What had happened between Davie's vision of three men, and *his* death?

She turned east on Upper Road until she reached the bridge over the Dorain. She stopped and peered down over the bridge railing. How could Angus have fallen, here? He'd have to have been well below the road, down by the steep banks of the Dorain. What took him there? Was he laying down the law to someone?

She looked downstream where the Dorain, sparkling in the sun, entered the distillery grounds. Which made her think of Fiona, which made her think of Reid Fleming, which made her think of Jennie. And that made her turn around and retrace her steps to the spot where the Fleming driveway left Upper Road.

* * * * *

Alice tapped on the ghillie's cottage door. Jennie answered, her face surprised. Jamie's round face peeked out from behind her legs.

"Hi!" said Alice. "I'm just out for a stroll and I wondered if you'd like to join me."

Jennie's mouth began to form a *no*—then she looked up at the blue afternoon and said, "Why not? It's early for our walk, Jamie and I usually wait until four, but this little guy's refusing to take his nap. I'd love some company." She picked up the little boy. "I'll put Jamie in the stroller and get Nana. I'm not allowed outdoors without

Nana." And indeed Nana, Jennie's collie, clearly understood the word walk and had moved close to Jennie, tongue lolling.

With Jennie's three-year-old in the stroller and Nana the collie trotting beside him, they made their way to the drive that led across the headland and into the heart of the Fleming property. "Want to see some of the Fleming place?" asked Jennie.

"I'd love to. I've never been past your cottage." And that suddenly struck Alice as quite odd. In her various visits to Broadview with Jordie and the children—a couple of Christmases, Easter, summer vacation—they'd never been in the Flemings' hunting lodge. Jordie had never mentioned hunting with the Flemings, even during the great August grouse shoot. Now that she thought of it, Gran had never invited any Flemings to the farm when Alice and Jordie were there. Why wouldn't the Flemings invite Gran, their neighbor? Conversely, why didn't Gran invite the Flemings?

She put the question to Jennie. Why would these neighbors not, after all these years, have some social contact? Christmas parties, and so on?

"I know," Jennie said. "The Flemings used to give a Christmas party every year, until they stopped coming north for Christmas. I remember the last one. But Kathy—your Gran—was not there."

"Maybe she was in Edinburgh?"

"Maybe," said Jennie. "However. The Flemings think they're lord of the manor here. Actually the Hardies—Gran's family—have been here much longer."

Alice shook her head, puzzled.

"And, for that matter," Jennie said, tilting her nose up, "my family's been here longer than the Flemings. Yet Samantha Fleming treats me like the backstairs maid. In fact, she insisted I help serve at that last Christmas party." She laughed a short laugh. "Must sound odd to someone from the States."

"Actually, I'm truly relieved not to have to deal with that sort of snootiness," Alice said. "At least not very often."

"Well," Jennie said, "I know who I am. I'm part of this place. Like this tree, that hill"—she nodded her head at Ben Cathair, uphill on the right. "I'm here. And I belong here."

"Would you ever move anywhere else?" Alice asked, curious.

"That would feel so odd, to live away from here. No one knowing who I am!"

"But people move all the time these days. And what about refugees?" asked Alice. "They have to reconstruct their lives. Don't they still know who they are, in a new place?"

Jennie shook her head. "Horrible. I'd feel lost." She reached down and patted Jamie's head, assuring herself that she was here on Scottish soil and so was he.

"But why would Samantha Fleming treat you like the backstairs maid?"

"She thinks she's posh, and I'm not. She thinks my accent's wrong, clothes, education, all wrong. She also thinks I could never be posh like her."

"Well, what about Robbie's friend Mae, who runs the Soup Plate? Where does she fit in?"

"She's from Glasgow. That accent! And her family's Irish! I don't know why she's here."

Ah, thought Alice. The ease with which we establish "otherness." How deftly we slot our fellow humans into pigeonholes. So devastating, so inescapable, our constructs that dictate why a particular person can never be part of "us."

"She'll never fit in here, then?"

"Oh, I don't know." Jennie laughed. "Her curried chicken soup is even better than Neil's wife's."

Alice and Jennie walked on up the drive, Jennie leaning forward to push the stroller. Nana was sniffing every shrub, every tree. "I'd never do this—take you up here—if the Flemings were here today," Jennie said. "For one thing, Nana hates a leash and loves to investigate, with her nose, I mean."

"She could probably tell us which fox crossed the road, which rabbit escaped and which didn't, and which hedgepig didn't make it home last night," Alice said.

"Absolutely."

"But why aren't you comfortable walking up here? Is this property supposed to look like the great English country estate with no pesky humans troubling the landscape? No strollers or other signs of human life? Just manicured lawns and stately oaks?"

Jennie laughed. Then she pointed at the overgrown grassy verge. "Not too manicured anymore, actually. Probably because this spring the Flemings laid off the groundskeeper, who'd been here thirty years, and hired the work out to some contractor in Newton Stewart."

"Why?"

"Cost cutting. Angus lost two of his best men at the same time. Men he'd trained. The younger generation of Flemings doesn't feel any loyalty, unlike Robert Fleming, who always saw the staff as part of his family. His two daughters, for example, they never come up. They spend all their time in the south of France. And you'd think his son, Robert Junior, would have some feeling for the place, but he apparently has no say, or gets no say. It's his wife, Samantha, who's running the show, now that Mr. Robert is gone and his wife is so ill."

"Reid is Samantha's son?"

Jennie nodded.

"Who does Reid take after?"

Jennie stared out at the horizon and pursed her lips. "He's a fairly nice boy. But just a boy. He got in trouble at school, we hear. Got sent down. Supposedly his grandfather Robert was very angry. Then he lost his place at the Ness of Brodgar dig up in Orkney. Reid told me about that himself; he said he didn't have funds to continue and that his grandfather was really not happy with him, and told him he would need to stay here and work for Angus this summer. Then Mr. Robert died, right after that. And he wasn't even sick for very long." She glanced at Alice. "Angus later told me he suspected Mr. Robert despaired of his family and just turned his face to the wall and decided to die. And he did."

"How does Reid feel about selling this place?"

"Hmm. I'd say, a bit sad. He did say once he'd be losing his heritage. But even if Samantha would let his dad try to keep the property, his dad can't buy out two sisters, and they all want the money. Reid did say, though . . ." Her voice trailed off.

"Yes?" Alice prompted. She didn't want Jennie to stop talking.

"He said he was looking forward to having his own money for a change."

"His own money?" said Alice. "Wouldn't it be inherited from his family?"

Jennie went on, oblivious to Alice's tartness. "He's a bit immature. Do you know what he said he wants?"

"No."

"He wants to buy a big Land Rover with a safari top and spend the winter down in South Africa, traveling, hunting."

"Nice work if you can get it! So, not looking for a job, is he?"

Jennie sighed. "Very unlikely." Jamie voiced discontent, twisting around in his stroller. Jennie handed him a cracker. "Unlike this little rascal, who will have to look for a job when he's big!" He smiled a wet smile at her.

They'd reached the top of the headland. For the first time Alice could see what lay hidden to the east, behind the north shoulder of Ben Cathair. Before her the ground swooped out and down, in a patchwork of sheep pastures, barns, and long, half-forested fields running downhill. "I never get tired of this view," Jennie said. "Look, a falcon." They watched the bird soar, then hover, then plunge toward a pasture.

Ahead and to the left, the drive branched. The short left branch led to a long stone barn, one story, with white trim and a gravel forecourt. No one was about. "That's the old stables," Jennie said. "Hasn't held horses for a decade. Now it's the estate garage."

"Are there that many estate cars?" asked Alice.

"Oh yes. There's the truck, and the big Land Rover, and the smaller one, and an old Morgan that Mr. Robert loved to drive. And one of those Gator things, to haul fence and supplies."

They walked on. Past the garage, the drive curved, and suddenly the steep roof and multiple chimneys of the hunting lodge appeared. The sun glinted off three stories of leaded glass windows. "Wow." Alice stared. "It's fairytale, almost." She felt a sudden desire to make her own grand entrance, walking up the wide stone steps leading to arched wooden doors, then turning to look out and down at the long view.

"Impossible to heat," Jennie said.

"But really pretty."

"Horrible kitchen and backstairs area."

"But what a view!"

"Think about laying fires in all those bedrooms."

"Surely you didn't do that, Jennie?"

"Once I did, in an emergency." She shook her head. "After that, no more." She turned the stroller around. "Hey, Alice, let's go. I'm not comfortable up here, just staring at the house."

"But no one's here, right?"

"Right. But still. It makes me twitchy."

Alice thought, Reid Fleming can waltz right through your back door, but you aren't comfortable walking your child on a road that passes your cottage.

Jennie picked up the pace. Alice tried to keep up. She was amazed at how much faster Brits habitually walked than Americans. Why? The garage was nearing—the elegant stone garage.

"Jennie. Didn't you say the Flemings had a big Land Rover? And another smaller one?"

"Yes. Angus used the big one for taking larger groups out to the fields. Grouse season, for example. And actually, he drove it all the time. The little Discovery—Reid drives that one and so does Samantha. She doesn't like the Morgan, it musses her hair."

They were near the garage now.

"I'd love to peek in, see the Morgan," Alice said. No, it wasn't a lie. She'd like to see the Morgan. What she really, wanted, though—

"Well, hurry," said Jennie. "I'm nervous. I'm going to keep walking."

Alice darted over to the garage. The doors facing the drive were windowless. She walked along the front, peering in the windows. The afternoon sun's glare made it hard to see in, and there was road dust on the windows. She trotted around to the rear, to a door. And pulled the door handle. And the door opened. She slipped in.

The stable stalls had been knocked down, creating a large room beneath the peaked roof. Parked on the flagstone floor stood the old green Morgan, a venerable Land Rover Defender, a smaller, newer Land Rover Discovery, a battered truck, and a middle-aged Bentley sedan. The Defender was big and gray. She needed to see its front fenders. She edged between the Morgan and the Defender and there . . . yes, she saw it. The right front fender held a big dent. She went closer, pulling out her cell phone. She took several pictures: fender, dent, grille (was that paint?). She peered in the back, curious about Angus's missing shotgun. No gun. She looked in the floor. No gun. Outside she heard "Alice!"

And the Discovery? She pulled the handle. Locked. She pressed her face to the windows. Front seat: no gun. Back seat: no gun. Rear: nothing.

"Alice! Where are you?"

She ran for the back door, closed it, and raced back around the corner. Then she stopped, took a breath, and strolled on out.

"What were you doing?" demanded Jennie. "I don't want anyone to see us prowling!"

"Just peeking," Alice said. "I'd love to drive that Morgan."

Jennie's shoulders relaxed but she didn't slow the stroller. "No kidding. Though I'd fancy something newer and zippier. Like an Aston Martin."

"Oh, you're not the mum in the minivan type?"

"Hardly!" Jennie pushed at the stroller handle. "You wouldn't guess it though. Miss Homebody. But I love to drive fast."

Okay, ask her. "Jennie, speaking of driving fast. Was it Reid who put that dent in the big Defender?"

"Oh yes. Angus was so angry. The big car's expensive to repair. Mostly I think Angus was furious that Reid had taken 'his' car instead of the little Discovery, which Reid usually would drive. Angus was very possessive about that Defender."

"How did Reid come to bash it?"

"He said someone hit it when it was parked at the grocery in Newton Stewart."

"And didn't leave a note?"

"Right."

"When did it happen?"

"Oh, last fall. About the first of November, or so. He was back home for All Souls'."

226

"Oh?"

"Yes. I remember because it was just before his grandfather Robert went in the hospital the first time."

"Did Angus ever mention his gun was missing?"

"No. He'd have had a fit." Jennie stopped suddenly, turned to Alice. "That means it happened after he died, the gun disappearing. Or he would have mentioned it." She glanced down at Jamie, who'd fallen asleep. "Alice, that scares me." Then, with heat, "What are you asking all this for, anyway? And making me worry? What do you care?"

"Well, I care who killed Angus. I care that he was trying to stop someone from doing something wrong. I care who killed Davie, too."

"What business is it of yours?"

"Because someone has threatened Gran, tried to run her off the road, and now poisoned her dogs."

"Poisoned her *dogs*?" Jennie stopped. "Are you serious?"

"Yes. The corgi died. But it looks like Sue will pull through."

"That's absolutely the lowest of the low." Jennie looked down at Nana the collie, who was looking back at her.

"Nana can tell something just upset you, can't she?" Alice said.

"Yes, she can." Her voice changed. "Alice. Why would someone threaten Kathy Greer and poison her dogs?"

"I've got to find that out." She looked at her phone. "But right now I have to run down to pick up smoked salmon. I'm getting addicted to the stuff. You know, Dougal's smoked salmon?"

Jennie, transfixed, slowly turned pink. "John Dougal? You've met him?"

"Of course. Gran sent me." The penny dropped. "Oh, Jennie. He's the one, isn't he. I mean, you're the one."

"I don't know what you mean."

"He said—well, he didn't really say, but it sounded as if he was interested in someone here when he came home from school, but it didn't work out. But I notice he still has stayed."

Jennie turned away, pushing the stroller. "He's very busy with his shop."

Alice couldn't resist. "Jennie . . ." But before she asked another question she caught herself. Surely John Dougal did not kill Angus. But let's confirm that. Time to leave, Alice. Leave well enough alone. "Jennie, thanks for the walk. I'll keep you posted if I learn who was after Gran."

Jennie nodded, waved good-bye, walked briskly back to her cottage. No promises of another walk, no mention of another meeting.

I'm as popular as plague, Alice thought, but I shouldn't try to spread infection.

Chapter Twenty-Six

Don't Mess *This* Up!

That afternoon Alice returned to Gran's room and looked for a long time at the old typewritten will in its frame. "The land, the house, and all that lies therein."

She was still thinking about her vision on the Sisters and the voice calling out, "Stay away . . . Hardie Farm!" If the dispute involved Hardie Farm, why was Angus's body found at the other end of Upper Road?

Davie said he'd seen three men upstream on the Dorain, "But—not Angus!" What if someone had moved Angus to the Dorain? To be sure, when she climbed down from the Sisters, she hadn't seen a single vehicle, nor heard an engine, or a car door. Nor had she seen any sign of an unfamiliar vehicle at Gran's when she arrived.

But she hadn't ever searched along Upper Road, where street after residential street ran downhill to the harbor. Crowded streets with small cottages, small drives, where a car or van could be parked. The prime candidate should be a blue van.

Alice slipped out and in her rental prowled systematically back and forth through Broadview. Neighbors gave her questioning looks as she puttered along at curbside. But she saw no blue van.

Why should she be able to find it if the inspector and his constable couldn't? Assuming, of course, that they'd tried. Discouraged, she drove back downhill and turned along Harbour Road. She pulled up at the Soup Plate and went in, cheered by Mae's smiling face. What exactly did a Glasgow accent sound like? Alice wondered. She couldn't yet tell the difference. "Coffee. Macchiato. Please."

She sat down in the corner, her favorite corner, back to the wall, where she could see everyone, and idly riffled through yesterday's *Herald* and *Scotsman*. The macchiato arrived. Some comfort, at least. She closed her eyes, sipping. "Ms. Greer?"

She looked up. The pretty girl from the tasting room. Fiona. "Could I speak to you just for a moment? I'm Fiona."

"Oh, yes." Alice nodded. "Of course I remember you. You work here, don't you?"

"Yes. I'm just coming off shift."

Alice moved the newspapers off the chair next to her, patted it. Fiona gave a quick look at Mae's curious face behind the counter, and sank onto the seat, turning so that she faced away from Mae. Then she turned toward Alice, fear in her eyes.

"Is it true that Davie—that someone killed Davie?"

"Yes." How could she even ask such a question? Surely everyone knew that.

"He didn't just have an accident? And fall onto the conveyor somehow?"

Not unless he arranged to fall backwards onto a dagger, Alice thought, and then turn on the conveyor and fall artfully onto it. "No, from what I know, he was murdered. Stabbed in the back."

Fiona flinched. She clasped her hands, put them between her knees, hunched her shoulders, staring down.

"Didn't you talk to the inspector about it?" asked Alice.

"He did come talk to me. He wanted to know what Davie said when he heard about Angus McBride, on Monday. That was after you and your friends had the first tour."

"Right. And you told him, didn't you?"

"I—I wasn't sure I remembered correctly. Davie said something about the afternoon before, but I—I was tending to the counter."

You're not telling me the truth, Alice thought. Why not?

"What did you tell the inspector?"

"I told him Davie looked upset."

"What else?"

"I told him Davie said something about the afternoon before, that he saw something."

"And what was it he saw?"

"I couldn't remember exactly how he said it. Something about the bridge."

You do remember, Alice thought. So why didn't you say?

"You remember what he said, Fiona. He said he saw three guys. Then he said, 'But—not Angus!' Didn't he?" Alice remembered Davie's white face as he clutched the counter in the tasting room.

And the girl turned bright red. "I'm so worried. I'm afraid I've done something wrong." She was trying to keep her voice down. Alice leaned toward her.

"You mean you didn't tell him all you heard?"

Fiona looked down, kneading white-knuckled fingers.

Alice pressed her. "You mean you didn't tell him Davie said there were three guys?"

Fiona just looked at her.

"Well, you can fix that; just go talk to the inspector and tell him everything Davie said."

"It's not just that."

Alice looked at this girl, this very pretty girl.

Alarms went off. "Did you tell someone else what Davie said?" guessed Alice.

Miserable, the girl nodded, kneading her hands together.

"Who?"

Fiona shook her head, tears spilling down.

"Fiona, what Davie saw may have gotten him killed." Rather, what he said he saw, she thought. "It's important for you to tell the inspector what you heard Davie say, and even more important to tell him who else you told. And when." When is critical, she thought, because someone had to find out between Monday afternoon and Wednesday. "And you must tell the inspector exactly what you told that person."

Silence. More tears.

"I can't. If I do he'll never—" And she put her hands over her mouth.

"Never what?"

And then she knew. She looked at Fiona, at the fashion magazine sticking out of her bag, at the careful makeup, the preppy flats and blazer. She thought of Fiona's mother, Maggie, vigorously local, unfashionable, shrewd and sharp-tongued.

"'He' is Reid Fleming, right?"

Now Fiona looked terrified. "You can't tell anyone! If you do he'll never—"

"Fiona. We're talking about murder here. You must tell the truth! If you don't, you will never be safe." She felt all her antennae quiver. "You think he's going to marry you."

"Yes! He—I mean, he didn't say so, but he's been talking about me coming down to London with him. And I could get out of here!

232

I could get out of this place! I could get away from—from everything."

"Like—your mother?"

"Yes! Well, maybe. But she wants me to move up in the world. She wants me to marry well. And I want out of here."

And Alice, looking at the desperate girl, felt the idea blossom. "Did Reid bring you to work Wednesday morning, at Uisge Dorain?"

"Yes!" Defiantly. Proudly. "Yes, he did."

"Came with you to the tasting room?"

"Yes! Why shouldn't he? People know he and I—that we . . ." She frowned at Alice. "Why are you asking that? Then he drove on to London. He had nothing to do with Davie, of course."

"Fiona. You have to tell the inspector what Davie said. If he finds out you didn't, you could be an accessory to Davie's murder. His murder!" Alice remembered how he'd looked longingly at Fiona. "And Davie—Davie was very sweet on you, wasn't he?"

"I can't! I can't!" Then she stood, shaking, and said, "Don't mess this up. Don't mess this up for me. You can't tell either!"

"I won't promise that. Fiona, think!"

But she was talking to the back of Fiona's blazer, which was disappearing out the door.

Alice stewed for a few minutes, then went out to the sidewalk to phone the inspector. "I'm afraid that what Davie Dockery saw—he told us he'd seen three men, not two—'But—not Angus!'—I'm afraid that's what got Davie killed."

"Why do you say that?"

"Because I'll lay you odds Fiona herself didn't tell those two yo-yos I saw in the mist what Davie said he'd seen. But Reid Fleming did know Davie had seen three men, because Fiona told him. And if Reid then told those two men Davie had seen them—I think that's what got Davie killed. So—I think you should talk to Fiona again. She'll hate me for calling you. But she'll be safer if she talks to you . . ."

"I wonder if she understands she's at great risk if she doesn't tell me," he finished. "Oh, and about that text you said Davie got, about going down to the malting floor just before he died: Maggie Smith says she never sent it."

"But is it on her phone?"

"We're asking her to give it to us."

"You might ask her how long she left her phone in her bag on the floor in the tasting room last Wednesday."

Alice shivered, thinking of men who would leave Angus to drown, who would stab Davie and load him on a conveyor belt, and also of Reid Fleming . . . who might decide Fiona knew too much.

Nosy

This is it, Alice thought. Already Thursday afternoon was nearly gone: her plane would leave on Monday. Time was running out. She felt sure the two men were hidden somewhere in Broadview. Keep looking . . .

Outside, sunlight had left; blue twilight had fallen. Alice left her car on Harbour Road, deciding to make a foray past the old stone building the Hardies had helped build before the Depression struck England.

She walked down the front side of the pier. No one was about. The art gallery was dark. A sign in the window at the Fibres Knittery read CLOSED; so did the sign at the pizza place. Lights were out at Kintyre Fudge and Ice Cream and Lighthouse Fly-Fishing Supply. John Dougal's shop was closed too. She looked up. No light gleamed from the second story. Keeping close to the building, she rounded the corner, where the sea crashed in on the rocks just below the pier. She nearly tripped in the growing darkness.

Now for the back of the building. A tall wooden fence, with interior fences dividing each store's back area, enclosed the entire rear yard of the long building, just high enough to frustrate Alice: she had to tiptoe to see over it. She peered over the fence into the yard behind John Dougal's place. A staircase ran up to his living quarters. His gate was chained shut, and the parking space was empty. He must be up in Glasgow or Edinburgh, doing Thursday deliveries, talking up his product, getting more orders.

Alice continued down the fence line, peering over into the back areas of the fly-fishing shop and the ice cream shop, with its faint sugary aroma of fudge.

Next came the pizza place. The rear area included a wooden carport. Halfway under the carport stood a blue delivery van, with a sign fixture on top. On tiptoe she looked over the top of the wooden gate, trying to read the signs in the growing darkness: the print on the side of the sign atop the van—a lighted sign, apparently—read HOT FAST PIZZA. Signs on the side and rear of the van said GET HOT—AND FAST! Hmm. Designed to appeal to . . . a yen for sex and pizza? They didn't go well together. Definitely not. A little tomato sauce stuck next to the mouth—not erotic. Wait. The signs weren't sitting quite straight on the van doors. Magnetic? And weren't all these signs, these lights, removable? She saw, leaning against the entry steps, two metal rasps. Files.

A curtain jerked at the back door. Someone flicked on the porch light, right into Alice's eyes. She ducked behind the gate, peeking between the wooden planks.

"Ha. Got the nosy bitch, don't we." Blocky Man stood at the top of the porch steps. Then he turned and called inside. "Come down! We got her!"

Alice darted left, back toward the end of the pier. She hoped they'd think she went the other way and was heading for Harbour Road so she could run to the police station for help. On the way she tugged at the gate behind John Dougal's. Locked. Now she heard the pizza place gate crash open, the thud of running feet, coming her way. She estimated the height. No way she could make it over Dougal's fence.

Where to hide? Desperately rounding the corner onto the empty pier facing the harbor, she saw a hundred feet ahead the gangway to the landing where the harbormaster kept his dinghy. She raced down the wooden ramp to the landing. One of the pier pilings stood right next to the landing, supported by two struts. She jumped with both hands for the strut attaching the piling to the pier, and then swung herself behind the piling, reaching out for the other strut with her left hand. Now she was hanging behind the piling, pressed against the wet creosote-smelling wood, holding on for dear life. If they looked down, perhaps they wouldn't see her. She craned her head back, looking at the streetlight shining down through the gaps between the wooden beams of the pier, listening to the footsteps come closer. The feet stopped, right over her head. She could see a glint of metal. "Where is she?" That must be the tall one.

"You check up ahead. I'm going down here," said Blocky Man.
Damn.

She slowly let herself down, sliding down the back of the mossy post, trying not to gasp at the chill of the water. Oh God, so cold, so cold. She let out her breath, sinking under the waves that slopped back and forth beneath the pier, and paddled underwater toward the end of the seawall below Dougal's place. She groped for the corner, pulled around to the end facing the ocean, and came up for a breath. Which way to go? Blocky Man was peering into the darkness under the pier, facing back toward Harbour Road, holding a long gun. Then he turned his head toward her, and swung around to face her.

Boom!

The blast hit the concrete corner of the seawall. Shards of concrete flew in the air.

Alice had backed around the corner just in time. Where now? Obviously not under the pier. But if she stayed round the corner at the end of the pier, the waves, slanting into the harbor, would dash her on the rocks or swoop her back to the shore. Or both. Like shooting fish in a barrel, she thought.

Alice took a big breath, dived under a wave, and started out to sea. Her gut heaved with the same sick feeling as when she'd swum in her one and only triathlon, which began with the ritual half-mile swim across a windy lake. You're going to drown, her gut had said. At least, she'd thought then, if I'm going to drown, I'll get it taken care of before I have to ride my bike and then run.

She was aiming for Gran's sailboat, tied to the last buoy in the basin, its navy prow serenely riding the waves.

Boom!

Now he could see her. The moon had escaped its cloud cover and flooded the harbor with silver. Alice gasped for a breath and dived under, managing to get rid of her shoes, and kicked again for the sailboat. Maybe if she faced out to sea her face wouldn't shine in the moonlight.

Thank God, a cloud. She kept her head down as much as possible, kicking, stroking, trying to surface in a wave trough where she could grab another gasping inhale of breath.

The moon danced out again. She dived.

Boom!

This time she thought the shot went nowhere near—what was a shotgun's range? Not this far, she hoped. He'd have to quit; someone at the police station surely would hear him. But Gran's boat was still two hundred feet away—a marathon, a trek, an impossible distance.

The moon slid behind the cloud. Alice floated a moment, tried to catch her breath, then started again, trying to stay under as long as possible.

She was close—only five feet to go—when a wave shoved her hard into the little mooring buoy, smacking her ribs. But she caught the buoy like a football, held it to her stomach, clung to it, gasping, shivering. *Now what?* She couldn't see anyone on the pier anywhere. But she couldn't swim in, she couldn't row in.

A voice in her head said, Sail her, Alice. Just take her around the point, onto Gran's cove. You can do it.

Untie first? Or get on the boat and then untie? She couldn't remember, but now it was coming back to her. She kicked away, to the seaward side of the boat. Easier to get aboard from the stern? She let a wave wash her toward the stern, gave a mighty kick, and tried to grab hold. She couldn't keep her grip, banged her chin and fell back in the water. She tried again, kicking madly, but a rogue wave swept her sideways just when she tried to grab her way on, left her choking on seawater. Desperation. Then she saw the faint whiteness of a trailing line, grabbed and tugged at it, hauled herself partway up, and fell over the transom, barking both shins as the boat rocked. She collapsed onto the stern seat.

Now what? Was there a motor? There was. But she couldn't get it started. Who knew when it had last turned over?

The tide felt as if it were beginning to turn, beginning to recede from the harbor a bit, merging into the swells rolling north, along the coast. Maybe she could somehow steer that way, into Gran's cove. Were there oars?

She crawled forward to the hatch under the bow and pulled it open. A flashlight was clipped to the inside wall. Good. But the battery was failing. In the wavery light she saw: A bailer. One oar. Life jackets. An extra-large anorak exuding a strong stink of mildew. Shivering, she put it on and tugged the oar out of the cabinet. She spied the bucket holding the safety kit. It held a reflective plastic packet containing an orange plastic signal flare gun with four orange plastic signal flares dangling from the attached plastic bandolier. She squinted in the moonlight at the price tag. I bet Jordie bought this over five years ago, she thought, hoping the flares were still good. She couldn't open the packet, finally had to bite it open. She stuck the flares and flare gun in one anorak pocket and the reflective packet in the other. Alone, alone, all, all alone. No, she had a phone. A very wet phone. Was seawater recommended? She pulled it out of her zippered hip pocket, punched the "On" button. Dark screen. Dark, even ebony screen, like looking into nothingness. Useless. She shoved it back in her pocket.

Could she unmoor and use the oar, quietly, to paddle out of the harbor?

Huddled low, she moved to the bow and uncleated the mooring line from the buoy and pulled it in. Now the waves had caught the boat, turned the bow, and started pushing her north, but into the harbor. She tried using the oar as a tiller, first on one side, then the other. Useless.

You've got to sail the boat, Alice! But too late she remembered Jordie's instructions: First raise the sail! *Then* unmoor!

The boat slopped up and down, side to side, in the waves. Somehow she managed to attach the halyard. Now to raise the mainsail. The sail flapped wildly. Then, hearing Jordie's voice the whole time— *"Point her into the wind! Into the wind!"*—she crawled back to the tiller, holding a line, dodging the erratically swinging boom, and stumbled onto the stern seat. The tide was going out, but the prevailing wind was blowing roughly from the southwest, toward Gran's point. How to manage? She frantically trimmed the mainsheet, trying to get some control.

Holding the tiller, she worked to point the sloop more toward the open bay. She was taking a risk, but it was her only option. She paid out the sheet a bit. A light, a bright flashlight, caught her, blinded her. She ducked down into the boat. Well, what if they knew where she was going? What could they do?

The wind finally caught. *"Hold onto the tiller!"* Jordie in her head again. *"Trim her!"* She trimmed the sheet. The wind was sporadic, gusty, but she was making way. Squinting into darkness, she tried to hold a line that would take her out of the harbor, northwest toward Gran's. The moon, fickle, curious, peered down, then retreated behind a cloud. If I could just make it around the point, into Gran's cove, she thought. Hear ye, ocean gods! I ask so little! Just a little push now, a little breeze, not too much . . . maybe the gods were at dinner, carousing around grapes and cheese and wine . . . she was cold, hungry, wet to the bones, and nearly becalmed.

Suddenly the wind picked up behind her. The boat bore down on the point. No, no! thought Alice. Not on the rocks! She needed to weather the point, then turn into the cove. But the wind refused to cooperate, blowing even harder, and to avoid the rocks she had to steer further out to sea. But that took her too far past Gran's cove. Now the wind was pushing her past the next point, covered in woods. I must already be at the Dorain Refuge, she thought. Ahead on her right, past the otter refuge, moonlight glinted off a small graveled beach. She'd have to gybe—the scariest maneuver to Alice, and one Jordie never made her try. Alice anxiously rehearsed the steps in her mind: tiller goes this way, pull the sheet to the other side, don't get hit by the swinging boom! And then Neptune smiled, or guffawed, or just winked, and the wind shifted, gusting strongly from the southeast, and shoved the *Lark* aslant, too fast. She ducked the wildly swinging boom, lost control of the sheet. The outgoing tide combined with the strengthening wind to rock the boat violently. *"The impervious horror of a lee shore,"* she heard in her head. *"Looks like an accidental gybe,"* Jordie commented. Nothing she did with the tiller worked; at least she would try not to smash the centerboard. She pulled it up just as the wind drove the sloop hard onto the graveled cove at the beach end of the Broadview Golf Course. The bow smacked into the gravel and the mast tilted, dragging the sail. The boat shuddered, slewed to starboard, and dumped Alice onto the beach.

Thank God Jordie didn't see that, she thought. And lord knows what Robbie would say about the *Lark's* condition. Alice righted herself, got unsteadily to her feet. Maybe someone was still at the clubhouse this late? Still in the borrowed anorak, barefoot, she picked her way gingerly across the gravel onto the sand, then up the steep slope to the tee box of the thirteenth hole. From there she looked back at the beach. The moon gleamed on the sodden mainsail, lying across the gravel like discarded laundry. Alice shook her head and continued on. Time to find a phone.

The first six holes at Broadview Golf Course ran from the south side of the clubhouse away from the sea and out toward the entrance on the road. Holes seven through twelve then turned back toward the sea, running down the northerly boundary of the course until the twelfth green, which sat above the beach. The thirteenth hole, with its strong sea breeze and stunning views, paralleled the ocean. Holes fourteen through eighteen returned to the clubhouse, parallel to a gravel road that divided the south side of the course from the otter refuge. Players having a drink inside the clubhouse could watch members trying to sink a last putt under watching eyes.

Alice so hoped someone would be there to help her.

She had only made it from fourteen to the tee box for fifteen when headlights moved down the gravel road to the otter refuge. The lights stopped at the refuge gate, then went out. She heard two car doors slam. She heard voices. "There it is. Right on the beach." Two dark shapes climbed over the fence from the refuge. She heard steps on the beach gravel. "Not here. Where is she?"

The moon came fully out from behind the clouds. Two men, one tall, one blocky, had just topped the rise from the beach. She slid behind a few rowan trees next to the tee box. Could she stay hidden well enough in the rough, dart from tree to tree, and make it to the clubhouse? She opted instead to try the clubhouse side of the gravel road, where trees and undergrowth provided some limited cover. But which way would the two men choose? Ah. They were marching up the middle of the course, heading for the clubhouse. Blocky Man still had a gun, that was clear. The moonlight glinted on it. *The moon was a ghostly galleon . . .*

Galvanized, the metallic taste of fear in her mouth, Alice crouched and ran from tree to tree, as quietly as she could in her bare feet, holding tightly to the anorak to keep it from rattling. If she could just get to the clubhouse before they did—but on the rise holding the tee box for the sixteenth hole, they finally saw her. *Boom!*

Alice ducked and crouched, then zigzagged frantically toward the seventeenth hole. Ahead one window glowed at the clubhouse. Was anyone there?

Seventeen—and her plan took shape. The green of the seventeenth hole lay atop another little rise, backed by a screen of trees. She dodged to the right, circling the rise, then began climbing up the back of the hole, in the trees. Out on the fairway boots pounded heavily, heading up toward the green. Standing behind an oak, Alice pulled the plastic flare gun from the anorak pocket. Fingers trembling, she pulled off a flare from the dangling bandolier, shoved it into the back of the barrel, and thumbed back the hammer. Was memory right? Did she remember exactly where she was?

Alice slid her head around the tree and peered up at the sky. The wind was blowing, blowing, and was about to blow a cloud right across the moon. She darted out onto the green, waving the reflective plastic pack in the air, then darted back, moving further into the trees. Yes, they'd seen her—she heard one yell "Hey!" Silently she crouched, holding the loaded flare gun. If they ran straight at her—

They did. She heard them both fall heavily into the pot bunker. She heard the shotgun go off. She heard the men. "What the fook! Get off me! Get off!"

Lights flashed on at the clubhouse. She must head off whatever innocent groundskeeper was still at the clubhouse, avoid getting shot herself, not let the groundskeeper get shot.

Alice pivoted and took a step but her feet met air and the earth disappeared. She thumped onto her back, five feet down, and an almighty flash erupted. Blinking, she saw her red flare soaring skyward. Great. Pinpoint your location in neon. She rolled to her knees. Something had knocked the air from her lungs. Finally she managed a breath, then another.

She heard the golf cart careening up the rise.

"All right, all right! Just what are you men doing?" A voice, out on the green, full of Scottish indignation at the violation of the sacred turf. "Oh no, you'll stay right here. Don't tempt me. I've called the police."

Staggering to her feet, then standing on tiptoe at the turf lip of the bunker, Alice could just see the moonlit characters at the foot of the green: three men facing Tall Man, who stood in the downhill pot bunker, groaning and leaning on his arms for support.

"And your friend is leaving you as fast as he can!" That was the head groundskeeper. He was pointing at Blocky Man, vaulting the fence to the road leading to the otter refuge.

"Don't let him get away!" Alice heard herself yelling. "That's the man who killed Angus McBride!"

Three moonlit faces swiveled. "You stay here with this one," said the authoritative voice. "Madam, what are you doing in that bunker?"

She had shoved the flare gun back in the anorak. She stuck up her arms. "If you could just give me a hand here—"

"Ms. Greer! Is that you?"

"Yes."

Alice noted a powerful reek of whisky as he hauled her over the lip of the bunker and onto the turf. "What the hell are you doing out here?" he demanded, then swung around, distracted by a new sight: "Fire!"

In the rough along the seventeenth fairway, yellow tongues of flame licked the dried summer grass, moved into the bracken, lit up and enveloped a gorse bush. Two of her three rescuers grabbed shovels and rakes from the golf cart and pounded toward the flames. The head groundskeeper kept one eye on them, one eye on the tall one, groaning as he leaned out of the pot bunker on the grass.

In her bare feet Alice could not help stamp out the flames, but with the flats of the shovels and the soles of their wellies, the two men subdued the flames.

Headlights on the otter refuge drive, heading back out to the road. "He's getting away!" Alice cried.

Head rescuer was calling the police again. "It looks like a van. It'll be coming out of the Dorain Refuge. You should see it if he heads for Broadview. How soon? And don't forget the ambulance." He listened.

"All right. They're on their way." He shook his head, staring at the charred moonlit area, gorse branches broken, grass consumed. "We'll have to deal with that tomorrow. It must be in order before the tournament." He turned back to her. "Ms. Greer, any explanation? Am I correct that the fireworks are your doing?"

She nodded, pulling the flare gun from the anorak pocket. "I had it in my hand when I fell in the pot bunker. It was on the boat and all I had."

"What boat?" he asked sharply, looking around for further incursions on his course.

"Those men shot at me down on the Broadview pier. I swam out to Kathy Greer's boat, and took it out of the harbor. It's on your beach."

Silence.

"They followed me by car. Then they saw me on the course, and were coming after me, and I remembered the seventeenth."

He nodded in approval.

Alice heard sirens in the distance.

Another groan from the pot bunker. Head rescuer and Alice walked over. Tall Man had relapsed and was flopped on the bottom of the pot bunker, one leg extended. "My ankle," he groaned.

The groundskeeper jumped down into the pot bunker. "Come on, man! Stand up!"

Tall Man: "No! Oh god. It's broken. I know it's broken." He sat, his torso rocking back and forth, clutching at one leg. And indeed his ankle looked peculiar. "Mikey landed on it with his damned heavy boots," he whimpered.

Alice thought she herself might throw up.

"Come on, man! We've called you an ambulance. Get yourself out of this bunker!"

With the tall man tottering on one foot, and the other three men grappling and boosting him to a standing position, they tried pushing him out over the lip of the bunker. He flopped forward, resting on his elbows. "Don't make me go further," he said. Nevertheless, they wrestled him back to a standing position and with a mighty heave shoved his torso up over the lip of the bunker, where he lay groaning, feet still dangling. One of the men, exhaling whisky fumes, grabbed the back of the man's belt and hauled his legs around and up onto the turf, then sat heavily on his back. "Until the ambulance gets here," he said.

"What's this I'm stepping on?" Head rescuer, still in the bunker, pointed his flashlight at the bunker floor, where the light glinted on the barrel of the shotgun. He picked it up. "Beautiful shotgun."

"Watch for fingerprints!" Alice said.

"Ah." Gingerly he laid the gun in the turf, pointed away from himself, and carefully maneuvered himself out of the pot bunker.

"I'm guessing that's Angus McBride's," she said.

"Angus's? But what does that mean? How did these men get it?"

"I'm sure the inspector will be asking exactly that!" Alice squatted in front of Tall Man, hot with rage. "Won't he? You murdered Angus McBride!"

"I didn't!" He pushed up on his forearms, shook his head. "I didn't!"

"I saw you two go after him up by the Flemings' property!"

"I didn't hit him! It wasn't me!"

"And you stabbed Davie Dockery in the back and put him on the conveyor into the flames!"

"No! I thought we were just going to make Dockery shut his trap."

"You already knew him, then? From Glasgow days."

"Yes, yes. But I didn't stab him, did I!"

"So it was your mate again. But you stuck Davie on the conveyor, didn't you! You shoved him on there!"

"I didn't want to. It wasn't my idea. But he was already dead!"

"Was he? Are you sure you didn't want to cook him to death?"

"No, he was dead, right? He said he was dead! I wouldn't have . . . He was already dead!"

"If it wasn't your idea, why'd you do that?"

"We needed more time, needed to put him somewhere. Look, none of this was my idea. You got to tell them I didn't stab him."

"You also moved Angus's body, didn't you? You took him over to the Dorain!"

He shut his eyes. "He made us. He said we couldn't leave him where he was."

"Who made you?"

A hunted look, a spark of intelligence in the eyes. "It's worth my life to tell you. Lady, make them go easy on me. It wasn't my fault! I didn't hit him!"

"You shot at me tonight. Why should I care what happens to you?"

"That wasn't me shooting! You know that! You know that wasn't me."

"And you poisoned Kathy Greer's dogs!"

"No! That wasn't my idea either!"

"But you were there, weren't you?" He didn't answer. "Tell me your name."

Long pause. "Joey Campbell," he mumbled.

"Tell me your mate's name. You said 'Mikey,' right?"

He shook his head. "He'd kill me. Honest, lady, you've seen him."

"Tell me who told you to move Angus's body. Was it your mate Mikey?"

He shook his head no.

"So who made you move the body?"

He shook his head, eyes closed.

"Well then, why did this mysterious person want you to move Angus's body?"

"To put him somewhere else."

"But why did you have to dump him in the Dorain? Wasn't it enough just to kill him?"

"We didn't!"

"What do you mean, you didn't kill him? He's dead!"

"It wasn't me that hit him."

"You kicked him, then!"

"No! And anyway, he was still alive."

"You mean, before you dragged him down to the water!"

"I tell you, that wasn't me! But he opened his eye. He saw us. With that one eye."

"He opened his *eye*?" Angus opened his eye and saw someone who didn't want Angus's body anywhere near his property . . . but wanted him dead. Who would want him dead? "It was Reid Fleming who made you take Angus to the Dorain, wasn't it?"

He looked up, terrified. "I didn't say that."

"But it's the truth." Alice stood up. The groundskeeper twisted around and stared down at Tall Man, then up at Alice.

"Reid Fleming?" he said. "Miss, you'd sure better know what you're talking about."

Headlights shone at the corner of the clubhouse. Doors slammed. The inspector strode across the lawn, followed by the constable.

"Ah, Ms. Greer again," said the inspector.

"Did you catch the other man? The one in the van?" demanded Alice.

He shook his head. "We saw no van on the road."

"He could have hidden the car in a driveway. Or maybe he went the other way. Can't you send people to check?"

"What people? You know how understaffed we are. What you see is who we've got."

"Well, here's one of your two, Inspector. He helped move Angus's body though he claims he didn't personally put his face in the water. He also helped put Davie on the conveyor after he was knifed in the back. He claims he didn't kill either of them, but that's not so."

"I didn't!" pleaded Tall Man.

Alice turned to him, furious. "Angus wasn't dead when you dumped him in the water."

"He made us!"

"Who's 'he'?" demanded the inspector.

"Ask him about Reid Fleming."

Mulish silence. Lights swept across the grass as the ambulance edged around the inspector's car.

"Stop!" yelled the groundskeeper, thumping toward the ambulance. "Stay the hell off my grass, damn it! This is a golf course!"

Obediently the ambulance backed up, retracing its tracks. The doors opened. The driver and technician started forward with a gurney. The groundskeeper ran right at them. "Stop there! Don't be running those wheels over my green!" He pointed indignantly at Tall Man, flopped over beside the top of the pot bunker. "This man can hop! Just hold him up, put your arm around his shoulders!"

The ambulance crew looked at the inspector. He nodded and said, "I'll follow you to the clinic. I'll talk to him there." He told the constable to ride with Tall Man. The ungainly trio, ambulance crew and the groaning Tall Man, hobbled past. Alice watched as they arranged Tall Man on the stretcher inside the lighted ambulance.

The inspector turned to Alice. "What else did he tell you? And what in the world are you doing here?"

What did he want to know first? Alice unfurled her story, starting at the back of the stone building on the pier, and ending in the pot bunkers on seventeen.

"So you've got to catch the other guy, the blocky one," she said. "You'll find his prints on the shotgun. Which belongs to Angus McBride, I believe."

The inspector picked it up with his handkerchief. Then he turned. Alice stood there, flummoxed. Did he plan to leave her in the middle of the night at the golf course? Apparently so.

"Inspector. I'd appreciate a ride back to Hardie Farm."

He stopped.

"It's not really safe around here for me, I'm finding," she said. "Particularly with the blocky guy still on the loose."

"All right." He didn't sound overjoyed. "Why didn't you pay attention to my text this afternoon? I told you to stay away from these men! We were trying to identify them!"

She held up her dead phone.

"Miss, what about your boat? Mrs. Greer's sloop?" called the groundskeeper.

"Do you mind getting a couple of lines and mooring it somehow?" Alice answered. "Robbie and I will get it in the morning. We certainly wouldn't want to mess up the view from the thirteenth hole."

The inspector spoke not a word as they drove around the back of Ben Cathair and rounded the curve heading back into Broadview. Then he said, "Where do you think he went? The, what do you call him, blocky one? We still haven't identified him."

"If you didn't see him, maybe he took the long way around—i.e., headed north from the golf course. He'll be hiding now that we've got his buddy. He's the strong one, he's the alpha dog, but he knows his buddy will talk, so I expect he's looking for some way out of the UK."

"I've alerted the ports and airports."

"At least you have my photo of him." She thought for a second.

"But he could make a run back here, if he left anything he needs at the upstairs apartment at the pizza place."

"What could he have left?"

"Passport? Money? Something valuable? Something he's hoping to sell when he gets out of the UK? After all, he's been out at Gran's with that metal detector. He might have found something he didn't mention to his boss, or bosses."

"And who might that be?"

Alice sat silent. Then she said, "That I'm not sure about. Reid Fleming made them move Angus's body. Reid Fleming made them put Angus where he'd drown."

She thought for a moment. "And Davie Dockery died because Fiona told Reid that Davie saw three men." But was it Reid who had them digging up Hardie Farm? She shook her head, puzzled. "What about the knife that killed Davie?"

"I meant to tell you. Ansley does have a knife. And it's Bronze Age, and corroded. So the pathologist says it's not the one that killed Davie. However . . ."

She waited.

"However, though he claims he's had it forever, the pathologist thought it was only recently dug up."

"I'll bet it came from Hardie Farm. It's Gran's." She turned to him. "Maybe if you lean on this tall guy, Campbell"—he'd been Tall Man to her for days; it was hard to give him his name—"he'll admit it's the knife they found and gave Ansley. Or maybe you can get it tested. Same dirt as at the farm? As to Davie . . ." What had Walter said? His hedge loppers were now "stupendously sharp." "Ask Joey what his mate was doing at the pizza place with those metal files, metal rasps, out on the steps." Had he been a customer at the museum store? "But I still don't know . . . what the engine was, that made all this happen."

He nodded, pulling into the drive at Hardie Farm. Suddenly Alice felt exhausted, entirely exhausted.

Gran and Robbie were standing on the front steps.

"I did tell you to be careful, you know," the inspector said.

She was too tired to answer.

"Where are your shoes?" Gran asked. She pointed at Alice's bare feet.

Alice could only laugh.

* * * * *

Early the next morning Gran called her to the phone. She heard Jorgé's voice.

"Hey! How are things at the Beer Barn?"

"Fine. We might be experiencing a little jet lag here. I hope I didn't call you too early." He sounded tentative.

"Everything okay?"

"Well, we need to get you back here, Alice, so you can get rolling on the distillery application."

"I should be back Monday. What's up?"

"The word is there's a new malt whisky distillery going in just down the road in Dripping Springs. We want to get ours built first. Birnbach has already ordered the pot stills and we've got a boatload of barley heading for Houston."

"Yikes. Let's get that application in. I can work on the draft before Monday."

"Great. And . . . uh . . ."

Long pause.

"Jorgé?"

"I've asked Robbie to come for a visit."

Alice stood up straight. "Nice! When's she coming?"

"She hasn't said yes yet. So I wondered . . . you know, if you might encourage her."

"You mean, talk about the live oaks and the barbecue and the secret springs and the strong, handsome men?"

"Yes. Not to put too fine a point on it. And with some emphasis on the strong, handsome man, singular, meaning me."

"I got it. And Jorgé? She's been kind of moping around since you guys left."

"Good."

"May I tell her you too are moping?"

251

"You may."

She hung up. Good grief. Her law school ethics course had said nothing about romance between clients and counsel's relatives. And look, she'd just offered to encourage the relationship. Shouldn't she think of the potential pitfalls?

Well, maybe not right now.

Right now she wanted another hot bath, a really hot bath. And how about a new phone?

Chapter Twenty-Eight

I Too Have
Run Afoul of
the Point

"And one tub of the spicy salmon," Alice said, trying not to salivate visibly as John Dougal wrapped the gleaming smoked salmon, such a delicious color.

"I heard about your nighttime sail," he said, with a quick look up at her. He weighed the tub of spicy salmon, marked it. "Why didn't you ask me to come along? We might have made a more graceful landing."

Smartass. "You didn't answer when I rattled the gate," Alice said.

"Sorry to miss you."

"Did you know those guys were there? At the pizza place?"

"I never really saw them. I heard folks coming and going in the back, the pizza van, the gate slamming, but I'm usually in the shop. The pizza place usually closes at the end of the summer, so I thought the owners were shutting it up." He stacked the tubs of salmon and began wrapping them in brown paper. "I'll tell you who I did see, though. You know the guy with the binoculars? He prowls around town wearing them, and climbs all over Ben Cathair, bird-watching? I think he's been staying with Walter McAfee, on Upper Road."

"Another client of yours? Walter?"

"Oh yes. We talk books a good bit. Anyway, his guest has been visiting the pier regularly."

"I'll bite," Alice said. "Not the knitting shop? Not the ice cream shop? Fly-fishing, perhaps?"

Dougal shook his head no. "A few times I've seen him stroll by the front of my place, then go round the end of the pier. Only tenants and fishermen usually go around to the back side. So I strolled out to my back gate to see where he was going. He'd stopped, more or less, outside the pizza place's back gate. He'd walk back and forth, make a phone call, send a text. That first time I was watching, he looked up and saw me, and left."

"An odd duck."

Well, thought Alice, would Ansley come clean to the inspector? Did the inspector now have some leverage over him?

Dougal handed Alice her wrapped purchases. "So your evening was pretty scary, right? I mean it, I'm sorry not to have been here to help."

"It was scary."

"But you made a daring escape, I hear."

"Could have used your help trying to weather the point," she said. "Could have used some nautical advice."

"I too have run afoul of the point." He smiled, and suddenly Alice liked him better, with his watchful eyes, his ironic smile. Lonely, a life of fish fillets. Didn't he want something in life besides fish? What about Jennie, then? She watched him pick up a CLOSED sign and walk around to hang it on the door, saying, "It's about time for my run. Running keeps me sane."

She cocked her head. "Do you ever run on the Upper Road, up where the Fleming driveway runs into it? I had a great walk up there just yesterday, with Jennie McBride. She takes her little boy walking with Nana the collie every day about four. You know Jennie, don't you?"

He nodded, silent.

"She's lovely, as you know. I just thought, when we were walking, that she seemed lonely," Alice said. She looked at the clock. "Oh, and it's almost four o'clock now. Well, I must go. Thanks again."

As she left she waved at John Dougal, still standing motionless inside, in his running shoes, staring out the door.

Well, Alice, you manipulative woman, she thought. But she felt not one whit of guilt.

* * * * *

Kinsear had sworn at her when she called him on Gran's phone, late Thursday night, to let him know about her sailing adventure. "Hey! I'm at least telling you!" she complained.

"Alice, Alice, Alice. It's just that I prefer you in one piece. Why didn't you call me to help?"

"Sea immersion. Bad for my phone."

"My life would be so much more serene if I hadn't gotten attached to a woman who prowls around the backside of a building looking for known murderers, and finds them."

Well, she had little to say on that point. He'd stated the facts.

"Just drive on up, big boy. I'll show you the town. The peaceful little town."

*****

But she didn't feel quite so cavalier on Friday afternoon, walking back with the smoked salmon, waiting for Kinsear to arrive. She slipped out the kitchen door and down the hill to the granite wall, climbed over it, and sat on the cold stone facing the sea. She'd sat here first with Jordie. Then they'd brought the toddlers to see Gran, to chase the sheep, to sit on the wall and watch the sun set. All those years . . . Jordie trying to teach her to sail, Jordie introducing her at the pub, Jordie teaching the children the names of the seabirds. Jordie singing harmony with Robbie at Christmas. Well. And now the children were launched, nearly launched. With this visit she'd grown closer to Gran and Robbie in new ways, independent of Jordie. She knew now she wanted both of them in her life for the long haul. Jordie, she said to the air, Jordie. All this was too hard to think about, and Kinsear would soon drive up. And he would be watchful, shy about this visit, shy on her behalf, not his.

No conclusion could she reach. So she got up and went inside, and heard gravel crunching under car tires in the drive.

Chapter Twenty-Nine

Air Full *of* Ghosts

ran had hauled out her silver tea service and made cake.

"Mrs. Greer, thank you! A real English tea!" said Kinsear.

"He means Scottish tea," said Alice. "You're getting the full treatment. Gran's cake and smoked salmon."

"At least she spared you oatcakes," said Robbie. "They're actually textured cardboard."

"Part of the hardy Scots nature," said Gran. "We pretend to like oatcakes. Some years, oats are all that would grow! Supposedly. However, here's my ginger cake with local clotted cream."

"And if she was somewhat extravagant in the matter of cream . . . ," said Robbie, passing around wedges of ginger cake topped by cumulus clouds of cream. Alice sighed happily. How she loved this ginger cake. Kinsear took one bite, leaving a trace of cream on his upper lip. He licked it thoughtfully. Then, brow furrowed in concentration, he took another bite. "Tell about the ginger, please, Mrs. Greer? You've used candied ginger but—is there fresh ginger too?" Kinsear, the recipe hound, was on the trail.

"Yes. It's a three-ginger cake. Powdered, fresh, and candied."

"But the texture! It's so moist." Kinsear would flatter until he got the secret.

"It's the Lyle's Golden Syrup," nodded Gran. "Absolutely required."

Silence while all four chewed contemplatively.

"If I could just have—" he began.

"One more slice?" chimed in Robbie and Alice, extending their plates.

* * * * *

After tea Alice walked Kinsear out the back door to the garden, chaperoned by Sue. The pink-and-white stock blossoms, luminescent in the long twilight, lent their clove perfume to the air. Taking Kinsear's hand, Alice walked him past the old sheepfold and down to the low stone wall, where she liked to sit above the pasture. "This is my favorite place out here," Alice said. "I like to look down this long slope to the sea."

Kinsear nodded. "I see why. The shape of the field, the far-off sound of the sea."

"But sometimes I think I almost hear the Vikings, yelling, pulling their dragon-headed boat onto the beach, racing up to kill, capture, smash."

"They were here, weren't they." It wasn't a question. He'd climbed up on the wall, gazing downhill, then back up past the sheepfold toward Ben Cathair.

"I assume so—didn't they maraud up and down the entire coast of Scotland? But how would we know? Are you a Viking? In a past life?"

"I have skipped the genotype test so far. I pretend to be descended from scholars, on all sides. Okay, Alice, show me where the detectorists were rooting around."

She pointed to the dug-up corner of the sheepfold, now disguised by the water tub and salt block.

"They were digging in the sheepfold when I saw them. But you know, the tenant described them as roaming the entire farm, all the way down to the copse by the beach."

"You haven't seen any more dug-up areas? What about along this—this berm?" He walked away from the far end of the sheepfold along a swale next to the slightly higher green-turfed curve of land that crossed the shallow crest of the headland. Sue trotted beside him, tongue out, glancing up at him from time to time.

"I don't know."

"Or out that way?" He pointed uphill at the point on the headland where the Hardie started carving the glen between Gran's farm and the Flemings' land.

She shook her head no.

"Well, it's getting too dark to see."

That night, Alice's narrow bed required them to coordinate if either wanted to turn over. They muffled their giggles, conscious of Gran across the hall.

"Is the air full of ghosts, whispering?" asked Kinsear.

Yes, there were ghosts. But Alice said, "No. That's the sea you hear."

And finally they were lulled to sleep, until the smell of Gran's butt'ries, toasting in the AGA, caused Alice to sit bolt upright and Kinsear to snort and crawl out of bed. "I wonder if she'd give me the recipe for those," he muttered.

Sun poured through the window, glinting on the painting Robbie had given Alice, propped on the dresser.

Kinsear stood looking at the painting. "What's that?"

"Robbie gave it to me. She's done a whole series of them. She calls them the 'bones of the land.'"

"It looks like . . . it looks familiar."

"It's the view from upstairs. From her studio."

"Is it! Would she let me see that view?"

"If you'll put some clothes on."

Alice found Robbie, who gave Kinsear a curious look when she heard his request. "Come on up," she said.

They climbed the hallway stairs to the studio. Robbie's landscapes now faced out, standing on the counter that ran beneath the windows and leaning against all the walls. Picture after picture, showing the view at sunset, at noon, early in the morning, in moonlight. In every one, Alice saw the slope to the sea, the lighter diagonal streak crossing the landscape, and the curves of paint crossing the field, sometimes dim, sometimes vivid. Kinsear paced slowly around the studio, scrutinizing each one. Then he went to the window. Alice and Robbie followed, squeezing in next to him, so that all three faced out. Kinsear pointed at the long curve, broken by the streak leading to the sea.

"Robbie, you always paint those two features."

"Yup."

"When you say, 'the bones of the land,' that's what you mean?"

"Yes, in the sense that they feel structural. They are what I hang the picture on."

"I think they are structures."

"Like—like a what?" asked Alice.

"I'm pretty sure that's a causewayed enclosure, or causeway camp. The causeway is the road that leads up from the cove. See that lightish streak, long and straight?" They nodded. Kinsear pulled out his phone and fiddled for a moment. "Here are some other examples on my phone. Look what you see in an aerial photograph."

They looked back and forth from the pasture to the group of images on his phone.

"Okay," said Robbie, squinting at his phone, and then at the landscape.

"So you have the causeway," said Kinsear, "but then you have the enclosures, which are, or were, ditches with embankments, berms, typically around the top of a hill, but broken by one or more causeways."

"Ah," said Alice. "So here the causeway is the old path or road from Gran's cove up to the top of the headland, and the enclosures are the swales and the adjacent little berms that curve around perpendicular to the causeway? So what is a causeway camp or causeway enclosure?"

"The origin is Neolithic—five thousand to three thousand BC, probably. No one knows why they exist. Theories abound: Were they settlements? Were they built for defense? Or to pen in cattle, or to keep out predators? Were they communal meeting places for feasting? Or for trade? Or for burials, or rituals? Definitely burials have been found, and deposits of pottery. Often, though, the picture is complicated by later Bronze Age use, such as the erection of stones at Stonehenge."

"Were there no buildings?" asked Robbie.

"Perhaps there were," Kinsear said. "But remains of timber structures are harder to find. What's been useful is aerial photography—you can see features that aren't apparent when you're walking the landscape. Especially where fields have been plowed for thousands of years."

"Neolithic," said Robbie. "Then Bronze Age?" Her eyes were drinking in the view, as if seeing it for the first time.

"Seeing something new?" Alice was curious.

Robbie nodded, with the faraway look of a painter envisioning the potential of a blank canvas.

"Well," Alice asked, with Kinsear still staring out the window, "does this help explain trespassers and metal detectorists digging up

Gran's sheepfold?"

"I'd heard about the burials, and the pottery, and animal bones, but I haven't heard of finding any hoards around here," said Robbie. "Metal detectorists are after treasure."

"But what if there were hoards?" asked Alice. "Maybe during the Bronze Age. Or later! What if this place was captured by Vikings? It's right in the path. You know they attacked Lindisfarne in 793 and Iona in 795."

"It's true I've always felt ghosts around here," Robbie said. "Or at least had the sense that the place has been inhabited for thousands of years."

Kinsear nodded. "I felt that last night by the stone wall, as if each step might be on broken pottery, or a burial, or an old bloodstain. But back to your question, Alice. Obviously the sheepfold intrigued your visitors. So something must be there, besides your blue beads. Did they get whatever it was? Or were they coming back for it?"

"I think coming back," said Alice. "They hit pay dirt somewhere because they gave a broken dagger to the anonymous 'him,' who turns out to be Ansley. He disparaged it because of the broken haft."

"Broken hafts are very common in bronze daggers with rivet holes," Kinsear said. "That's a common place for breaks. But that doesn't mean the dagger wasn't valuable."

"What we need," said Robbie, "is a metal detector."

"Let's ask Gran," Alice said. "She'll know someone."

Fortified by butt'ries and jam, bacon and eggs, they tackled Gran on the subject.

"Of course," said Gran. "Walter has one. I wish I'd thought of that earlier."

"The minister has one?"

"Think about it, Alice! He has to locate graves, and look for the odd lost earring or fountain pen. His is old, though. He says the new ones are much more sensitive. You'll likely have to buy some new batteries. I'll give him a call."

* * * * *

Kinsear squinted at the faint undulations across the surface of the pasture, then turned to Alice and Gran. "I think we could start looking in the ridge just below the sheepfold. Unless you want to go straight to the corner of the sheepfold where you and Gran were digging. Does that sound okay?"

Gran nodded.

He tossed some change on the dirt and turned on the pastor's metal detector, then began waving it slowly from side to side, watching the meter. *Beep!* "It looks like it works okay. Let's try it out! Gran?"

"I give you the honor."

He started along the slight ridge below the sheepfold, guiding the metal loop back and forth. Nothing. He crossed the faint straightness of the causeway, starting down the ridge on the other side. Alice trailed along at his side, rapidly becoming bored. She'd thought the entire pasture would start the detector dinging.

"Maybe it's all Neolithic, with no metal?" she said. Kinsear waltzed the awkward metal detector around the sheepfold, with Gran and Alice, carrying trowel and shovel respectively, following.

"Maybe." But he kept on to the end of that ridge. Still nothing. He walked back to the sheepfold.

"Either there's nothing there or we need a better detector," he said. "Well, what about the sheepfold?" They'd returned to the corner by the garden. Kinsear and Alice lugged the water tub off to the side. Kinsear rolled the salt block away. He approached again with the metal detector. *BeepbeepbeepBEEP!*

"Heavens," said Gran.

Alice handed the shovel to Kinsear. "Are you going to show us how you learned to dig in archeology class?"

"I am." He inserted the tip of the blade gently, pried away some soil, repeated again, and again, and again.

Alice took the metal detector and moved it back and forth over the soil. Result: a string of *beeps.*

Gran brought over her narrow weed blade and the trowel. They all knelt and began moving dirt away.

Clink! Alice turned up a small blue bead. "Trading bead," said Kinsear.

Using only their fingers they dug, dug, dug. Alice turned up another bead. Nothing else.

Kinsear picked up the metal detector. This time the *beep* indicated they should move close to and partly beneath the biggest stones, the lowest course of rocks making up the sheepfold. Again they resorted to the shovel, gently prying up small clumps of dirt, following up with the trowel and weed blade. Every few minutes Alice waved the metal detector near the excavation. The *beeps* kept them going. Finally, twelve inches down, Gran's weed blade hit metal. *Ping!*

And there it was, waiting for them: a wide-mouthed bronze jug, only nine or so inches high. The mouth of the jar was plugged with a wad of cloth—"Linen," interjected Kinsear, pointing to the weave, still visible. Alice and Kinsear sat back, waiting for Gran. She gently picked up the jar and levered out the linen. Then she said, "Do you reckon no one has looked in here for over a thousand years?"

They all leaned forward and peered into the depths of the jar.

Inside lay six tiny golden coins and two gold wire earrings, with dangling green beads. "Ooh, Gran, those would look lovely on you," said Alice.

"Fat chance," Gran said. "I expect Her Majesty will want those. Alice, the Queen's Remembrancer?"

"I guess so."

Kinsear said, "With the leaping horses, I'll bet the coins are Celtic staters. Maybe one-quarter staters, given their size. They're beautiful, aren't they."

"But—that's all there is," said Alice. "Don't you think there used to be more in this jar?"

"I'd lay odds on it," Kinsear said. "Especially since we found the loose beads. This was disturbed at some point."

"'The land, the house, and all that lies therein,'" said Alice, watching Gran. "Do you think an earlier visitor had to use part of the hoard?"

Gran nodded. "Maybe they left a bit in the jar, just in case of emergency." And she went off to the kitchen to stash the bronze jar.

Well, thought Alice, maybe the Flemings, decades ago, had indeed seen something from their superior position on the headland.

Maybe they'd seen someone digging. Maybe they'd just speculated as to how the Hardies got the last bit of wherewithal to pay off the loan and keep the farm. And maybe—her mind ranged. Maybe, and it was a big if, maybe Reid, hearing the old family tale, and then seeing the two metal detectorists prowling at Hardie Farm, thought he could siphon off the best, have first call on whatever treasure the detectorists turned up. And he'd likely be in a hurry. Once Mr. Zhou bought the Fleming land, Reid would be homeless in Broadview. So he had to get in ahead of Ansley, he had to grab it now.

But how did he persuade the two men to let him in? Did he buy them off? No, Alice thought, maybe he wouldn't need to. Maybe he let them know he'd seen them prowling the farm, then told them they could park the blue van up on the little mud track leading off the Fleming driveway, so they could walk down onto the farm un-observed. And maybe in the same way he knew of their fight with Angus, made them move the body to the Dorain. And maybe then, hearing what Davie said about "three men," he told them Davie could describe both men and blackmailed them into killing Davie. She would call the inspector . . .and he would point out the highly, the grossly, speculative nature of her theory of the two murders.

Gran had returned. "This is great fun," she was saying to Kinsear. "I put the bronze jar in the cabinet with the best teapot. Now what? Would the sheepfold have been at the top of the causewayed enclo-sure? Before it was a sheepfold? For example, if it originally was built as some sort of hall?"

"That's the logical place for a big hall or ritual space," he said. "But we don't know its vintage, do we? I'm really interested in this slight embankment—maybe it's a berm, maybe not—on the uphill side of the sheepfold. I'm wondering if it was part of some sort of enclosure around whatever this sheepfold once was."

The detector beeped on the little curved berm that ran along the uphill side of the sheepfold next to the causeway. Several strong beeps, in one location. Alice retrieved the shovel and trowel and brought them over.

"This is more or less where those two men were when Sue was barking at them, the night Robbie and I chased them," Alice said.

"They didn't have time to dig here, though."

He slowly rocked the shovel tip into the dirt, then picked up the soil and started the process again. Alice brought over the metal detector. "Good idea. Let's check where we are," he said.

Beep beep! "That's close!" said Gran. On her knees, she carefully inserted the weed blade and pulled it back, gently.

"Careful," said Kinsear. "You may have to dig around the edges first."

Gran pried more soil loose, then started working with her fingers, revealing buried metal. "It's a handle! A knife, a dagger," she said. "A long dagger, like a dirk. It's at least, what, fourteen or so inches long?"

"Gran, go really slow. The blade may have corroded," Kinsear said.

She used her fingers, and in a few minutes the thing lay bare before them, old, lost, lethal. Corrosion stained the blade blue-green but did not diminish the beautiful curves of the handle.

"Bronze," said Kinsear.

"Now what?" asked Alice.

"It's not precious metal," Gran said promptly. "Is it treasure trove?"

"It still might be 'precious,' especially if found with precious metal objects," Alice said. "And it's ancient and rare, too."

"There's something more," Kinsear said, kneeling next to the shallow excavation. "Look."

Alice could see an interruption in the soil, something dark, thin. "Is it leather? Wait . . ."

Very gently with his trowel tip, Kinsear tapped away nearby soil from something thin, something that might have been leather, once . . . and they saw lying there next to it three pieces of ivory, now darkened, yellowed. And unmistakable.

"Bones," Kinsear said.

"Finger bones," Alice said.

"We need to let this lie, not to mess anything up, Alice," Kinsear said. "We need to rebury it. And don't anyone touch these bones; it could contaminate them for DNA testing. Gran, do you agree? It looks as if someone's buried inside this berm."

"All right," Gran said. "And I do feel like a grave robber. But how do we protect it—him, maybe?—in the meantime? And what about the dagger?"

"First, Alice, take a picture." She did. Then Kinsear pulled an old blue bandana out of his pocket. "Always carry one," he said to the air. "One thousand and one uses for a used bandana." Avoiding entirely the area of the finger bones, he picked up the bronze weapon with the bandana, wrapped it carefully, and presented it to Gran. Then he gently reinterred the finger bones with several more shovelfuls of dirt. "Makeshift," he said. "We need to call your favorite university right away. Alice, take another picture, would you?"

"Well, we also need to call the Queen's Remembrancer, actually," Alice said. "But only for the dagger, not the bones, because . . ."

"The Queen's Remembrancer does not have jurisdiction over bodily remains," finished Kinsear.

Later they would call both. But at the moment they stood over a grave, each thinking about the man in the berm, a man who once had a voice, a name, a dagger, now bones. A ghost and his weapon, from—"Would you say at least 1000 BC?" she asked Kinsear.

"It could be 3,500 years old, the dagger. And the man."

"Aren't you curious about him? Who he was, where he was from, why he's buried here?"

Kinsear nodded. "Oh, yes. And how did he die? In at least one of these berm burials, the bones had been murdered. But why? By whom? No one's telling. But these bones can tell us part of the story."

Alice stared down at the dirt he'd replaced over the finger bones.

"These metal detectorists," Kinsear said, "in a way, they're like the Vikings in your bad dreams, Alice, the ones racing up from the sea, destroying a village, a monastery, in a way that makes it hard to reconstruct history. Archeologists find gold ornaments ripped off missals and testaments and turned into earrings and gifts for Viking ladies, hundreds of miles away . . . so that gives us interesting information about raiding and trading, but we've lost the information on the testament or missal. Frustrating. And look at us: here we are with a metal detector, and it's thrilling, undeniably, when it goes *beep beep* and we find something! I get it, I do."

Gran and Alice nodded. That *beep* was thrilling, compelling, almost addictive.

He went on. "Certainly there are hobbyists who do no harm, and help build the historical record. On the other hand I've read online comments where a detectorist says, 'These artifacts were in the ground before the owner ever owned this land, so I say the owner has no claim at all!'" Kinsear turned to Gran. "Moral: we need to be cautious that we don't talk about this, don't let the news out, until the site is safe."

Gran frowned. "Well, for goodness' sake, we'll certainly not go broadcasting this all over town! I don't want to be invaded by random detectorists from all over Britain!" Reflexively she glanced up at Ben Cathair. "Which reminds me of Mr. Ansley and his binoculars."

"Exactly," he said. "We've got to be careful that no one we notify mentions the location and that nothing we do here turns you into a news item."

They all stood, worrying about the implications.

"Well, I'm just grateful those guys didn't have time to dig here," he said. "And now that Gran has the dagger, maybe there's no more metal in that berm to attract a metal detectorist. But imagine if someone had torn up the site, with bones and artifacts dug up, stolen, scattered? Think of the incalculable loss to our knowledge of human history! From the DNA in his bones we can learn who this man's people were. From his teeth we can tell where he grew up, what water he drank. We can look at the skeleton and figure out his age and some of his history. And what about that gorgeous weapon? Where did he get it? Had he killed with it? Who made it, and when, and where?" He smiled. "We may actually find out!"

"I have another job for you right now," said Gran to Kinsear.

"Of course!"

"Come help me order my own metal detector."

They stared at her.

"I've had a grand idea!" Her face was alight, her eyes sparkled. "You know how the ghosts seem to always crowd around us outside? Stone Age, Bronze Age, Iron Age. Celts, Irish monks, Vikings. Well, I am going to map the farm!"

"Map the farm?"

"Yes! Map the farm! With my metal detector! We've already found Celtic coins, and a Bronze Age dagger, and trading beads from somewhere. I'm positive we'll find something from the Vikings. They were all here, all those people, and I want to create a huge wonderful map, showing the entire farm, trees, copse, cove, pasture, showing what we found and where."

They stared openmouthed at her fierce enthusiasm. "It's brilliant," Kinsear said. "Brilliant!"

* * * * *

Just before noon on Saturday, Kinsear disappeared with Gran into the kitchen.

In a bit he found Alice, waiting out on the front porch. She was still thinking how odd it was to have spent the night with another man in Jordie's house. Kinsear kissed her good-bye. "I've got to pack up and head for Heathrow." He had a morning flight back to Austin. "I'll call you."

One more kiss. "Your Gran. I do love that woman. She's invited me to come back during the excavation of her Bronze Age man. Of course I said I'd stay at the pub. I think I'll do it." His eyes sparkled. "I never thought I'd see anything like this!"

Gran came out to wave good-bye. And then he was gone.

Without looking at Alice, Gran said, "Good man, that. And really quite a cook. Do you know he guessed the secret of my butt'ries?"

"Did you give him the recipe, Gran? I thought it was a state secret!"

"It would have been rude not to, Alice, after he guessed the secret. But you'll have to ask him what that is."

C h a p t e r   T h i r t y

For a' That

"**A**lice. Come help me with these paintings. I need to move the big ones close to the door. You've convinced me it's time to show my 'bones of the land' canvases. And an Edinburgh gallery said yes!"

"Excellent!" Alice extended her palm to high-five. Wait, did they do that in Scotland? Robbie did.

Upstairs in the studio, three tall paintings stood propped on the counter, next to the stone chimney that rose through the studio from the downstairs hall.

"I need to get those down."

Alice had always liked what she thought of as Robbie's abstract landscapes, though now she could see that each had what Alice now recognized as the causeway and enclosures. "Robbie, does it make any difference to you, knowing those are Neolithic constructions?"

"Not really. I thought about mentioning that in the catalog for the show, but to me, really, they're just shapes and colors, the bones of the land. Of course now I know there are bones in them . . . but still. Do you know the scene in *To the Lighthouse* where Lily Briscoe, the spinster painter, is trying to find just the right shape, in just the right place, to paint the last few strokes and finish her painting?"

"I do," said Alice. *To the Lighthouse* had been her favorite book since college. "That description was the first time I felt even a vague understanding of what it might be like to be a painter, to have a vision and try to capture it on canvas."

"Right. That is what it's like, you know. When the right shape, the right shadow, falls in the right place. It's probably the same feeling as when a musician captures harmony. Or a poet finds the precise word and the line falls into place. Alice, you climb up on this stool and grab those paintings and hand them down to me."

Alice obliged. She handed down the first, then the second. The third slipped and the corner hit the side of the stone chimney five feet above the counter.

"Yikes! Is it okay?"

They looked at the painting.

"It's fine," Robbie said.

"Thank goodness."

"But look at that stone."

Now a rectangular-shaped stone stuck out at an angle from the side of the chimney.

Alice climbed back up the stool, put one foot gingerly on the counter, and leaned sideways, pushing the stone. "It's loose." She poked the one above it. It moved as well.

"If I pull these out, will the chimney fall down?"

"It's on you, Alice!"

"Well, wait. Will this counter hold me?"

She climbed atop the counter and stared at the chimney. She could see only darkness behind the angled stones. She handed both stones down to Robbie. Then she reached into the cavity but felt only stone.

"Robbie, you should be the one up here. It's your chimney."

Alice got down and Robbie climbed up. She reached back as far as she could into the empty space. "I can't feel anything back there."

"The stones aren't mortared. How long do you suppose they've been sitting there loose like that?" asked Alice.

Robbie clambered down. "I have no idea. There's no gap, because they fit so well. You can't really tell they aren't mortared unless you're up on the counter looking straight at them. I do wonder, though, how Jordie missed them. This was his room."

"Well, who put in the counter?"

"I did. After I moved my studio in here. So unless Jordie was shinnying up the side of the fireplace, he wouldn't know."

They heard slamming doors and happy voices downstairs. As of one accord they hurried to the kitchen to find Gran, Ann, and John. "Hi, Mama!"

"We need you kids upstairs," Robbie said, after a moment. She motioned them up the staircase, then followed. Alice and Gran, waiting below, heard voices, questions, silence, a whoop, then feet pelting down the stairs.

"So we both climbed up on the counter in Robbie's studio—," John said.

"And then John reached way back to the back, and found there was a drop-off in the back—"

"About four inches by twelve inches," said John.

"And he said, 'I've found something!'"

"And I pulled it out—"

"And here it is!" they said together.

John handed Gran a small metal box. "Oh," she said, "oho. Now I remember!"

"What?" said the two.

She opened the lid. And there, lying clean, dustless, as fresh as they'd been thirty-five years ago, were—

"Flies!"

"Your dad tied those himself," said Gran. "That's his first one, the Royal Coachman."

John and Ann stared at the little fuzzy fly with its red body.

"That next one is his black shuttlecock. And look, this one's his coch-y-bonddu beetle!"

"Gran, are you making these names up?"

"I am not. You should try these first thing in the morning," Gran said. "I'll help you if you want."

"How old was Daddy when he made these?" Ann asked.

"Hmm. Eleven, when he tied his first fly. He was quite good, actually."

"Did these work?" asked John.

"Oh yes. See the dung fly?"

"The *what?*

"Dung fly. That's a useful one. I know Jordie caught a big trout with that because—well, we all remembered the name of the fly, didn't we?"

Robbie rolled her eyes.

Alice thought, Jordie would have loved this, the kids finding his fly box. Let's see what they do with it. Treasure trove.

* * * * *

That night Gran and Robbie and Alice, with John and Ann carrying their instruments, walked down to the Sisters. They'd be playing with Seaheart. Sunday night: the pub was filling fast.

Alice watched as Gran introduced John and Ann to her friends. Over by the bar Seaheart's fiddler was tuning. John pulled his fiddle out of the case and walked over to stand next to her, listening, tuning, both faces intent on their instruments. Ann bounded onstage, her bodhran drum in hand. The four musicians conferred, looked down at a set list, looked around at each other, nodded. The pub patrons hushed. The music began.

At one point Alice, as in a dream, saw Neil Gage rest his elbows on the bar, chin on his hands, his eyes on the musicians. Then he closed his eyes. She'd never seen him other than erect, eyes alert, hands busy, washing, wiping. Now he was as still as if he were caught in an enchanted forest. Gran sat immobile, her eyes like forest pools, reflecting her grandchildren and their music. And Robbie—Robbie was checking her cell phone. Ah. Jorgé, I'll bet, Alice thought.

"Ae Fond Kiss," Ann announced, smiling at the crowd. And her soprano soared up: "Ae fond kiss, and then we sever, ae fond kiss, alas, forever . . . ," followed by the fiddles, harmonizing with each other. "And now, 'The Bob o' Dunblane,'" she said, getting laughs with her eye-rolling delivery. Later, "My Love's in Germany," said the guitarist. "Bring him home, bring him home . . ."

So could the American siblings sing? They could. Did Ann's voice blend with the guitarist's? It did. When he sang again "Lassie, Lie Near Me," Ann came in straight and true on the second verse. "A' that I hae endur'd, lassie, my dearie, here in thy arms is cur'd. Lassie, lie near me . . ."

Alice saw Gran's eyes were suspiciously bright.

It was getting late. Ann took a step forward. "For Davie Dockery and Angus McBride."

She sang the question:

Is there for honest Poverty
That hings his head, an' a' that;
The coward slave—we pass him by,
We dare be poor for a' that!

The crowd answered, "For a' that, an' a' that, a man's a man for a' that . . ." They sang all of the verses, every one, and at the end were standing up and singing, "For a' that, an' a' that, a man's a man for a' that . . ." The fiddles played low, the guitar beat the rhythm, the voices sang strong, and on the last verse, no instruments, just voices.

Not a dry eye in the house.

Certainly not for Alice. Davie, so young, so proud of his new job, so in love with the unattainable Fiona. Angus, so experienced, so strong, such a leader . . . and perhaps, though he knew his duty, as he said, and loved Jennie and his Jamie, perhaps he'd also loved Robbie almost as much as she wanted, almost as much as she needed. Well, Alice thought, let's just see what happens next.

Chapter Thirty-One

Couching *at the* Door

Early on Sunday Alice and Gran took John and Ann off to church. Gran's face glowed as they walked down the aisle to her customary pew. "I've got my tribe surrounding me," she whispered.

Walter McAfee preached that morning on Cain and Abel. He read aloud the short passage from Genesis. "Is this a story that suggests our eternal human desire to understand tragedy?" he began. "So much is left to our imaginations. We aren't told how exactly Cain killed Abel. We aren't told of the grief of his parents. But we can all imagine finding one of our children—perhaps the one who filled you with calm joy, or perhaps the other?—lying dead. Cold, gone, eternally nonresponsive.

"We aren't told of the parents' agony when their child Cain, after the murder, is exiled to the wild lands. Did he ever return? Send birthday cards, call home? Did he come back just close enough to stand on a far-off hill and wave at Eve?

"We aren't told how Cain felt about Abel, or Abel about Cain. Did they love the same girl? Had they skirmished from childhood or was this rivalry new? We aren't told how desperately each son wanted his offering to be the one whose smoke rose straight and high. That son might have said something like, 'My burnt offering pleased the Lord, but yours didn't.'

"The wandering Israelites, when they settled down, planted grain and orchards. Did Cain chafe as he worked the crops while Abel and his flocks walked the hilltops?

"Cain founded a city, we're told, and his descendants were urbanites, metalworkers." Alice perked up.

"So is this just a myth of the pastoral versus the urban? Of the coming of the ages of metal, copper, bronze, iron? Of more and more weaponry? Of our violent mining of the planet, our extraction of gold, silver, diamonds, and other gems from the earth? Or is there more to this story?

"The Lord tells Cain that if he does well, he will be accepted. But the Lord also warns Cain that if he does not do well, 'sin is couching at the door; its desire is for you, but you must master it.' That's an older translation; the newer one says 'lurking,' but I like 'couching' because it sounds as if sin has such a comfortable place, lolling at the door, sleeping at the door. At any rate, Cain hears the warning. But instead, Cain says to Abel his brother, 'Let us go out to the field.' And we know the rest. Sin was 'lurking at the door,' and Cain did not master it. Perhaps that is all it tells us, this foundational story of human tragedy, that sin sits ever waiting at the door. When we do not master it, we can, and sometimes do, kill each other. And when murder happens, we confront grief, immeasurable grief. Staring at, and bearing, that grief is the audience's eternal share in this story of Cain and Abel. That role is assigned to all of us."

And Alice thought of Angus, of Davie, and of the grief for them. Grief grows exponentially, she thought. Not in a straight line, but up and off the charts. The ripples spread, and spread . . . She thought of the child's dagger at the museum, called only a "grave good." But the grief . . . And the murdered bones belonging to the Bronze Age dirk buried in Gran's berm? Someone had mourned those bones too.

Alice wondered if that was Hamlet's despair, the impact of killing another human? "The beauty of the world! The paragon of animals! And yet to me, what is this quintessence of dust?" Wanting to be a paragon, he struggled to decipher whether the ghost spoke true, whether Claudius had indeed murdered his father, and, even if he had, whether Hamlet's killing him would be honorable vengeance, or further sin. Whether wreaking vengeance on Claudius would mar this paragon with the mark of Cain. What a piece of work are we . . . we humans, for whom sin is 'couching at the door'?

Come on, don't overcomplicate it, Alice, she told herself. In her limited experience, the murderers who infested her dreams did not engage in Hamlet's anguished debate. Instead, they struck and killed because it was "all about them." Maybe *that* was the sin couching at the door—letting everything be all about you and what you want, right that snatching minute. And yet, whose names lived on in our hearts? Not always the names of the murderers . . . but the names of the victims? Ollie. Cassie. Alex. Blanton. Annie. Their names lived on. That struck her as ironic. Did murderers know they'd be forgotten? If they did know, would that have made a difference? No, she decided, not in the pressing moment when sin sat couching at the door, no, not at that moment when they said, instead, "Let us go out to the field."

Gran nudged her. Everyone but Alice was standing up to sing the final hymn. Alice was still staring forward, sitting on the rock-hard pew, the penitential uncushioned best-of-British-oak pew of the Church of Scotland, thinking about murder. In relief she stood to sing . . . enthusiastically but out of time, since British hymn tunes apparently marched to different drummers. Then, Lord be praised, came Walter McAfee's benediction, and an escape down the aisle to an exquisite August noon.

Chapter Thirty-Two

A *Few* Loose Ends

The inspector asked her to stop by after church. "Just a few loose ends," he said. "You understand we will need you to testify when those two come to trial?"

"I'll come back."

Blocky Man had been caught trying to board the ferry to Norway.

"What's his name?"

"Mikey Goss."

She rolled the syllables on her tongue. "Sounds threatening."

"He is. Turns out he's wanted in Glasgow for a particularly vicious robbery that went very badly for the victim."

"Does he say his mate did it? Joey Campbell?"

"Mikey's not talking. But Mr. Ansley is."

Alice sat up, interested. "Ansley admitted he'd been at the distillery the day Davie was killed?"

"Yes, finally. First we asked him what possible claim he thought he had to a knife that was likely illegally dug up at Hardie Farm. He hemmed and hawed and said something about protecting treasure trove for the Queen's Remembrancer and preventing a valuable artifact from being sold out of Scotland, like he was keeping it in trust."

"Oh, please."

"Right. Clearly that was precisely what he himself planned to do with it. Then he did admit he'd asked the two men to conduct a search for artifacts at Hardie Farm. He actually called it the 'Hardie Farm Project.' He said he only wanted them to locate artifacts 'in situ,' as he called it. He appeared to be concocting a grandiose scenario about making a significant discovery 'to advance the cause of Scottish history.' Of course he glossed right over the fact that he has no right to conduct his so-called 'project' on Mrs. Greer's farm. Anyway, he was concerned about their possible involvement in Angus's death. He overheard you telling Walter McAfee what you'd seen. The two men weren't answering his messages. He'd looked for them at the pizza place and couldn't find them, but then he saw the blue pizza van parked on Wednesday morning on Distillery Road, right by a climbable fence on that side of the distillery, and thought he'd better find out what they were doing."

"So he saw us, on the day of Davie's death? He knew I was there?"

"Yes. It gave him quite a start to see your group that day. But he claims that he never saw Mikey Goss and his mate there."

"He must have just missed them," Alice said. "I saw him at noon, and right about then Davie would have been walking into the malting floor. And after that?"

The inspector nodded. "They were there."

"Did no one see them leave? I guess they had those blue shirts on."

"Apparently not. And unfortunately, you were asleep." He lifted an eyebrow.

She thought about that and shook her head. "Did Ansley get those two men involved after he visited the pastor in June?"

"Yes. He'd had some prior dealings with them on a smuggling deal; they were part of a ring that brought non-precious metal antiquities from Scotland to England where they could be sold because they didn't have to comply with the Antiquities Act."

"Because they weren't precious metal, you mean?"

"That's it," said the inspector.

"Did Ansley have any idea about Reid Fleming's role?"

"I don't think so. I think Reid Fleming had successfully inserted himself between Ansley and the two men. Reid could freeze out Ansley and Ansley wouldn't even know he'd been supplanted, unless the two men told Ansley, which he claims they didn't. Reid could blackmail the two men into doing what he wanted, after they killed Angus—they claim that Angus attacked them, by the way, and that they struck back in self-defense."

"That doesn't explain why they turned Angus over into the water so he drowned," Alice said.

"Oh, they say Reid did that."

"And Reid? Where is he?" asked Alice.

"He's 'lawyered up,' as I understand you say in America. He's not speaking to us. He'd disappeared to London the day Davie was killed, before you had your sailboat adventure."

"And did Reid Fleming give Angus's shotgun to those two?"

"They say so. Of course Reid is denying everything."

"Will the two men testify that he's the one who sent them after me? Not Ansley?"

"I think so. Joey Campbell, at least, will say that Reid told them you were the only one who could tie them to Hardie Farm, you were the only one who could tie them to Angus."

"What about Fiona? Does she realize that Reid could try to shut her up too?"

"She's just feeling resentful," said the inspector. "Resentful of you for meddling, for investigating, for pursuing Reid's involvement in both deaths. I pointed out that often a murderer will commit a second murder of a person who has learned, or who suspects, what he did. She's still refusing to accept that Reid was involved in Angus's death, or that he persuaded those guys that Davie must die."

"And Davie loved her," Alice mused.

"What?"

"Oh, he told me he had no chance with Fiona."

The inspector shook his head, staring off at his filing cabinet. "It was no fun, having to talk with Davie's mum about her son's murder."

This time they both shook their heads.

"I'll definitely come back," Alice said. "And you've got my statement."

He nodded, and stood to shake hands.

"Please give my regards to Mr. George Files," said the inspector.

Well. She would, too.

* * * * *

Ann and John wanted a family climb up to the Sisters before they left for Edinburgh. The sun warmed their backs as they climbed from Upper Road up the steep path to the stone circle. Ann flung her arms wide and pirouetted. "So beautiful! Look, Mama! You can see Ireland today!"

They stared west.

"If you look really hard, and squint your eyes," said Alice, "you can see Coffee Creek."

"And not two, but three burros," John said. "Waiting for you to show up with their carrots. Braying when you drive through the gate."

But Alice had turned, and was looking at the rockfall, the granite boulders sparkling in the sun, the gorse sending heady coconut perfume across the green turf. There she had crouched, gorse prickling her neck, watching Blocky Man appear in the mist, clutching the drain spade, a murder weapon that had smashed Angus's temple, leaving only the one eye to stare accusingly when they moved him to the Dorain. Angus. Robbie's love. Jennie's love. Jamie's dad.

She turned back to her children.

John said, "Mama. Tomorrow I'm meeting at the University of Edinburgh with my favorite professor from last year. He's got some ideas he thinks might be useful for my senior thesis this fall. And after I graduate I might try to get into the master's program the following year at the University of Edinburgh. He wants to talk to me about that too."

She'd felt it coming. The thought of her boy spending another year on the other side of the Atlantic . . . such a wave of loss rose in her chest that for a moment her heart hurt. But you had to let the arrow fly, you had to let the fledgling flutter off the edge of the nest, all the time thinking, Fly, damn it! Flap your wings! Well, all right, he was flapping.

And what was Ann thinking? Ann, whose phone calls—all beginning with that excited "Mama!"—reliably pulled her out of any office funk. This past year, with both of them in Edinburgh, she'd sometimes felt so bereft driving down her long driveway to an empty house . . . well, her children were not going to hear her whine, ever.

"It wouldn't be for another year, Mama. And Ann and I will both be back home in two more weeks." She knew that. They'd be back just in time to pack up and leave for school.

She hugged him hard, looked deep into the eyes, the eyes waiting for approval.

"I'm so proud of you." That was all she could say. "I'm so proud of both of you."

They had their usual scrum, the three-way hug, and took pictures of themselves with the Sisters, who stood quietly, making no comment on human hopes or foolishness.

Then they climbed back down the hill to Gran's. Packets of cake to take along. Last hugs.

And then they were both gone. Flapping, flapping.

* * * * *

Now the house was quiet. Robbie had driven Gran to Newton Stewart, to call on Davie's mom. Alice stood in the small guestroom, packing to leave.

Kinsear called. "Alice. I'm at Heathrow. I'm sitting in this vast perilous room where you have to wait before your flight is called and you can finally trudge off to the gate. I'm surrounded by Prada, Ferragamo, Hermès, Burberry. Intimidating. And Harrods. What should I get for my clerk at the bookstore? I have to bring her something."

"Harrods," said Alice. "A tote bag from Harrods."

"Excellent. Listen, Alice, I'm ready to go home and ready for you to come home too. And Alice, I have got to have some barbecue."

"Oh." She thought about it. "At Shade Tree?"

"Yes. I want the brisket-sausage combo. And sides, of course. I'll have the green chile black-eyed peas. Also Mexican-German potato salad with chorizo instead of bacon."

"Oh, Lord," said Alice. She swallowed. "I'm ready. What is this, barbecue porn?"

He laughed.

"But I think I'll go with straight brisket, sliced just so, on a flour tortilla, fresh of course, with green sauce, not too much, and decorated with some fine-sliced coleslaw, no mayo, just a really good vinaigrette on that coleslaw." She thought for a moment. "And after I finish that first tortilla"—she could almost taste it, but only almost—"then on the second tortilla I just want the green sauce, and the most perfectly sliced outside pieces of brisket, with plenty of brown. And also . . . a Negra Modelo Especial, on draft if possible. Extremely cold."

"Alice, it's indecent, talking like this. The phone lines are melting. Don't stop."

"Mmm." She shut her eyes, took a breath. She wasn't just thinking about barbecue.

Nor was he. "And, listen, Alice. Barbecue is not all I'm thinking about."

"Ah. Well, I need to make that flight home tomorrow night."

"Yes, you do. I'll meet you at the airport. I'll be waiting at the bottom of the escalator."

T H E   E N D

GRAN'S BUTTERIES

Ingredients:
2 ¼ cup white bread flour
½ tsp. salt
5 level tsp. active dry yeast
½ tsp. sugar
6 oz. tepid water (about ¾ cup)
3 T. lard
9 T. unsalted butter (1 stick plus 1 T.)

Yield: 2 dozen crispy buttery square-ish rolls. The technique resembles easy puff paste. These are quite delicious. You can use all butter (12 tablespoons total) but lard makes a significant improvement. Total time: you'll pay attention on and off for about 4 hours but actual time spent on the process is minimal.

1. Put butter and lard in mixing bowl to soften. Put flour and salt in another large mixing bowl. Put yeast in small bowl. Sprinkle with the sugar, and pour over the yeast the tepid (never hot) water. Leave for 20 minutes while the yeast activates and puffs up.

2. Pour the yeast mixture over the flour and mix with a wooden spoon. Your goal is a fairly sticky but not wet dough. You will need to add, tablespoon by tablespoon, more water (between ½ cup and ¾ cup), stirring it in as you go. Don't overdo the water (but if your dough gets too sticky, add a tablespoon or two of flour). The amount of water you'll need varies with flour, temperature, humidity, etc.

3. Let your dough rise, covered (plastic wrap or damp towel) until the dough has doubled in size—40 to 50 minutes.

4. Meanwhile, whip the butter and lard until fluffy. Divide roughly into three portions.

5. Take the risen dough and, on your heavily floured counter or pastry board, roll the dough into a long strip, about 4-5" wide and about ¾" thick. With a spatula, spread 1/3 of your butter/lard mixture fairly evenly on the entire strip. Now, as if folding a business letter into thirds, pick up one end of the buttered dough strip and fold it over the middle one third. Then fold the other one-third of the buttered strip over the middle one third. Leave the dough for 15 minutes, to let the gluten relax.

6. Repeat step 5 twice more using the remaining two portions of whipped butter/lard.

7. Roll out the dough about ¾" thick. Using a sharp knife cut it into two-inch squares (I get about 2 dozen). Place them about 2" apart on nonstick baking sheets or on baking sheets lined with parchment paper. Let rise about 40 minutes. Heat oven to 400.

8. Bake in middle level of oven for 20-25 minutes until slightly golden. They can overcook very quickly so watch them like a hawk. Let them cool on a wire rack. Restrain yourself and others from eating them for 15 minutes or until they are just warm.

9. These freeze beautifully; reheat gently at 275 for 15-20 minutes.

GRAN'S THREE-GINGER CAKE

This looks pretty made in a 10" spring form bundt pan. Whatever cake pan you use, butter it heavily, then add 2 T. of flour to the pan and turn and shake it so your pan is buttered and floured.

Ingredients:

1 c. (2 sticks) unsalted butter
1 c. dark brown sugar
½ c. molasses
½ c. Lyles Golden Syrup
2 eggs
½ c. chopped candied ginger
   (1/4" pieces)

3 c. flour, plus 2 T. flour for ginger
2 tsp. baking soda
1 c. buttermilk
½ c. fresh ginger root, peeled and
   minced
½ tsp. salt
4 tsp. powdered ginger

Secret ingredient: Lyle's Golden Syrup, a British ingredient. If you can't find it use Karo's clear corn syrup, but try to find Lyle's, which makes the cake moist and irresistible.

Cream the butter. Add the sugar and beat until fluffy. Add the molasses and Lyle's Golden Syrup (I butter the inside of the measuring cup so they'll pour out more easily). Beat in the eggs, then the salt, baking soda and powdered ginger. Add 1 ½ c. of flour. Then add ½ c. of buttermilk. Repeat, beating well and scraping the bowl. Sprinkle the remaining 2 T. flour over your minced fresh and candied ginger (this helps suspend the pieces in the batter). Briefly beat in the fresh and candied ginger.

Bake at 350 in middle rack of oven until just done, about 40 minutes (baking time will depend on whether you use a tube pan). Let cake cool 10 minutes before unclipping spring form and placing cake on serving dish. If possible, cover and wait to serve until the next day. Serve at room temperature with a dollop of whipped cream.

THE GREEN SAUCE

When you have the archetypal beef brisket, smoked for a dozen hours over a parsimonious little fire, an option is to slice the meat on the bias, put the brisket slices on warmed flour tortillas, and add a cautious smear of green sauce. I learned this recipe on the square at Fort Davis, after the Fourth of July parade, from the lady at the brisket truck.

Ingredients:
8 jalapeños

Put the whole jalapeños in a non-reactive saucepan; cover with water. Boil about 35 minutes. Drain and cover with cold water. You may want to wear gloves for the next step. When the jalapeños are cool, pull off and discard the stems, slit the jalapeños, scrape out and discard the seeds, and put the jalapeños in a blender jar. Add ¼ c. water and 1 tsp. salt. Blend. Stand back when you take the top off the blender, and serve forth.

Cyprian Broodbank, *The Making of the Middle Sea*, Thames & Hudson Ltd. London 2013. Broodbank is Professor of Mediterranean Archaeology at the Institute of Archaeology, University College, London. Here he synthesizes new thinking and data from many disciplines (geology, climate, anthropology, archeology), describing early human history and migration, the competition and clashes of Neanderthal and modern humans, the origin and human impact of farming and metallurgy, and the rise of the civilizations. If you wonder why humans migrated east across north Africa, when humans began sailing west, what urban life meant, why hunter-gatherers adopted (or rejected) agriculture, that and much more awaits your eyes. Warning: "weighty" describes this book. If you read in bed, don't let it fall on your nose.

Robert Burns, poems selected by Don Paterson, Faber and Faber 2001. I discovered some love poems I didn't know, including "Lassie Lie Near Me," and "Oh Wert Thou in the Cauld Blast."

Barry Cunliffe, *Britain Begins*, Oxford University Press 2012. Sir Barry Cunliff is Emeritus Professor at the University of Oxford. I liked the photographs and the graphics (especially maps showing how styles of artifacts migrated around Europe and the British Isles). He describes bronze weapons, and their mass production. The aerial photographs of earthworks and archeological remains will make you want to fly low over Britain in a small plane, looking for barrows, causewayed enclosures, and hill forts.

William Letford, *Bevel*, Carcanet Press Limited, Manchester 2012. Letford's a roofer as well as a Scottish poet. His poems about physical work, outdoor work, grab me. Sometimes he writes straight English, sometimes he invites you into the sound of Scottish pronunciation, with grand results. The words spring to life. See, for example, "Taking a headbutt."

Adam Nicolson, *The Mighty Dead: Why Homer Matters*, Henry Holt and Company LLC 2014. Nicolson's thesis is that Homer reflects the experiences of the migrants from the Europeans steppes who brought their warrior horseback culture to Attica and became the Greeks we see in the *Iliad* and *Odyssey*, which describe their epic competitive collisions with the rich urban cultures of Anatolia and Egypt. In particular, Nicolson focuses on the role of bronze weapons in the rise of a warrior culture that spread across the northern Mediterranean, responsible for the burial steles in Spain, engraved to memorialize the brief triumph of a warrior's life, with his lyre, his comb, his mirror, his sword and his shield. I couldn't stop thinking about this book, with its penetrating appreciation of Homer, and its wrestling with the impact of Bronze Age warrior culture on our own lives today.

Finally, significant inspiration came from Professor Michael McCormick, and the Harvard Initiative for the Science of the Human Past with its projects and studies, described online, which absolutely fire the imagination. http://sohp.fas.harvard.edu/

This book would not have taken shape without the collaboration, brainstorming, and support of Larry Foster, Sydney Foster Schneider, Drew Foster, and my sister Grace Currie Bradshaw. Nor could this book have hatched without the creative and generous comments and encouragement from friends and family: Carol Arnold, Ann Barker, Dr. Megan Biesele, Boyce Cabaniss, Elizabeth Christian, Ann Ciccolella, Keith Clemson, Josh Feldmeth, Nancy Willson, Suzanne Wofford, and Stephenie Yearwood. What friendship! Heartfelt thanks to all of you.

For superb advice from Bill Crawford and Aaron Hierholzer (editor nonpareil) and for Bill Carson's cover, layout, craftsmanship and sheer professional brio, thanks and more thanks!

Any errors are mine.

ABOUT THE AUTHOR

Helen Currie Foster writes the Alice MacDonald Greer Mystery series. She lives north of Dripping Springs, Texas, supervised by three burros. She is drawn to the compelling landscape and quirky characters of the Texas Hill Country. She's also deeply curious about our human history, and how, uninvited, the past keeps crashing the party.

Find her on Facebook or at www.helen.currie.foster.com.

Thank you for reading Ghost Dagger! If you enjoyed it, please consider rating it or leaving a short review at the site where you bought it. Your review, which could be just a few words, can help the success of this mystery series.

If you have comments, questions or suggestions please email me at TheAliceMysteries@gmail.com. You can subscribe to the mailing list at www.helencurriefoster.com.